FIRST SALVO

For a moment Natasha was grateful to Major Cameron Talbot when he rescued her from his rakish cousin Charles. But that feeling faded when Cameron dryly remarked, "He won't marry you, you know. Charles is hunting an even greater heiress than you."

"I have no thought of marrying Charles," Natasha choked out.

"It merely amuses you to have him kiss you."

"It did *not*. He caught me by surprise."

"It has always puzzled me that women who invite unwanted embraces by going off alone with men invariably declare themselves astonished to receive those embraces," the major observed.

A black rage such as she had never experienced before engulfed Natasha's whole body and propelled the hand that lashed out at the major . . .

. . . which should have been the end of everything between them, instead of just the beginning. . . .

DOROTHY MACK is a native New Englander, born in Rhode Island and educated at Brown and Harvard universities. She now lives with her husband and sons in northern Virginia.

SIGNET REGENCY ROMANCE
COMING IN JANUARY 1989

---•---

Emma Lange
Brighton Intrigue

Jane Ashford
Meddlesome Miranda

Mary Jo Putney
The Controversial Countess

---•---

The Steadfast Heart

by

Dorothy Mack

A SIGNET BOOK

NEW AMERICAN LIBRARY

SIGNET TRADEMARK REG. U.S. PAT. OFF AND FOREIGN COUNTRIES
REGISTERED TRADEMARK—MARCA REGISTRADA
HECHO EN CHICAGO, U.S.A.

SIGNET, SIGNET CLASSIC, MENTOR, ONYX, PLUME,
MERIDIAN and NAL BOOKS are published by
NAL PENGUIN INC., 1633 Broadway, New York, New York 10019

First Printing, December, 1988

1 2 3 4 5 6 7 8 9

PRINTED IN THE UNITED STATES OF AMERICA

1

Spring's first incursions on the winter-deadened landscape were making themselves felt in the coppice, but the girl hurrying along a path spared scarcely a glance at a scattering of jewel-bright violets nestling in patches of sparse grass. Her purposeful stride soon took her out of the trees and into the warm sunshine. The path led down a gentle incline for a few hundred feet to where a stream swollen from recent rains rushed between grassy banks before disappearing around a bend where a stand of birch trees hid its progress from view. The girl headed directly for a willow tree near the stream but remained in the sunshine outside the perimeter of its drooping boughs sporting the tender yellow-green fuzz that preceded full leafing. She pulled the gray woolen shawl from her shoulders and cast it to the ground, dropping onto its protecting folds with a little sigh of satisfaction as she looked about her with quick appreciation of the lovely scene before drawing an envelope from a pocket of her gown. The air of purposefulness about her movements, oddly at variance with the idyllic setting, was accounted for as she proceeded to tear open the letter with impatient fingers.

Her eyes sought first the date of the epistle. Written from Saint-Jean-de-Luz late in February, and it was now mid-March. So the news would be old, what with the London papers full of what was confidently expected to be the final campaign in the long Peninsular War.

My dearest Tasha,
    First I must apologize for my long silence, but this has

5

not been like other winters here with an extended stretch of inactivity while the field marshal got in his hunting. I know how very disappointed you were that I could not wangle leave, especially since I wasn't able to get home when Grandmother died last spring, but you are aware that Wellington is notoriously unreceptive to requests for personal leave beyond the occasional weekend pass.

There has been little letup in the fighting since we crossed into France. The French still hold Bayonne, but our engineers have been busy bridging the Adur, so we'll soon have them surrounded. The weather has been uniformly foul; gales of wind and rain blow in from the bay to make our task harder, but there is no doubt we have them on the run. It may all be over by summer, but that won't do you any good as far as your come-out is concerned. There was no question of it, of course, after Papa died two years ago, but now Grandmother is gone too and you are virtually alone in that vast barracks of a house. Great-aunt Mary can scarcely be considered fit company for a young girl. It's bad enough that she's deaf as a post, but those startling conversations, not to say arguments, she holds with God at the drop of a hat would drive me into Bedlam if I had to bear witness to them with any frequency. In view of this, I have made arrangements for you to be brought out this season by Mama's cousin, Edwina Taylor. Her daughter Lucretia is only a year younger than you, so you girls will be good company for each other.

At this point in her reading, Natasha gave an audible gasp and lowered the letter to her lap while her eyes darted about among the trees along the bank on the opposite side of the brook in an involuntary display of agitation.

Peter couldn't do this to her! He must know how much she'd dislike being consigned to strangers, even if they were relatives, like some unordered package. Oh, it was too bad of him! What did it matter if she waited one more year before appearing in society? When had she ever evinced the slightest desire to live amid the hustle and bustle of a dirty city? Her eyes fell to the sheets, which she had crumpled inadvertently, and she took a steadying breath while her fingers smoothed the letter before returning her attention to its dismaying contents.

My dear impulsive little sister, before you protest that you are unacquainted with Cousin Edwina and would prefer to postpone your debut until I return to England, let me assure you that I would infinitely prefer to supervise your initial bow to society personally, but you would still require the good offices of Cousin Edwina to procure vouchers for Almack's and to act as chaperon, you know. There is no escaping that. You must have the sponsorship of a respectable matron. I can almost hear you arguing in that husky little croak of yours that next year will do just as well, but the plain truth is that it won't, my dear.

Natasha smiled to herself at this evidence of her brother's knowledge of her temperament, but his next words drove the smile from her lips.

I have hesitated about sharing this next development with you but have concluded that ignorance could be more than somewhat awkward. I have received a request from Rupert Carteret to pay his addresses to you.

A shocked exclamation broke from Natasha's lips and again she glanced wildly about her for a few seconds like a hunted animal before bringing her eyes back to Peter's difficult scrawl.

I have every respect for our worthy cousin and owe him a debt of gratitude for taking over the running of the estate at Papa's death, but you shall not pay my debt. In any case, as my heir he is aware it is in his own best interest to see that Springbrook continues to thrive in my absence. If I have anything to say in the matter, your fate shall not be a widower nearly twice your age and already saddled with three children. I have refused him in no uncertain terms but am concerned lest you find the situation awkward in consequence. Thus the arrangements with Cousin Edwina.

Peter's letter went on to explain his arrangements for her immediate future in some detail and finished with a description of the current military situation as the army lay within the gates of France, impatient now to finish off the task of defeating the man who had held all Europe in thrall for so many years.

Natasha, usually so avid for news of all her brother's actions and adventures, read through to the affectionate salutation at the end with something less than her customary concentration. Her fingers refolded the sheets of paper and replaced them in the envelope with precise controlled movements that were the antithesis of her chaotic thoughts. The one insistent theme that reiterated through the mass of unconnected mental fragments was that her life had suddenly undergone a radical change without her participation or knowledge.

Here she was, seated in this familiar spot made dear through countless pleasant hours spent dreamily watching the little stream's rushing journey. The scene was unchanged, she was unchanged, but nothing would ever be the same again. This morning she had arisen at the usual hour and performed all the usual morning tasks that awaited her execution before stealing away to read one of the eagerly awaited letters from Peter that constituted the most significant and welcome break in the quiet routine of her days. It seemed incredible that a few words in her brother's nearly illegible scrawl could spell the end of the only life she had ever known, but reduced to the most basic terms, that is what had just happened.

This letter might easily have been lost in transit. If she were to drop it into the rapidly moving waters of the brook, would that mean that everything would go on as usual?

Natasha shook her head to clear it of the fanciful drift her thoughts were taking. Peter's letter had been all too illuminating about the plans he had set in motion from faraway France, plans that were well under way even as she sat here trying to force acceptance upon her unwilling senses.

For the plain truth was that she did not wish to go to London to dwell among strangers. She did not wish to plunge into the social life of the city. The social life of the country suited her very well. She knew every living soul on her brother's estate from old Grandfather Morestem, a toothless wizened nonagenarian with a tongue still as sharp as a razor, to the newest inhabitant, a baby girl who had put in an appearance just three weeks ago during the last snowstorm of the winter. She had been the first visitor to the cottage the day after the birth, bearing gifts of food from the big house and a soft woolen shawl knitted by Great-aunt Mary for the baby.

She appreciated Peter's concern for the lack of companions of her own age, but it had always been thus. Springbrook Hall was fairly isolated, and she had only once had one female friend in any case. That friendship had perforce been interrupted when Susan had married and left the area three years ago. It had been a wrench, and Peter's long absences left a terrible gap, but while her grandmother had lived, Natasha had never felt a need for companions of her own generation. And in the last two years there had been Rupert and the children.

Rupert Carteret. As an image of their cousin came into her thoughts, Natasha shifted her weight uneasily on the shawl, which did nothing much to reduce the discomfort of the uneven ground beneath her. Peter's disclosure with respect to Rupert had come as an unwelcome surprise, not to say shock, but honesty compelled her to admit that she had not been quite so comfortable in Rupert's presence just lately. Their acquaintance had begun on her father's death and had progressed rapidly (but not too rapidly, for Rupert was a man of deliberate habits) from formal cordiality to a genuinely warm alliance as Natasha made friends with his motherless children and helped ease their adjustment to a new home in the dower house of Springbrook. She and their father had dealt together on the easiest of terms as he began to fill in some small degree the place left by Peter's absence. He relied on her intimate knowledge of her brother's tenants in smoothing the takeover of the estate management, and Natasha had good cause to be grateful for his conscientious performance of unaccustomed duties. Theirs had been a pleasant partnership on behalf of the absent owner and a personal friendship that she had taken for granted.

It struck Natasha all of a sudden that she was already

thinking of her relationship with their cousin in the past tense. Her first impulse was to blame her brother for spoiling matters, but long habits of disciplined thought instilled in her by her father made nonsense of such wayward emotional reactions. The truth was that the situation here had been inexorably changing and Peter's letter had merely defined it in a way that demanded her reluctant acceptance. She had noticed an added warmth in Rupert's manner toward her of late that made her faintly uncomfortable.

And how had she dealt with her observations? By refusing to acknowledge or examine them with her intelligence, that's how! Her father would have roundly condemned as moral cowardice such tactics to avoid possible embarrassment. She had hoped, of course, that by ignoring the signs of a growing attachment on Rupert's part she might avert a declaration that would require her to wound him. For all her fondness for her cousin and his children, she knew herself unwilling to succeed to the place vacated by his dead wife. Without ever having formed a mental picture of the man she would marry one day, she wished to feel more for her husband than lukewarm affection and a mild desire to be of service. This mixture of undifferentiated irritation and anxiety that was churning in her bosom at present must be the result of a guilty knowledge that her nature was not unselfish enough to enable her to make of herself a willing sacrifice in a worthy cause.

Peter's prompt action in refusing Rupert's request had removed the burden of inflicting pain from her shoulders but not, as he himself had suspected, the resultant awkwardness of her situation at home. Even if Rupert never opened his lips on the subject the awareness of it would lie between them from this moment. Fortunately, if she read his character correctly, his sense of propriety was so strong she need have no concern that he'd continue to press his suit when she attained her majority this summer. Although she didn't question the sincerity of his sentiments, she doubted if his feelings for her went very deep. Two years' opportunity to observe their cousin as he went about his work and among his children had shown her an estimable man who took his duties seriously, one who was moderate in all his emotions and prudent rather than passionate in his affections. Her own sense of guilt must be alleviated by this knowledge.

A slight chill shivered through Natasha's body. The sun's rays were not entirely adequate this early in spring. A strange disinclination to get on with the day slowed her movements as she struggled to her feet and bent to retrieve the shawl. Its warmth across her shoulders was comforting and she lingered by the stream watching the rippling waters with wistful pleasure until a dog's insistent barking brought her mind back to the present. Her eyes remained on the dancing iridescence for another second or two until her ears and then her mind recognized the distinctive bark-whine of her great-aunt's small terrier, Frisky. The little scamp must have followed her, though she had not been aware of his presence when she had left the house in a great hurry to read her letter.

With a sigh of resignation Natasha left the sunny stream bank and reentered the coppice to search for her aunt's pet. As she suspected, he had come to grief among the thorny bushes, and his frantic exertions to free himself had been entirely unavailing.

"Yes, yes, I realize you are happy to see me, you perpetual nuisance," she scolded, trying to fend off the pup's exuberant greetings while she worked to extricate his paw from the spiny branches. "When will you learn that you are a lap dog, not a hunting dog? You've been chasing rabbits again, have you not? Don't you know that no self-respecting rabbit would allow himself to be caught by such a foolish animal as you?"

Frisky's sharp bark-whine noisily refuted this charge.

"Quiet!" Natasha ordered in firm tones. "How can I free you if you keep wriggling? *Ouch!* There, see what you have done? Now I've scratched my finger on your behalf. Thank you, I appreciate the thought, but I'd prefer you not to lick my wounds," she added, succeeding at last in releasing the pup's paw. She was scooping him into her arms when a voice behind her spoke.

"Need any help, miss?"

"Goodness, you startled me!" Natasha came to her feet and spun around in one swift motion to find a strange young man smiling at her in a fashion that caused a slight prickling of the hairs on her arms. His teeth were brilliantly white in an olive-complexioned face and curly black hair fell over his broad brow in a careless manner that would no doubt excite much admiration among the girls in the village.

"No, thank you," she replied politely, bending to rescue the shawl that had fallen from her shoulders during her efforts to free the dog, who now lay quiescent in her arms.

Lithe as a cat, the young man swooped on the shawl and had dropped it over her shoulders before she could straighten up again. She ignored the familiar squeeze his hands administered to those same shoulders during the process, moving away with what she hoped was a casual turn as she headed back through the trees to the path.

"Thank you," she murmured with automatic civility, disquieted but unsurprised to find the stranger still beside her as she walked with a lengthened stride. She was aware of the appraisal in those bold black eyes of his, aware too that since the curtailment of her dancing lessons on her grandmother's death she had gained a few pounds and that her old cotton dresses stretched rather tightly across her breasts these days. None of her instinctive uneasiness was permitted expression on the impassive features she turned toward his as he spoke again.

"That was a mighty cool thank-you just now, I'm athinking, missy."

"Yet adequate to the service performed, you will agree," she returned pleasantly, quickening her step a trifle.

"Well, now, I'm not certain that I do agree. A kiss would be a much warmer thank-you."

Natasha feigned obliviousness to the hint of coercion beneath the wheedling tone and maintained her air of cool unconcern. "It would, of course, but apart from being excessive to the occasion, would also be totally inappropriate between strangers."

"Ah, but we're not going to remain strangers for long, missy." The strong fingers that seized her arm, stopping her progress, did not relax when the dog she was holding bared his teeth. "Quiet, you," he commanded sharply, and the incipient growl degenerated into what Natasha in her exasperation could only deem an ingratiating whine.

"Since you are not of a mind to volunteer a proper payment, I reckon I'll just have to collect my own reward." The man's perfect teeth were very much in evidence as he came closer to carry out his threat.

Natasha managed to subdue her natural annoyance and trepidation at the situation, keeping her expression serene despite the firm pressure of calloused fingers imprisoning her chin. Her eyes never shrank before the masculine triumph illuminating the boldly handsome face approaching hers as she reverted to his earlier statement. "You are correct that we are not destined to remain strangers if you are, as I suspect, the new groom at Springbrook Stables."

The black eyes nearing hers narrowed at her words, and the pressure on her jaw relaxed somewhat as a slight wariness entered his manner. "Now, just how would you be knowing who I might be? I haven't even been nigh the village yet."

"I don't come from the village. I am Miss Phillips of Springbrook Hall."

"The *devil*, you are!"

Natasha, taking advantage of his initial chagrin to slip out of his grasp, had no difficulty in interpreting the expressions racing across her antagonist's face, and to a certain extent she could even sympathize with his plight. It struck her from the shocked incredulity in the eyes that raked her person that much of the blame for the unsavory episode could be laid at her own door. With a wry twist to her lips she acknowledged mentally that she did not present the appearance of a Miss Anybody from Anywhere in her faded, outgrown gown, utilitarian shawl, and worn half-boots. In her haste to leave the house she hadn't bothered with a hat, and her unmanageable hair was, as usual, escaping from the inadequate confinement of braids and pins.

"A thousand pardons for my familiarity, Miss Phillips," declared the groom, who had himself well in hand by now, though those black eyes still snapped wickedly. If there was an element of mockery in the graceful bow he swept her, Natasha thought it expedient to ignore it. "Michael O'Rourke at your service, ma'am. May I carry the little dog for you?"

At her service perhaps, but far from servile, concluded Natasha, declining his offer civilly. Together they walked the rest of the way through the stand of trees in a silence seething with unspoken thoughts. It was probably a moot point who was the more eager to bury the late incident in decent oblivion, though Natasha, stealing a look at the arrogant profile of the vital figure beside her, had a sneaking suspicion that amusement was greater than embarrassment in her companion's reaction.

They parted shortly thereafter when her path took her around the side of the house and he branched off toward the stables. His reply to her formal wish that he should find his life at Springbrook congenial was politely acknowledged and contained nothing she could label familiarity. Neither did it contain a trace of servility. There was a thoughtful cast to Natasha's features as she watched his departing figure in breeches and top boots striding confidently away before she took up her own path.

A dangerous young man that, unless she was very far out in her reckoning, to the peace of mind and continued innocence of the village maidens. Rupert had been loud in his praises of the new Irish groom's way with the horses, but having had a sample of his way with women, Natasha decided it might be well to drop a hint in the ears of local parents before she left for London. She was under no illusion that she would have been able to prevent him from carrying out his intentions just now had she been other than his employer's sister. The only comfort she could salvage from the incident was the satisfaction of having stood her ground and revealed no fear in the face of his obvious attempts to intimidate her. There was no denying that she had indeed experienced a twinge of fear at the thought of a man's disproportionate strength. It was a new and most unwelcome discovery.

Natasha sighed gustily and stroked the hairy head in her arms. "Perhaps Peter is right, Frisky. It is time I widened my experience of the world, and more than time that I made some acquaintance of a more genteel nature."

A rough tongue on her hand and a wriggle of ecstasy signified the little animal's agreement that the time for change was ripe. As Natasha speeded up her steps to seek out her great-aunt to deliver the news of the imminent changes in her life, she reflected with relief on the growing affection between Aunt Mary and Rupert's elder daughter. Her own departure would mean a number of necessary adjustments at Springbrook, but at least she would have the comfort of knowing her elderly relative would not be entirely bereft of company once she was gone.

2

*A farmhouse outside of Toulouse, France
April 13, 1814*

Before the red-coated officer could swing himself down
from his horse, the door to the farmhouse burst open and a
fresh-faced young man erupted into the yard, grinning
broadly.

"I heard you ride up, my lord—leastways, I figured it
was your lordship again."

"Good news, Walker?"

"Yessir! The major has been conscious since shortly
after daybreak. He's almost like his old self, sir. Claimed
he was starving, first off, and he'd scarcely bolted down
the lot the Frenchie's wife what owns this place cooked up
when he made me shave him, and now he says he's getting
up to go find his unit. I'm right relieved to see you here,
sir. He won't listen when I tell him the doctor's ordered
him to stay put till he examines him again, nor when I tell
him it's rumored the war is over."

"Getting above himself is he, Walker?" A responsive
smile spread across the captain's face as he turned the
bay's reins over to the batman. "He'll listen to me, have
no fear. I'll keep him on his back till the doctor gets here if
I have to give him another concussion to do it. When he
sees this"—holding up the bottle he had been cradling—
"it might not even be necessary to take such stern
measures."

"Very good, sir. I'll just give Fiero here some water if
you like."

The officer, already halfway to the door, waved his
hand in acknowledgment and entered the cool interior of
the farmhouse. He headed directly for the small back room

16

where Major Cameron Talbot had been carried, bleeding and unconscious, after falling in the Easter Sunday battle for Toulouse. The impatient muttering coming from within intensified to a snarl as his footsteps approached.

"Is that you, Walker? God's teeth, you had best not show your ugly face in here unless you have my clothes! Oh, Peter, hello. I thought you were that rascally servant of mine."

Captain Lord Phillips paused in the doorway to survey the scene before him. He had spent a number of anxious hours within these four walls since learning of his friend's fate, and his eyes didn't linger on the dusty boxes and impedimenta of the erstwhile storeroom that had been hastily jammed into corners to make space for the cot in the center, but immediately sought its occupant, who was easing himself back down onto his pillow, his pale face shining with sweat and taut with the effort of controlling the pain such movement cost him.

"Your lungs appear to be in good form this morning, Major," the visitor remarked judiciously, dragging up the room's only chair, a deformed object, every broken slat of which had impressed itself upon his anatomy on previous visits.

A weak chuckle akin to a groan greeted this sally as he cautiously seated himself. "Then they have the distinction of being the only part of my body that could be so described," admitted the invalid. "I'm glad to see you, Peter; I can't get any sense out of that buffleheaded man of mine. Is it true that we won the battle?"

"So we claim, though our losses were high, higher than the French, I shouldn't wonder. In any event, we drove Soult out of Toulouse. It's over."

"The war? There is a peace already?"

Captain Phillips leaned over to restrain the injured man's instinctive efforts to rise onto his elbow. "Napoleon has abdicated. Colonel Cooke arrived with the official dispatches during the big dinner Nosey gave at the Prefecture in Toulouse last night."

"Abdicated? When?"

"On the sixth. Cooke left Paris at midnight on the seventh. I'll wager the white cockades will be out in force at the theater tonight. It seems Fat Louis will get his crown, after all."

Major Talbot paid no attention to this frivolous comment. "The sixth," he repeated, bitterness edging his tones. "Then the war was already over when we fought on Sunday. My God, the waste!" He lapsed into silence, staring past his friend, reliving a soldier's private agony at seeing comrades fall in battle, the sweat gleaming on his forehead.

"I know the Third was badly decimated," Captain Phillips said sympathetically. "It's being said Picton disobeyed Wellington's orders to feint and pressed on ahead."

"The general saved a lot of lives by disobeying orders at Vitoria when we took the bridge at Mendoza instead of waiting for Lord Dahousie to arrive," Major Talbot riposted in quick defense of his commander.

"Of course," the other agreed. "When have there not been costly errors and miscalculations during an action? We all know victory and defeat often hinge on the pettiest of accidents. Like it or not, it has to be accepted that all the careful planning in the world can be overset by some unforeseen mischance. But what of you, Cam?" he inserted, bringing the conversation back to the personal. "The doctor was more concerned over the knock on your head than your shoulder wound, though the ball was in deeply enough in truth."

For the first time a faint smile trembled briefly on the lips of the man on the makeshift bed. "The Scots are a hardheaded race, even half-Scots, ye ken, but I don't mind admitting that I'm not precisely in prime twig at the moment."

Captain Phillips, scrutinizing the weary face beneath him, knew that for a classic understatement. The hint of austerity in his friend's finely chiseled features was heightened by the discomfort he was bearing, and his habitual pallor was intensified. Difficult to remember that

Cam was half-Scot. There was nothing about him of the rawboned, high-colored aggressiveness so characteristic of His Majesty's Highland troops. Though possessed of a strong pair of shoulders and a taut well-muscled body, he stood an inch or two below Peter's own six-foot stature, carrying his supple frame with an indolent grace that belied a quick and active intelligence. Only the clear green eyes and a touch of red in the brown hair betrayed his Scots ancestry—physically, that is. Now that he came to consider it, there was more than a bit of the Puritan about Cam. In the midst of a general licentiousness spawned by wartime conditions, he remained true to a rigorous standard of personal conduct and demanded similar self-control from the officers and men under his command. It said much for his qualities of courage, leadership, and loyalty to his men that they remained devoted to him, taking a perverse satisfaction from serving under such a strict disciplinarian. A man couldn't ask for a better comrade in war or peacetime, Captain Phillips acknowledged to himself, though his affection for his friend was scarcely apparent in his laconic speech.

"You'll mend," he predicted with cheerful callousness. "You're too mean to die in bed. And to speed up the healing process, I have brought with me today a bottle of the finest French champagne, liberated from our late enemy and saved for just such an auspicious occasion." He reached behind his chair for the bottle he had placed there on settling himself and produced it with a theatrical flourish that brought a smile to the green eyes watching him from the cot.

Hearing Walker without, Captain Phillips ordered him to fetch glasses from the farmer's wife. He left the man-servant to open the bottle while he assisted the wounded man to a half-sitting position, shoving a rolled-up blanket behind him for support.

"This won't do your aching head any good, but it'll do wonders for your spirits," he promised, handing his friend a glass. He raised his own.

"To victory."

"To peace," amended Major Talbot.

Captain Phillips shot him a quick look before lowering his eyes to his glass, where they remained for a few seconds after he had savored the first taste of champagne. "As to that," he began, shattering the appreciative silence, "I fear it will be a while yet before I shall be able to drink to peace." He glanced across at his friend, whose expression became alert.

"America?"

Captain Phillips nodded. "I would say it is almost certain. The last time I was in Fuenterrabia to visit some of my men in hospital the rumors were flying around. The War Office feels Jonathan wants a drubbing. Our former colonists are getting too big for their breeches. What about you, Cam? Will you sell out? That shoulder will be some time healing."

The injured man shifted position, grimacing as the motion jolted the shoulder strapped tightly to his body. "I have had my fill of fighting, and I'm sick to death of dirt and poverty. It's been four years since I was last home. I long to see an English spring, or what's left of it. Yes, I'll go as soon as I'm allowed to travel."

Neither man spoke for a time, hindered perhaps by the suddenness and enormity of the change about to take place. Long years of traveling with the army, often under deplorable conditions of privation and exposure, had bred a camaraderie that was strong and satisfying and would be much regretted. Each had seen close friends cut down swiftly in battle with no opportunity for farewells, but farewells came no easier now that there was time aplenty. They drank again and their eyes met and slid away, aware of the inadequacy of words at such a moment, but still seeking some that would ease the awkwardness. Captain Phillips cleared his throat.

"I would, if I may, beg a service of you when you reach England."

"Anything," promptly declared his friend.

"Perhaps you'd best hear me out before you volunteer so rashly. You are aware, I think, that I have a young sister who has been living on my estate."

"I am aware that you receive a lot of letters written in a feminine hand that you claim are from your sister."

"And so they are, worse luck. Not but what I'm glad enough to have any letters over here to remind me there are places where people can live without fearing an army will appear on their doorstep one day." Noting the other's sudden stillness and recalling that he seemed rarely to receive any correspondence, Captain Phillips hurried on.

"My father died the winter we took Ciudad Rodrigo. I remember I got back here just in time for the finish, but a deuce of a time I had of it getting leave at all. The Peer let me go only because I had to arrange for someone to manage my inheritance or sell out on the spot. That was the last time I was home. Tasha's had a pretty thin time of it since and I—"

"Tasha?"

Captain Phillips grinned at his friend's puzzled expression. "My sister—for Natasha—we had a Russian grandmother. *She* died last spring, and now the cousin who's running the estate for me wants to marry Tasha." He fell silent.

Major Talbot, having noted the exasperation in his comrade's voice, waited for him to resume, which he soon did.

"The man's a good enough sort, but he's already been married, has three children to prove it, and is nearly forty. My sister is only twenty and hasn't even had a London Season yet. Not that she ever complains, mind you, Tasha's not that sort. She can always find something that needs doing about the property. She probably could have managed the place herself, but she had enough responsibility during our grandmother's final illness without carrying that burden too."

"I take it your sister doesn't wish to marry her widowed suitor?"

"Of course not! And he isn't a suitor at all. I will say for him that he had the decency to apply to me for permission before speaking to her."

"As well as the damned effrontery to think of her at all," put in the major slyly.

Captain Phillips' expression grew sheepish as he realized that his grudging praise had failed to conceal his indignation at the situation. "Yes, well, at least it made me take stock and do some planning for Tasha's future. The first thing was to arrange for her to make her bow to society this spring, no easy matter, I can tell you, when one is as short of relatives as we are, at least of the kind who could be of any use in this matter. I had to cudgel my brains to dredge up a cousin of my mother's who lives in London. A regular harridan from what I remember, but she has the entrée everywhere. She's a widow in reduced circumstances since her husband turned up his toes."

"Which should operate in your favor."

A grim little smile played about his friend's lips as he nodded. "Metternich could take lessons from Cousin Edwina in negotiating. I had to agree to underwrite all the expenses of her own daughter's come-out too—a flat sum with no accounting due—before she would consent to take Tasha under her wing. I was prepared to outfit the girl for the Season on a par with my sister as a matter of course, but the old witch held me to ransom. If she doesn't break out with a new carriage and four and have her entire house redecorated from cellar to attics with what she screwed out of me, you may call me a Chinaman. It goes against the grain with me to enrich the old harpy by so much as a groat, but she had me in a cleft stick—and she knew it. In appealing to her womanly sympathy, of which quality I should have recalled she was woefully short, I committed the error of letting her see how anxious I was to get Natasha out of Devonshire this spring. That woman has the soul of an East India merchant cloaked in pious platitudes."

"And yet you would have her take charge of your sister?"

"What choice have I if Natasha is not to languish another year in the country? She's older than most of the girls already. It's more than time she was settled. And that's where you come in."

Increasing wariness had become naked alarm in the eyes

of the man on the cot. "Oh, I say, Peter, dear fellow, you know I would do anything in the world for you, but—"

"Lord, I don't expect you to *marry* the girl!" exclaimed Captain Phillips as comprehension dawned. "Don't be such a gudgeon. Tasha won't lack for suitors. She's not enough of an heiress to attract the gazetted fortune-hunters, but she's well-dowered, and London is going to be as full as it can hold of Peninsular heroes this spring if I'm any judge. I'd just like you to keep me apprised of anyone who looks like winning her confidence. And perhaps head off any of the less savory sort."

"But surely your cousin will not permit any acquaintance that is likely to be harmful to your sister."

"She no longer has a husband who is likely to hear things of that nature at the clubs. Besides, my sainted Cousin Edwina won't care a fig what happens to Tasha so long as she don't cause any scandals that rebound on her or her daughter."

"Is . . . is your sister likely to cause any scandals?"

Captain's Phillips' bright-blue eyes twinkled with amusement at his listener's obvious discomfort. "Not knowingly. Tasha's not spoiled or headstrong. She's not one of your proud beauties who can't bear to be eclipsed and so must play all sorts of female games with their suitors; she's too genuine for that. But," he went on more slowly, seeking words to describe his sister to his wary friend, "she's impulsive and warmhearted, her instincts are to aid the underdog, no matter how undeserving, and damn the consequences to herself. She's not addlepated, she's extremely commonsensical, in fact, and a shrewd judge of character, but she has practically no experience of the sort of people who inhabit the so-called polite world. I'd be surprised if she didn't fall into a scrape or two, given her temperament. That's why it will relieve my mind tremendously if you will keep a brotherly eye on her for me. You *will* be fixed in London for a time, will you not?"

"Yes, my estate is let until the fall. Naturally, you may count on me to do everything in my power for Miss

Phillips, but I must warn you I am not much of a hand with the ladies. She may not take to me."

Miss Phillips' brother hooted at this. "I haven't noticed any conspicuous lack of success with the ladies of Lisbon or Madrid."

"It's different with women of that stamp, of course. After weeks of marching and camping, often in the worst of conditions, to say nothing of the actual fighting, I sometimes feel I'll go mad or turn into some kind of insensate animal. At least a woman, any woman, talks of something other than war. It restores one's sanity just to look at them, to feel their softness."

"You've done more than look," put in his friend dryly.

"Sometimes. One isn't a saint, after all, but it means nothing, and that's not something to be proud of either."

Watching the tide of red recede from his comrade's cheeks as he made these admissions, Captain Phillips reflected, not for the first time, that Cam Talbot was a far cry from the typical soldier. He didn't possess that useful knack of living from day to day with the senses alert and the mind suitably subdued. He persisted in thinking, in trying to reconcile what was happening around them with some higher moral or intellectual rationale. Small wonder he suffered more than most from the cruel madness that was commonplace in wartime. In four years he hadn't grown a protective shell to enable him to live comfortably armored from the immediacy of the prevailing lunacy.

The two years' difference in their ages was the wrong way about; *he* felt like the elder. It struck him anew how little he had actually learned of Cam's previous life, of the factors that had bred in him the reserve and reticence that kept even good friends at a distance.

"We are what we are," he said, shrugging off any philosophical ramifications. "These women know what they are about. We don't take advantage of them, the other way around, I often think. And fundamentally they aren't so very different from their respectable sisters either—in their basic natures, I mean," he amended as Major Talbot seemed about to enter a caveat. "You have no need to mistrust your ability to deal smoothly with a set of tonnish London females. There's no fault to be found with your manners or your conversation. And remember, lad, most women have a soft spot for a redcoat. A temporarily stiff arm, acquired in a suitably heroic fashion, will do you no harm with the gentler sex either,'' he added with cheerful cynicism, noting with satisfaction that Talbot was smiling, albeit unwillingly, at his nonsense.

Peter extracted himself from the dilapidated chair and refilled their glasses. "To the ladies—God bless them all,'' he intoned, downing two-thirds of his champagne in one gulp. A memory nudged him and he spoke with all the impulsiveness previously attributed to his sister.

"When you first came out here I seem to recall hearing that you were betrothed. Obviously you got along with at least one female. What happened in that quarter, or shouldn't one ask?''

In the following uncomfortable seconds Peter concluded that one shouldn't, but eventually the man on the cot, unsmiling now, reported, "Shortly after I arrived out here I was wounded by a lucky shot from a French vedette while leading a scouting party. I had gotten separated from my men, who subsequently found my horse a long way from where I had fallen down a steep incline. At least that's what the Portuguese peasant who found me deduced. I don't remember anything about the incident; in fact, I didn't know my own name for weeks. The Portuguese got me onto a mule and took me to his house, and he and his wife somehow kept me alive until the wound healed and my memory returned.''

Cam's fingers absently traced the path of a scar at his temple. "I was reported missing, you may recall. By the time I had recovered and the official accounts had been corrected, Priscilla had married someone else. She was—is —extremely beautiful, and there were any number of hopeful candidates flocking around her when she accepted me. I heard later that she married one of them, which was only to be expected.''

Any thoughts that occurred to Captain Phillips on the nature of the lady's constancy, he kept to himself, merely offering with understandable awkwardness, "I'm sorry, Cam; I never knew the story at the time. For that matter, I scarcely knew you then, either."

"No one knew the story, including me. I found out when her father returned my letters several months later. I never told anyone the details, just allowed the engagement to be forgotten."

"So you have nothing much to go home to. I know you have no immediate family. Do you have any plans?"

"Well, I've thought since I've become involved with this war that I might like to go into the Foreign Office. My uncle is a crony of Castlereagh's. I'll go to see him once I'm settled in England."

"Meanwhile, you have taken a huge weight off my mind by agreeing to look after Tasha. I want to see her happily established in a home of her own."

"You are very fond of your young sister, I collect."

"Oh, yes. Tasha and I have always been great friends despite an age gap of nearly seven years. There were just the two of us, you see. She always wanted to do everything I did, and I must say she kept up fairly well for a girl. She even joined me in studying under my father's direction, and when I went off to Cambridge, she continued with him. My father was always more scholar than landowner, and he wasn't best pleased when I went into the army without taking my degree. Said I was a useless fribble and mourned that Tasha should not have been his son."

"She sounds a rather unusual girl."

Hearing a certain reserve in his friend's tones, Peter laughed with real amusement. "Well, I must admit she's not just in the common style of females, but you'll like my little sister," he predicted. "Everyone does. You won't be able to help yourself." The flashing smile that lit up his face was very much in evidence as he admitted, "It has relieved my mind enormously to know Tasha will have at least one real friend in London."

3

London, England
May 20, 1814

Major Cameron Talbot, late of his majesty's forces in the Peninsula, strolled down a city street leading to one of the residential squares developed in the last quarter of the previous century, his gaze seeking number thirteen in a row of nearly identical terrace houses of gray brick. On spotting an acquaintance, he doffed his hat, an elegant gray beaver purchased just last week from Messrs. Lock of St. James's Street, hoping he did not look as self-conscious as he felt in the still-unfamiliar civilian attire he had been at pains to acquire during the fortnight since his return to England.

The smile with which he had exchanged pleasantries faded from his lips and his eyes sobered as he proceeded on his way to Mrs. Taylor's residence to fulfill his promise to Peter. To begin to fulfill the promise, he amended, uneasily aware that he could not share his comrade's confidence that he and the unknown Natasha would become bosom friends. Impossible to explain to a doting brother that a man of nine-and-twenty, newly home from four years of fighting, could have little in common with a young lady enjoying her first London Season, even if the man in question had grown up with a pack of sisters, which was decidedly not the case. His attempts to warn Peter that he was never really comfortable in feminine society had been casually brushed aside by that happy-go-lucky individual. The young baron had the happy facility of approaching the future unencumbered by any anticipation of difficulties, a trait he himself did not possess.

He could foresee all sorts of difficulties, not the least of

27

which was the persona of the young lady he was about to meet. Nothing in Peter's description of his admittedly unusual sister had imbued Cam with a matching confidence that they should become fast friends. Though he had not previously given the matter any serious consideration, he was pretty certain that he much preferred to associate with women of a more traditional bent, like his own mother. When one came to think of it, there was something definitely off-putting about females who invaded the realm of male scholarship, though in this case the blame was clearly to be laid at the door of Miss Phillips' eccentric parent. He must make allowances for an unconventional upbringing, and it went without saying that he would do his duty by Peter's sister no matter how uncongenial he might find her personally.

With this noble resolution taken, Major Talbot found himself in front of number seventeen and was forced to retrace his steps. Number thirteen, a narrow house of three stories like its neighbors, had a black door sporting a shiny brass knocker. Both the door and the iron railing across the area way gleamed with fresh paint, and eyeing them, Major Talbot was reminded of Peter's complaints that his widowed cousin had extorted a sum of money sufficient for the refurbishing of her house from top to bottom. His mood lightened somewhat at this evidence of his friend's omniscience, and there was something approaching a smile in his eyes as he presented his card to the soberly dressed individual who opened the door to his knock. He was invited to follow the butler up the staircase immediately, a likely indication that his name was not completely unknown in this house, although the middle-aged man leading him upward had the quiet assurance of an old family retainer long accustomed to exercising his own judgment in admitting callers.

The front apartment into which he was ushered was occupied by two ladies, who put aside their handwork as he was announced. A quick glance about was sufficient to reveal that this room had also received recent attention; the walls and ceiling were newly painted and some few of the furnishings were recent acquisitions if their air of not quite belonging to the whole was to be credited.

It was equally apparent that the girl he sought was not present, for the two women gazing expectantly at him could only be mother and daughter, so strong was the family resemblance right down to identical expressions of restrained curiosity—or was it suspended judgment?

The elder rose unhurriedly and came to meet him, fingers extended, a polite smile on her lips.

"How do you do, Major Talbot? You see we have already heard of you from dear Peter, who wrote that he had commanded your good services on his sister's behalf."

"The pleasure is entirely mine, ma'am. And Peter had no need to command my services, they were willingly at the disposal of Miss Phillips."

"How very gallant of you. Not that it will be a chore at all. Natasha is such a dear girl at heart, though a trifle ill-at-ease yet in our little circle—most understandable, you will agree, considering she has grown up entirely in the country."

He was spared having to comment on this apparently artless disclosure, since Mrs. Taylor turned at once to her butler to request that Miss Phillips be sent for and refreshments brought up. Her voice was like her appearance: cool, distinct, well-bred, and unrevealing of any emotion. Her natural good looks, which derived more from a regular arrangement of features than any one distinctive asset, had been carefully preserved into middle age and were enhanced by the elegance of her toilette and the assurance that comes with maturity. Of a good height, she carried her beautifully proportioned figure proudly and turned now with a graceful economy of motion to present the visitor to her daughter.

As Major Talbot indicated his pleasure in making the acquaintance of Miss Lucretia Taylor, his initial impression of similarity in the two women was both confirmed and amended. She had her mother's fair hair and coloring, the same light-blue eyes, and long straight nose, but her mouth was softer and fuller and her chin was less decided.

The bloom of youth was on her skin and she was slighter in build than her parent. Though not particularly striking in appearance, Miss Taylor would pass anywhere for a pretty girl. She could not yet hope to equal her mother's presence, but she possessed a deal of countenance for such a young lady. There was nothing in her manner in greeting him that bespoke the shy uncertain miss, a breed he found disconcerting at best. Her voice was well-modulated and she met his glance unshrinkingly.

"Natasha will be here directly," Mrs. Taylor assured him when all three had settled into chairs. "At this time in the morning she is generally to be found in the schoolroom with her two youngest cousins. She is wonderful with the children, quite one of them almost," she added with an amused tolerance before going on to inquire after her male cousin.

"Peter is in fine health and spirits, ma'am, though naturally disappointed not to be present for his sister's Season. He is very grateful to you for accepting the charge of Miss Phillips at this important time," he improvised unblushingly in the interest of promoting good feeling.

"Nonsense," Mrs. Taylor disclaimed graciously. "What are relatives for if not to assist each other in times of need? I should have considered myself a monster of selfishness had I refused to take that poor girl under my wing. She has had so little in the way of feminine companionship or example up to the present. One cannot wonder at it that she is a trifle . . . unusual, but altogether delightful . . . so spontaneous," she added with what sounded to him like trumped-up enthusiasm. Apprehension settled over him like a cloud.

"Do you intend to make a long stay in London, Major Talbot?"

"My future plans are still uncertain, but I shall remain for a couple of months at least."

"Your home is not in London, then?" she probed delicately.

"No, I have an estate in Wiltshire—not a large place," he qualified as if correcting any false impressions that might have arisen. Peter's comments on the avaricious nature of his mother's cousin had alerted him to the wisdom of concealing his own comfortable circumstances if he did not wish to feature prominently in any match-making plans she might be hatching with respect to her charge or her own daughter.

"Do you have any acquaintances in London at present? Or perhaps you are very newly arrived?" inquired his hostess, continuing her polite inquisition.

"I have had the good fortune to meet a number of former friends in the week or so since I landed. I would have called on you sooner had it not been imperative to replenish my wardrobe before I was fit to be seen in a lady's drawing room. You may imagine what a state it was in after four years in the dust, mud, heat, and snow of the Pyrenees," Major Talbot explained, smiling impartially on his audience.

"Oh, but many returned soldiers are seen about the town wearing their uniforms," Miss Taylor put in, speaking for the first time.

"Yes, you need not have scrupled to present yourself to us in uniform," her mother said. "You must regard us as Peter would while you are here."

"And so I might have, ma'am, had I been able to assemble a whole uniform that wouldn't disgrace me," he returned lightly before addressing Miss Taylor, who had been somewhat neglected up till now. "Have you and Miss Phillips been enjoying a busy round of parties and balls?"

"Yes, we go out a great deal, but what I like even better than parties is—"

A slight stir outside the door prevented Miss Taylor's disclosure.

"I'll open that door for you, Chudleigh," declared a husky feminine voice that brought three heads around to witness the stately entrance of the butler carrying a silver tray and that of a young lady who seemed to materialize out of the ether, so quickly did she whisk herself into the room.

"You sent for me, Cousin Edwina?"

Even standing still, the girl seemed to radiate energy. Major Talbot, on his feet for the expected introduction, scarcely heard Mrs. Taylor's conventional phrases as she performed the social ritual. He was staring at the newcomer, hoping his initial reaction had not been evident to anyone present as he struggled to overcome a natural resistance to the idea that this little *dumpling* of a girl could be sister to the slim, long-limbed Captain Phillips, who somehow contrived to maintain an air of elegance even after a day-long battle. It was almost beyond belief that the same two people who produced the fair-skinned, blue-eyed Peter could also have been the parents of this little dab of a girl with her gypsy darkness. To his eye, brother and sister did not possess a single feature in common.

In the next instant after reaching this conclusion, however, he was forced to repudiate it as the girl smiled delightedly on hearing his name. Just so did Peter's smile flash suddenly across his face, changing it out of all recognition.

Major Talbot mastered his emotions and bowed gracefully. "How do you do, Miss Phillips?"

He found his hand gripped firmly and actually squeezed briefly as she wrinkled a small straight nose in protest. "Oh, please, do call me Natasha. Peter has written me about you and warned me that I am to treat you as if you were standing in his shoes. How is he really? He is most maddeningly reticent about himself—he is always fine, his health is perfect, he has not suffered the slightest scratch in any action, et cetera and so on until I could scream with frustration. Oh, and how is your wound healing? Is it this arm?"

The major blinked as the eager words came tumbling out in a torrent that made any response impossible until she stopped for lack of breath. "Yes, my left arm," he said at that point, electing to start at the end. "It is completely healed except for some little stiffness."

She nodded sympathetically. "I thought it must be the left from the way you moved."

"Natasha, my dear, one doesn't make personal references," warned Mrs. Taylor. "Major Talbot will think you very badly brought up."

"Oh, I do beg your pardon, sir. Indeed, I didn't mean to be presumptuous, only that Peter has told me to regard you as his substitute, but . . . but perhaps *he* was presuming too much on your friendship."

As her voice trailed off, Major Talbot took pity on her scarlet-cheeked embarrassment. "Of course it isn't presumptuous of you to regard me as you would Peter," he said reassuringly, though he had been thinking just that until her cousin rebuked her. "It is my earnest desire to be of service to you in whatever way possible."

"Thank you," she said quietly, giving him a searching look from dark eyes that were set on a slight upward slant in a heart-shaped face. She seated herself next to her younger cousin on the settee and repeated, though without the earlier animation, her request for information about her brother's well-being.

The conversation became general once he had minimally satisfied her as to Peter's health and spirits and apologized for having no confirmation of an assignment to America beyond what was rumored when he had taken leave of Captain Phillips almost a month before to sail home from Pasages.

Mrs. Taylor firmly guided the subsequent talk into social channels, checking out mutual acquaintances with an eye, as he was aware, to taking full advantage of his professed desire to be of service to Miss Phillips. That young lady, though her manners could not be faulted, sat beside her cousin in a self-imposed restraint that tried her to the core. He, a stranger, could feel the waves of passionate protest that emanated from her rigid form, and he wondered that her relatives could remain oblivious to the firebrand in their midst. Once again his reluctant sympathy was aroused by her plight. At present he was her sole contact with a beloved brother, and she was constrained by convention from pursuing a singleminded desire to mine him for any scraps of knowledge he possessed that could help renew a bond that absence was withering.

Meanwhile the time limit on a first call was fast approaching, so he shortly took his leave of them, wishing he could both convey understanding and counsel patience with his valedictory smile for Miss Phillips. Something of his intention must have reached her, for he was treated to another of her radiant smiles on his departure.

It was a pensive man who walked back toward St. James's, where he had taken a set of rooms. The English half of him had never credited the claims of second sight common among his mother's people, but from this vantage point his instinctive reluctance to meet Miss Phillips looked like a case of premonition. Not that he cared a fig what the girl looked like, but how could brother and sister be so dissimilar? Of course, the drawling languid Peter, who lounged so indolently around quarters, could when the occasion demanded be roused to quick, definite, and very efficient action, but this sister of his was pure quicksilver and as unlikely to be contained within conventional bounds.

As far as appearance went, Peter was very nearly a dandy, while his sister in her fussy little muslin gown with her black hair escaping from an old-fashioned arrangement of pinned-up braids had seemed positively dowdy in comparison with her well-groomed relatives. It was not that she was unattractive—that quality of intense vitality was arresting if nothing else—but one had the feeling that little thought had gone into her appearance. Those enormous dark eyes in their slanted setting under soaring brows that enhanced the exotic aspect of her heart-shaped face would no doubt have their masculine following, though for his part, he had seen enough dark-eyed beauties to last a lifetime. The typical English style of good looks was a refreshment to his eyes these days. To one who preferred tall, willowy women, Miss Phillips seemed deplorably lacking in the requisite inches, and while it would be unfair and inaccurate to call her plump, one could never term her willowy.

Miss Phillips' looks were a minor consideration in his disappointment or whatever this uneasy feeling was that pricked at his nerves. It was the delicacy of the situation that really bothered him, of course; his was the natural unease of the stranger cast in a role that really belonged to someone of her own blood. His spirits began to revive with the distance he put between himself and his newly acquired "sister." In all probability there would be nothing required of him beyond the expenditure of a certain amount of his time in a manner that he had hitherto not found altogether congenial, but it would not hurt him to do the social rounds for a time. Certainly it would make a change from the drabness of his recent life, and it would be a source of satisfaction to know he was contributing to his friend's peace of mind.

Major Talbot remained uplifted by the knowledge of his own self-sacrifice until his second visit to the Taylor home two days later for the purpose of delivering a number of gifts Peter had entrusted to him.

The occasion began fortuitously enough with his finding Miss Phillips alone in the saloon awaiting the imminent return of her cousins from a morning errand. She put her book down and rose with a glad little exclamation when Chudleigh announced him.

"Major Talbot, how nice to see you. My cousins will return directly, but before they do, I wish you will tell me about the last weeks of the war. Peter leaves me hanging so often in his letters."

Among other specifics he found himself explaining the mechanics of the bridging of the Adur under Sir John Hope, the army's chief engineer, though he could not afterward recall how he had been enticed into such a strange conversation with a female. In the next few minutes he was able to remedy the omissions of their first meeting. She listened with concentrated attention to his account of the last days of the campaign. The impropriety of such a conversation with a young lady did not come home to him until she mentioned that she had been haunted for weeks by Peter's description of the soldiers' using piles of dead bodies for windbreaks as they had huddled down in the intense cold of the night that followed the battle of Salamanca.

"But those horrors are not for a female's ears!" He was aghast that Peter should have reported such details to her.

Her chin went up defensively. "I must differ with you there. Females inhabit the same world you do, and it is foolish to expect that they can go through life wearing blinkers like a cart horse, even if that were desirable. I doubt the ordinary Portuguese and Spanish women were spared the atrocities of this war."

He clamped his teeth on further argument and sought a change of subject, saying as his eyes fell on the large package he had placed beside him on the settee, "Peter has made me the bearer of gifts for you and your cousins. Will you like to open them now?"

She gave him an enigmatic look but reached obediently for the bundle and accepted his clasp knife to cut the string with the crisp motion of one used to handling tools. In the next instant she was entirely feminine, squealing in delight at the beauty of the lace fabric revealed when she removed the wrapping paper.

"How exquisite!" she breathed, lifting the top piece with reverent fingers and releasing the folds. "Is it a scarf?"

"It can be used as a scarf or stole certainly, but the Spanish women wear them on their heads. They call them *mantillas*. The white ones are worn by unmarried girls; Peter sent the black one for Mrs. Taylor."

"How on their heads?" inquired Natasha, lifting the cloud of white lace to drape it across the top of her head. "Like so?"

"No, they are generally arranged over a comb. I believe Peter sent you a couple, also two or three fans so that you may make your cousin a present of one if you wish."

Her hands were rummaging in the package beneath the folds of black lace even as he spoke, and emerged holding a tall comb beautifully carved in an openwork pattern. "How gorgeous! Show me how to arrange the *mantilla* over it—please."

The polite afterthought tacked onto her eager command brought a faint smile to his lips. "They stick the comb in their hair and place the lace over it so that some comes forward to the hairline while most of it falls across the shoulders."

There was no mirror in the saloon. Watching her awkward attempts to afix the unwieldy comb in her hair, Cam said suddenly, "I believe they anchor it rather farther toward the back of the head. Perhaps if you were to stick it in your braid it would hold." He hesitated a second, then took the comb she held out to him and secured it where her hair was thickest. "There!" When she presented the length of lace to him, he accepted it too and draped it as near as he could remember after the fashion of the *señoritas*, arranging the folds evenly about her shoulders with both hands while she stood patiently unmoving in front of him. "There!"

"Really, Natasha!"

The censorship in the cold syllables got through to Major Talbot, who dropped his hands and stepped back quickly, though he could have kicked himself the next moment for behaving as though caught out in some disreputable conduct.

Natasha turned a beaming face to the door and said excitedly, "Cousin Edwina, look what Peter has sent to me from Spain. Is it not beautiful? There is one for Lucretia too, and a black one for you, since you are a married lady." She executed an impromptu pirouette with her hands gracefully outflung to display the effect from the back and then seemed to become aware of a third person in the doorway behind her cousins.

"Oh, Captain Standish, how do you do?"

"Miss Phillips, it is indeed fortunate there are no Spanish ladies present to see how much more becoming the *mantilla* is on you, for they would no doubt set upon you in a jealous frenzy."

Natasha's laughter bubbled up, though she shook her head at such blatant flattery.

Mrs. Taylor frowned repressively at the girl. "I think you might reserve your finery for a more appropriate moment, my dear child." She turned to Major Talbot, whose eyes had narrowed on spotting the tall blond officer resplendent in the uniform of a hussar. "May I make you gentlemen known to each other? Major Talbot, Captain Standish."

In her determination to bring the small assemblage within a conventional social format, she barely gave the men time to acknowledge the introduction before herding everyone into chairs. Miss Phillips lost no time in removing the headdress that seemed to have offended her cousin's aesthetic sensibilities. She sat in demure silence, as near, that is, as one with her very expressive countenance could come to this desirable quality, and spoke when spoken to. The gentlemen made polite noises at each other, discovered some mutual acquaintance among the returned military personnel in the town, and took each other's measure while following Mrs. Taylor's conversational dictums.

Major Talbot was first to propose himself as escort to a party the ladies planned to attend the next evening, an offer that was graciously accepted by his hostess. Not to be outdone, Captain Standish sought the pleasure of undertaking this duty for the Friday-night assembly at Almack's. His petition was unopposed, since the major had neglected to procure a voucher of admission to this hallowed precinct, a mistake he vowed to rectify as soon as possible.

For the rest of the social call Captain Standish devoted himself to entertaining the young ladies while Major Talbot's energies were mainly focused on a study of the captain. This officer, who was some two or three years junior to Major Talbot, was seen to possess a splendid set of large white teeth, which he displayed rather too frequently for the latter's approbation. Though his remarks were addressed impartially to both girls, the caressing light in his fine hazel eyes was reserved for Miss Phillips, who was, in her brother's estimation, well-dowered enough to make her personal qualities of lesser importance than her fortune in some men's eyes. With no knowledge of Captain Standish beyond what a few moments' observation offered, Major Talbot could not dismiss the thought that his unofficial guardianship of Miss Phillips' interests had already begun.

With this in mind, he issued a friendly invitation to the captain to walk along with him when they left the Taylor residence. While he was still mentally framing a tactful question to find out how Captain Standish had met Miss Phillips, he was himself asked the same question outright.

"Her brother asked me to look her up." When this flat statement brought no immediate response, he added as one making dutiful conversation, "Is that the way it was with you?"

Captain Standish hesitated a second before admitting he was personally unacquainted with Captain Phillips. He had been presented to Miss Phillips at a ball, and she had right away inquired whether he knew her brother. From what he had seen so far of Miss Phillips' unnervingly direct style, Major Talbot could well believe that was her first question to each new member of the military who crossed her path. A sudden picture of himself vetting every former soldier dallying in London this Season served to depress his spirits thoroughly.

"She's a dashed fine girl," Captain Standish was saying.

"Both Miss Taylor and Miss Phillips appear to be charming young ladies," Major Talbot agreed.

"The cousin's too prim and proper, if you want my opinion. I prefer girls with a bit more life to them, like Miss Phillips. And by Jove, didn't she look a picture in that Spanish getup. What magnificent eyes!"

The major left Captain Standish to the pleasures of his reverie, wishing his own thoughts were half as gratifying. On the one hand, he was fairly certain he could acquit the captain of making a deliberate dead set at an heiress. His admiration for Miss Phillips was patently genuine. On the other hand, this did not automatically make him an eligible suitor. Checking into the officer's background would be his first priority in the next few days, along with equipping himself with a voucher for Almack's. The first would be accomplished in due course by dropping the captain's name among a number of former comrades-in-arms to see what kind of reseponses it provoked, but the other would require a social call on one of the patronesses of Almack's, probably Lady Castlereagh, who had always been well-disposed toward him.

He parted from Captain Standish on the corner of New Bond Street with every evidence of goodwill on both sides, but his own goodwill could not be said to extend to the person for whose benefit all his machinations were intended. After two meetings with Natasha Phillips, he was forced to the reluctant admission that his reaction to her was one of profound irritation. He had not expected to like her but had hoped they could rub along well enough together in the typical superficial manner one developed within a social circle. Had Peter's sister been like Lucretia Taylor, this would have been a reasonable expectation. But Miss Phillips, with her outlandish name and painfully direct nature, seemed incapable of recognizing the accepted social distance. Look how she had inveigled him, of all unlikely people, into arranging that *mantilla* on her head at the exact moment when her chaperon should appear to misconstrue the situation. He had nightmare visions of every rattle in a red coat who preferred females with "a bit of life to them" queuing up to pay court to her. The possibilities for disaster were infinite.

On this gloomy note Major Talbot took himself off to lunch at his father's old club in the soothing company of a set of predictable males. He would banish the incalculable Natasha and her probable followers from his mind until the moment when he would be forced to deal with her in person again.

4

Lizzie, the cheerful parlor maid recently promoted to waiting on the young ladies, fairly bustled about the small back bedchamber, folding and putting away discarded clothing and gathering up soiled linen for the biweekly visit of the laundress. Time was passing and Miss Taylor would be ringing her bell any minute now. Not liking to be rushed in her toilette, she had elected to receive the dresser after the latter attended to her cousin's needs. The arrangement had worked well during the past five or six weeks—since Miss Phillips was not one to dawdle over her dressing—unlike Miss Taylor, who had been known to reject an entire outfit after what should have been a final check in her mirror. Nor did the visitor require much assistance from the maid, preferring to do her own hair, which was a pity, for Lizzie's fingers itched to see what they could make of that lustrous but neglected dark mass.

Tonight was another story, however. Miss Phillips, still in her shift, stood staring into the open armoire where her gowns hung. She hadn't budged a muscle for a full five minutes, long enough to have memorized every ruffle and tuck of every dress, though it was Lizzie's guess that what she was there for had gone clear out of her head by now. The abigail cast a harried glance at the clock on the bedside table and ventured a soft cough.

Miss Phillips started and her eyes flew in turn to the clock. "Oh, heavens, look at the time! I'm so sorry, Lizzie, to have kept you here so long. Do no bother about me, I can manage by myself. You must not keep my cousin waiting."

"Now don't you be in a fret, miss. There's plenty of time to do you up before I go to Miss Taylor. Shall it be the blue dress tonight?"

"I . . . Yes, the blue will do fine, thank you, Lizzie."
Natasha raised her arms while the dress was slipped over
her head, and remained motionless until all the buttons
were done up, instinctively responding to the motherly
note in the maid's voice. Neither seemed to find this odd in
one who was actually a couple of years younger than her
mistress. Unused to city ways, Natasha had found the
accommodating Lizzie most helpful from the first days of
her stay in the Taylor household. It was thanks to her
unobtrusive suggestions that some few gaucheries had been
avoided these last weeks. Now she glanced over her
shoulder and smiled. "Finished? Thank you, Lizzie, I shall
do splendidly now. You hurry along to Miss Lucretia."

The maid bobbed her head, her red curls dancing under
the huge mob cap as she smiled widely, displaying the gap
between her two front teeth. "Your pearls will look a treat
with that dress, miss, or that silver filigree pendant with
the blue stone. Mind you don't forget to do your hair,"
she cautioned as she edged over to the door with reluctant
haste.

"Yes, nurse," Natasha promised impudently.

"Well, your mind is somewhere's else tonight, and
that's a fact, miss," declared the maid, having the last
word as she closed the door behind her.

With a sigh, Natasha conceded the accuracy of Lizzie's
observation as she sat down at the small dressing table that
doubled as a desk, and mechanically began to rebraid her
hair. Before ever leaving Devon she had decided to regard
this visit to London as a temporary interruption in her
ordinary life, an interlude of city living and societal
activities that might provide her with considerable enjoyment so long as she didn't lose sight of her real life in the
midst of temporary pleasures. And if it happened that the
difficulties outweighed the pleasures, she had resolved to
take that in her stride too. She could put up with anything
for a few months, and all experience was to be valued.

This saving attitude had served her well so far. It
enabled her to dwell amicably in her cousin's house,
responding to the surface cordiality and concealing her

instinctive knowledge that she was merely tolerated here, not really liked or welcomed despite Cousin Edwina's invariable practice of prefacing her name with an endearment. Unconsciously, she must have cherished hopes of making a friend of Lucretia, judging by her continuing disappointment that this happy state had not been achieved. Her cousin was unfailingly polite, but she reserved her confidence for her mother. A repeated lack of encouragement from the younger girl had finally cured Natasha of seeking out Lucretia's company. Fortunately, the children's warm acceptance of their new cousin and Lizzie's helpfulness served to redeem the chill atmosphere of the house to a considerable degree.

When would she learn that it did not pay to expect too much of others? Natasha demanded of herself as she jammed another pin into the thick arrangement of braids. She recognized at last the cause of this latest disappointment. She had done it again. Peter had written so enthusiastically of his friend Cameron Talbot that she had allowed herself to hope that he would become her friend also. After two meetings with Major Talbot she had reluctantly abandoned this comforting illusion to which she had been clinging for the past month. He was very kind—she had realized this by his unobtrusive support in the face of Cousin Edwina's little public digs at her—but *au fond*, she sensed the same disapproval of herself in him that existed in this house.

What was there about her that alienated people? She stared despairingly into the glass, seeking an answer. Puzzled, hurt dark eyes stared back. Her looks were rather alien in England, to be sure, but too many gentlemen had indicated their admiration for her coloring for that to be the answer. She was fairly certain that Major Talbot was not among the number of her admirers, though he revealed little of his thinking behind that handsome countenance. She had expected to like him on Peter's recommendation and was most sorry to be unable to do so unreservedly, but his cold correctness was repelling. There was no other word for it. Well, she must simply keep in mind that he was Peter's friend and wished to befriend her despite little natural inclination in her favor. That at least was in *his* favor, that and his extraordinary good looks, she amended, smiling impishly all of a sudden.

Peter had not prepared her for this Adonis with rich red-brown hair and amazing green eyes under a wide intelligent brow. The sculpting of his head was spare and beautiful, and although not quite so tall as Captain Standish, he had a finely muscled body that showed off the tight fashions of the day to great advantage as well as an innate grace that appealed to the dancer in her. If she could not like him wholeheartedly, at least she would derive immense pleasure just from looking at him and be grateful that they were to have such an impressive escort.

With her natural optimism somewhat restored, Natasha rooted through her jewel case for the pendant Lizzie had mentioned. She spared scarcely a glance for her gown as she fastened the chain about her neck. Why bother? She had a half-dozen such gowns, very nearly identical, in all the pale pastels decreed by the fashion arbiters as suitable for a girl in her first Season. Cousin Edwina had nearly jumped down her throat when she had indicated a preference for a length of fabric in a vibrant wood violet shade that they had come upon in one of the shopping arcades. She knew better now but still found the acceptable choices boring in the extreme, at least against her own dark coloring. Lucretia managed to look quite attractive in the pale pinks and blues she always affected. Cousin Edwina had made an amusing little story out of her cousin's mistake that had her friends tittering at the ignorant country mouse. It was possibly not done in a spirit of unkindness, and she had already adopted a "this too shall pass" attitude toward such incidents.

Natasha went downstairs a few moments later, bolstered by the knowledge that if Peter had not produced a friend for his sister, he had certainly conjured up an enviable escort. That should please Cousin Edwina, who had previously bemoaned the lack of any natural protectors available to a widow without grown sons.

Three hours later, Natasha was whirling happily around the crowded ballroom of a large mansion in Grosvenor Square, reflecting with satisfaction on the plural benefits of possessing a presentable escort. Not that she or Lucretia had ever been subjected to the mortification of being long without a partner at a ball, but it was easy to see that girls with brothers or suitors in their train had an initial advantage over the rest in sheer numbers. To the degree that they could manage it, this pool of potential partners was jealously guarded and shared among their intimate friends only. Up to now, Natasha and her cousin had remained outside these charmed circles, but tonight two popular young ladies who had previously limited themselves to smiling bows in passing, though their mothers were on visiting terms with Mrs. Taylor, had made it a point to stop and present their partners to the cousins. In her naïveté, Natasha had later communicated to her cousin her pleasure in what she interpreted as advances toward friendship, whereupon Lucretia had promptly undeceived her with a pitying smile. According to Miss Taylor, their newfound attraction in the other girls' eyes could be summed up in two words—Cameron Talbot.

Though a trifle disconcerted for a moment, Natasha had rallied quickly, more than willing to accept what the gods—and Peter had provided. It had certainly been pleasant to have the first dance bespoken by Major Talbot, whose dancing skill had lived up to her expectations. Pleasant also to have been presented to several of the major's friends, who had promptly solicited dances from herself and Lucretia.

Natasha looked up, her face breaking into laughter at a nonsensical remark of her partner's, and encountered the interested glance of a gentleman in the next set. The contact was broken off immediately as each turned away with the requirements of the dance but not before she realized with a little ripple of curiosity and feminine satisfaction that here was the same man, unknown to her, who had previously caught her eye several times in the course of the evening. She concentrated her attention on her partner's lively conversation and didn't permit her gaze to stray to where she knew the stranger to be, but if the truth were told, she was secretly reveling in the undisguised admiration she had read in his blue eyes. She chuckled at her own vanity but could not deny that the pleasures of knowing one had excited masculine admiration, though fleeting and perhaps valueless, were nonetheless sweet and heady.

Her present partner, Lieutenant Seagrave, was an acquaintance of Major Talbot's and had actually met her brother on one occasion in Spain. He had a rollicking sense of humor and kept her in a constant ripple of laughter throughout the dance. This was turning out to be one of the most delightful evenings she had spent during her stay in London. It was true that once or twice when she was struggling to keep her mirth under some control, she had happened to catch sight of Major Talbot standing under one of the arches formed by a line of columns running down the length of the room. His expression was gravely polite and unrevealing, as was generally the case, but again she sensed an underlying disapproval of herself that had the effect of sending an uncharacteristic surge of reckless defiance along her nerves. What ailed the man? Did he never laugh at a joke? Unconsciously, her small pointed chin lifted as though answering a challenge. She was not going to allow her brother's humorless friend to dampen her spirits on this of all evenings. She slanted him a final look from the corner of her eye and was thus privileged to witness the major's loss of his customary equanimity.

He was standing alone, partly hidden by the pillar, gazing onto the dance floor when a woman walked past him. Natasha saw her glance in his direction and then stop abruptly. She must have spoken to Major Talbot, for he turned quickly and then jerked to a halt, the color draining from his face as he remained motionless with his profile toward Natasha for a fraction of a second longer. She had to turn away herself for the final steps of the dance as he began to move slowly like a man in a dream toward the woman who waited for him in silence. As the music wound down to a close, Natasha saw Major Talbot carry the woman's outstretched fingers to his mouth and release them lingeringly.

"Shall I bring you back to your cousin?" asked her partner.

"I don't see her at the moment, but Major Talbot is just over there, and I believe he is my next partner," Natasha replied shamelessly, curiosity making her tug delicately at her escort's sleeve to direct his steps. He switched direction obediently, and as Major Talbot had his back to them, Natasha was able to study his companion without seeming rude while she and Lieutenant Seagrave strolled up to the pair. That the young woman was well worth studying was instantly apparent even at a distance, for she eclipsed every other female in the room *au fait de beauté*. Tall, ethereally slender and delicately made, she exactly fitted Natasha's mental image of a fairy-tale princess with her shining gold tresses piled high on her head except for one or two ringlets falling over one shoulder. She was speaking in a serious vein to the major, for her lovely features wore a slightly wistful cast that was echoed in grave blue eyes of extraordinary size and brilliance. Natasha's attention remained fixed in fascination on the unknown beauty until Lieutenant Seagrave hailed his acquaintance in hearty tones that caused Major Talbot to start. He gazed on them with eyes in which recognition was slow to dawn.

"Miss Phillips tells me you are slated to be her next partner, sir, so I have brought her to you."

"Partner? Oh, yes, I see. Yes, of course. Thank you." The major drew himself up formally. "Lady Frobisher, may I present Miss Phillips and Lieutenant Seagrave?"

The ladies murmured gently and smiled at each other, Natasha with lively interest and Lady Frobisher with an inexplicable air of sweet sadness, while Lieutenant Seagrave's slightly vacuous countenance took on a look of reverent admiration as he swept the beauty a low bow. The silence that ensued after the formalities might have struck an awkward note had not Natasha offered a comment on the heat of the rooms. Lady Forbisher, who was languidly plying her lace fan, concurred. Major Talbot's conversational talent seemed to have atrophied, and Lieutenant Seagrave's ready tongue must have been struck to the roof of his mouth in admiration. Natasha then summoned up an approving comment on the music, to which Lady Frobisher merely smiled her agreement. Valiantly the younger girl persevered, complimenting the other on her stunning gown. Too late she realized that the all-white costume that so became the golden blond fairness was heavily appliquéd with alençon lace that must surely have been smuggled into England if she had obtained it during the last few years of wartime.

"You are very kind," murmured Lady Frobisher, disposing of that subject with another of her sweet wistful smiles.

Natasha was searching her brain for something to say about the ballroom's decor when rescue arrived in the person of the gentleman who had been watching her all evening. He had approached the quartet unseen and now addressed Major Talbot.

"Well, coz, so we meet at last! Father told me you were back. Accept my felicitations on surviving the war undamaged, or nearly so, if I understood my parent correctly."

Major Talbot's eyes narrowed and his lips compressed briefly, but the recent air of mental vacancy vanished. "How do you do, Charles? Yes, I am, as you see, quite whole."

When he did not immediately launch into an introduction, his cousin, who had already bowed to Lady Frobisher, said smoothly, "Lady Frobisher and I are old friends, of course, coz, but I have not yet the pleasure of this lovely lady's acquaintance, or that of the lieutenant."

Natasha thought she detected a faint hint of reluctance in the major's polite compliance with his cousin's request, but she was too interested in Mr. Charles Talbot to give it more than passing consideration. The cousins were nearly of an age, though she judged Charles Talbot to be slightly younger. To her eye there was no discernible family likeness. Mr. Talbot was shorter and slighter than his relative, with brown hair worn fashionably tousled and merry blue eyes. His countenance was made up of good features that were assembled into a pleasant rather than a distinguished whole, and his style of dress was very unlike that of his military cousin, favoring as he did a more extreme fashion. He wore the correct black-and-white evening ensemble, but his waistcoat was a pale pink rather than the chaste white most men adopted nowadays and his cravat was so wide and intricately tied that even the inexperienced Natasha placed him in the dandy class. A large ruby pin held this creation in place. Another ruby adorned his finger while a third hung on a fob dangling beneath his waistcoat.

Mr. Talbot bent over her hand, his blue eyes caressing her brazenly. "At last we meet, fair lady, after an interminable evening of admiring you from afar. Please say you will dance this waltz that is just striking up with me."

"You are very kind, sir, but I'm afraid this dance is promised to your cousin."

"Oh, but what is a little friendly piracy between relatives?" The irrepressible Mr. Talbot seized her hand. "In addition to which, my cousin and Lady Frobisher have several years of gossip to catch up on. I am persuaded they will shower us with gratitude for our tactful removal from the scene. What about it, coz?"

It was not gratitude that looked out of Major Talbot's green eyes at being placed thus in an untenable position, but no one was to know what his reaction would have been, for Lady Frobisher here intervened to say hesitantly, laying a white hand on his arm and smiling appealingly at Natasha, "If you really would not mind, Miss Phillips?"

"Not at all." Natasha's brilliant smile was all for the other woman as she avoided the major's glance and whirled away in the arms of the quick-footed Mr. Talbot. Before they were swallowed up among the twirling couples, she saw Lieutenant Seagrave excuse himself and walk away from the other two.

Mr. Talbot turned out to be the best partner she had ever had in the waltz. He guided her expertly through a series of intricate turns before the floor became too crowded for such daring maneuvers. As they settled into a more circumspect pattern, he looked at her with triumphant satisfaction. "Your dancing is everything I expected it to be—in a word, perfection."

Natasha smiled up at him. "And yours, sir, far surpasses my more modest expectations."

"We were meant to dance together. It was ordained from the beginning of time."

"You have a rather grandiose idea of our place in the natural scheme of things," she protested laughingly.

"Nonsense, the entire world revolves around us. Just look about you." Since he had slowed their steps down considerably as he spoke, the other couples on the floor were whirling by them.

"Quite literally true," she conceded, dimpling at him.

"Why have I never seen you before tonight? Who are you and how do you come to be acquainted with my worthy cousin, who, to my certain knowledge, has not been back in this country above a fortnight?"

"I am merely a visitor to your city, staying with some relatives for the Season. Major Talbot happens to be a close friend of my brother's. Peter, my brother, asked him to call on us. He did so and very kindly offered his services as escort to my cousins and me tonight. A very simple tale."

"I see. At long last I have something for which to be grateful to my cousin. It's plain as a pikestaff that the fair Priscilla still exerts her fatal fascination over him. The immediate future seems fraught with interest."

"I beg your pardon?" The abrupt change of subject left Natasha confused. "Who is 'the fair Priscilla?' "

Mr. Talbot seemed to recollect himself as he stared down into puzzled dark eyes. "No, I beg *your* pardon for speaking in conundrums. Can it be that you were not aware that my worthy cousin was once betrothed to Lady Frobisher?"

"*No!*" Natasha mastered her initial shock at this piece of news and continued in even tones. "I am really only slightly acquainted with Major Talbot. I know nothing of his personal life." Having done her best to discourage gossip, she proceeded to listen avidly to Mr. Talbot's subsequent explanation.

"About four years ago, just before he was scheduled to sail to the Peninsula, my cousin met Priscilla Fanshawe, as she was then, and was completely taken in by her helpless-little-female-in-need-of-a-protector act. He tumbled into love with her face, which I grant is exquisite if you've no objection to insipidity, and proposed within a sennight. The surprising thing was that she accepted him under such conditions, except that he was, and is, a rich prize."

Natasha did not miss the slight hardening of the light tone in which his narrative had been crouched, but she made no comment, allowing him to take up his tale after they had executed a few more waltz turns.

"The fair Priscilla came to her senses the minute the troop carrier sailed out of sight and accepted Frobisher before it ever reached Portugal, although I believe she set it about that it wasn't until Cam was reported missing and presumed dead that she defected." A malicious little smile appeared on his lips as he said gaily, "That is the end of the story up till now, but I daresay we are just in time for the sequel. The next few weeks should prove most entertaining."

Natasha digested this as they continued to move about the floor in perfect accord as far as the music was concerned. At last she looked into merry and mischievous blue eyes and said quietly, "Your cousin seems an honorable man. I would not expect that he will provide the gossips with much entertainment."

"Wouldn't you? But then you do not know the dramatis personae of this little comedy—or tragedy, as you will. Now *I* expect to be vastly amused. My cousin is, as you say, a man of honor, and Lady Frobisher is a respectable married woman, though hers was no love match. She opted for a title in the hand, if you will pardon such coarseness of expression. If I know anything of the lady's nature, she will employ all her arts of fascination to keep Cam at her side. She won't be able to resist trying to attach such an impressive cicisbeo.''

Natasha was glad that the music came to a halt just then. What had begun as an exhilarating sensual experience had degenerated in the last few moments into a mildly distasteful conversation. She would have preferred to dispense with Mr. Talbot's company altogether, but he insisted on returning her to her cousin. As luck would have it, Lucretia was sitting with her mother, so Natasha was constrained to present her partner to her relations. She left him exercising his considerable charm of manner over them almost at once when her next partner stepped forward to claim her.

Natasha was not to know that Mrs. Taylor was employing her own wiles during this period to find out more about the man Peter had landed on them. Although one or two persons had spoken well of the Talbot family in general, she had not been able to ascertain anything relevant to the major's personal financial position. She had learned that his father had been the younger son, and that Sir Humphrey, the present baronet, though well-connected in government circles, was not believed to possess a great fortune.

Mrs. Taylor found Mr. Charles Talbot much more forthcoming on this delicate subject. She had merely to make an ingratiating reference to his cousin's kindness in putting himself at the disposal of his friend's family for Mr. Talbot to respond carelessly, "Oh, yes, it isn't just his wealth that makes my cousin such a prize on the marriage mart. He'd walk over the proverbial plowshares if duty called. A veritable pattern card of responsibility is my worthy cousin.''

Such frankness did not at all suit Mrs. Taylor's book, especially accompanied as it was by a knowing smile that raised her hackles.

"Indeed,'' she uttered repressively.

Mr. Talbot was not to be repressed so easily. "Yes.'' He

nodded solemnly. "Besides being as rich as Croesus, thanks to having been his Scots grandfather's sole heir, Cam is also the possessor of every manly virtue—I have this on the authority of my own father—and"—he turned to the silent attentive Lucretia—"is thought by most members of the female persuasian to be extremely well-favored personally. Ah, I see you agree with the consensus," he added, noting the blush she was unable to prevent. "In fact," he continued, with an assumption of guilelessness, "the sole disqualifying feature is his avowed disinclination to enter the holy state of matrimony. Once bitten, twice shy, they say. Now if you charming ladies will excuse me, I see an old friend across the room who has been trying to attract my attention. *Au revoir*."

Before the astounded Taylor ladies could recompose their features, Mr. Talbot had bowed with careless grace and walked away.

"Well, what a singular young man, to be sure!" exclaimed Mrs. Taylor in tones of strong disapproval.

"Singularly confiding, I would say."

Mrs. Taylor regarded her daughter thoughtfully. "At least his confidences were to the point. I might have guessed that Peter Phillips would not have made such a point of sending a poor man to befriend his sister. You may depend upon it, he intends Talbot for Natasha."

"Major Talbot may have other ideas on that score."

"Yes, I would not say that he is noticeably taken in by all that wide-eyed interest she affects in every member of the military, which I would rather call forwardness. Major Talbot is a true gentleman, and one of his correct bearing and nice discriminations would naturally prefer a more gently reared female who will not put him to the blush with awkward enthusiasms."

Mother and daughter exchanged a look of perfect understanding before an acquaintance came up to speak to Mrs. Taylor.

The returning party was not nearly so talkative when they assembled to await the arrival of the carriage Major Talbot had hired for the conveyance of his guests.

Natasha's earlier ebullience had abated, though she warmly echoed Mrs. Taylor's expressions of gratitude to their escort.

After civil inquiries into the ladies' comfort, the major initiated no conversation and replied rather absently to Miss Taylor's tentatives remarks on the success of the ball, so that she too lapsed into a silence that lasted until they entered Manchester Square. Mrs. Taylor then reiterated their gratitude and, as the major handed down the ladies from the carriage, issued a general invitation to him to consider himself always welcome in her house. While Major Talbot bowed and responded appropriately, Lucretia ventured to inquire if they would see him at Almack's on Friday. His affirmative reply elicted smiles from Mrs. and Miss Taylor and a quick speculative look from Natasha before final good-nights were uttered all around.

5

The ball in Grosvenor Square marked the beginning of what almost seemed a threefold increase in social engagements for Mrs. Taylor's charges. Where before they may have spent two or three evenings a week at home, now there were times when they had to choose between two or three invitations for a certain date. And it was not just in the number of evening parties that there was a noticeable increase. The girls found their circle of intimates among other girls making their come-out widening also, which meant more daytime calls, enlarged shopping expeditions, and group excursions to beauty spots like the gardens at Kensington Palace. As June advanced, bringing better weather with it, Natasha and Lucretia enjoyed their first al fresco breakfast party on the wide terrace of an old property that sloped down to the busy Thames. Each week a number of eligible gentlemen sought their company, singly or together, for drives in the park at the fashionable hour; in short, the cousins were everywhere to be seen at the height of that busy London Season.

This geometric increase in social activity was not accompanied by a corresponding increase in contentment as far as Natasha was concerned. She was aware, of course, that the upswing in their popularity was due in large measure to their association with Major Talbot, whose social consequence was obviously enormous, far beyond what Peter could have anticipated when he had requested that his friend act as his sister's unofficial guardian. Natasha's gratitude for finding herself dwelling under the mantle of his magnificence was strongly tempered by what she perceived as an unsatisfactory relationship obtaining with the major. They were no closer to becoming friends than on the day of their first meeting, though a week never passed with fewer than four or five encounters, if one included those of a purely accidental nature. His manner toward her was still as formal as if they had met yesterday, and Natasha, when she remembered to do something so alien to her nature, was careful to maintain a distance on her side also. Not if her life depended upon it would she put herself in the position of having a third request to call her by her Christian name ignored, though she and his cousin had gotten upon first-name terms almost at once. She sensed no abatement in the major's inexplicable disapproval of her, though on consideration, "inexplicable" was very likely an imprecise term, since she was fairly certain a significant proportion was directly attributable to her advancing friendship with Charles Talbot.

The coolness between the Talbot cousins had not escaped Natasha's perception. Charles was possessed of an irreverent and amusingly acerbic wit at all times, but he reserved his most acidulous tones for the seeming tributes he paid to his cousin's probity, the quiet preciseness of his dress, and the nicety of manner that did not permit him to rid himself of bores in an expeditious fashion. Major Talbot said nothing at all about his cousin for the ears of his friend's sister, but it had gradually dawned on her that the most effective means of bringing herself to the major's notice was to engage in a lengthy tête-à-tête with Charles Talbot at some social affair or other. If he didn't invite her to dance himself, he appeared with an acquaintance in tow who was desirous of being presented to her. Natasha would have been considerably amused by these transparent tactics designed to curtail the time she spent with Charles had there not existed within her a little residue of hurt that her conscientious guardian's interest was solely attributable to his sense of duty to her brother. She had so wished to regard Peter's friend as her own.

Major Talbot's attentions to the young ladies in Manchester Square were regular but strictly impartial. Not the most lynx-eyed of the tabbies who prided themselves on being first to spot the various attachments being formed among the younger set each Season could detect a shade of distinction in his attitude toward the cousins. If this was disappointing to Natasha, she quickly realized it was equally so to Lucretia. The two girls had never been confidantes, but Natasha's powers of observation were keen and she was not unaware of the subtle stratagems by which Lucretia contrived to remain always within the major's orbit. She availed herself of every opportunity to engage him in private conversation within a social grouping and ended up sitting by his side in the carriage more often than not. The girl was attractive and conversable with a good understanding. She was musically accomplished, and her well-bred manners, though a trifle formal, were such as must universally please. Natasha privately thought she would be much improved by an infusion of a little human warmth, but the major was a cool reserved person himself, and she might have wished her cousin good hunting had she not discovered that her relatives were not above engaging in deceitful practices to secure their ends.

At least once a week Major Talbot punctiliously invited the girls to drive with him in the park. On one such occasion early in their acquaintance he had observed Natasha's wistful sigh when a mixed party of riders passed them heading for the Row.

"Would you like to ride with me sometime?" he had inquired solicitously at a moment when Miss Taylor happened to be monopolized in conversation by the occupants of another carriage that had paused beside the major's barouche. "I would be most happy to procure hacks suitable for a lady."

Natasha had glowed with pleasure at the promise of some real exercise until she recollected that the city-bred Lucretia did not ride. Concealing her disappointment as best she might, she had regretfully declined his invitation. "I'm afraid my cousin does not ride, sir. It would not be seemly of me to engage in an activity in which she may not participate."

Major Talbot had accepted her refusal with an

approving comment. That was actually the sole occasion upon which Natasha felt she had ever aroused his approval.

A week or so later during a dance at Almack's he had expressed a formal regret that she had been unable to join her aunt and cousin in a drive to Kensington with him that afternoon. "I understand you were already promised to Captain Standish for a drive," he remarked.

"Why, yes, I did drive out with the captain today, but I do not recall any mention of a trip to Kensington," she had replied, meeting his eyes, a puzzled frown in her own.

"Do you not? I daresay you ladies receive so many invitations a few must be declined of necessity."

"Well, yes, of course, but I still do not recall hearing—"

"It is of no significance whatever," he had said dismissively, but Natasha had been left with an odd conviction that he did not believe her.

The obligations of the dance drove the incident from her mind until later, when riding home in the carriage the major had put at the ladies' disposal, she had recollected it and declared impulsively, "Major Talbot told me you drove to Kensington with him today, Cousin Edwina. I do not remember hearing talk of such an excursion."

There was a short pause before Mrs. Taylor said smoothly, "It must have slipped your mind, my dear girl—not surprising, I declare, with scores of invitations arriving every week."

Natasha had had her lips open to protest that in order for something to slip one's mind it had to have been there at some prior time, when a clear recollection of herself passing on Captain Standish's invitation just yesterday to Lucretia popped into her head. Her cousin had demurred, saying she had some personal tasks to perform and urging Natasha to go without her, since it was her company the captain obviously desired. She had even laughed about not wishing to play gooseberry.

For the second time that evening Natasha became the unwilling recipient of a full-blown intuitive conviction. Lucretia had lied to her yesterday. Unless Major Talbot's offer had been extended sometime today, which was highly unlikely, her relatives—or at least her young cousin, with her mother's tacit approval—had willfully concealed the invitation so that Lucretia might enjoy the major's company under more private circumstances than was generally possible.

Natasha wondered dispassionately if her cousin had found her deception rewarded by an advance in friendship, but she was of the opinion that Lucretia was throwing her cap over the windmill in attempting to attract Major Talbot's romantic interest. Although the Taylor ladies had been presented to Lady Frobisher, they had not had any sustained conversation with the beauty and could not be expected to know of her past relationship with the major. Natasha, with more knowledge and thus more inclination for observation, was fairly certain that Major Talbot was still emotionally enslaved by the lovely and unattainable Priscilla. It crossed her mind to acquaint her cousin with the situation as she knew it, but apart from an inherent dislike of spreading gossip, she remained too ignorant of Lucretia's real feelings and the major's future matrimonial intentions to depart from the safe policy of minding her own business. Major Talbot might be hanging out for a wife, and Lucretia might meet all his requirements in that direction. It was not her place to meddle.

Though her personal relations with those closest to her could not be considered gratifying, Natasha was far from immune to the excitement in the air that month. All London was alive with gossip surrounding the ceremonial visit of the Allied sovereigns following the defeat of Napoleon. Emperor Francis of Austria had sent his minister, Metternich, in his stead, but King Frederick William of Prussia had come in person, accompanied by his chancellor, Prince von Hardenberg, and Field Marshal Blucher. The Londoners were most interested in the romantic figure of Tsar Alexander, whose sister Catherine, the Grand Duchess of Oldenburg, had been in town since the end of March as the guest of the Russian ambassador, Count Lieven, who had hired the whole of the Pulteney

Hotel for her use at a cost of over two hundred guineas a week. This undiplomatic lady had greatly offended the Prince Regent by her interest in his estranged wife and her sympathy for Princess Charlotte, whose betrothal to the young Prince of Orange, promoted by her father, was said not to be to her taste. If the grand duchess's demeanor toward her royal host was embarrassing to the Lievens while she was alone in England, they had infinitely more to contend with after the tsar's arrival with the other distinguished guests at the end of the first week in June.

The English regarded the tsar as a savior and hero and lined the streets to cheer him on his arrival, but he eluded them and the Prince Regent, who had gone out to Shooter's Hill to welcome him. Changing his route, he went directly to the Pulteney, where his sister persuaded him to remain with her during his stay instead of using the accommodations prepared for him at St. James's Palace.

The Regent's popularity was at such a low ebb at that time that he did not dare to brave the crowds to drive to the hotel to welcome his guest but was forced to undergo the humiliation of asking the tsar to come to him at Carlton House hours later, where an uncomfortable first (and last) private meeting took place. This unfortunate beginning to the visit was quickly known about the town, of course, but the gala plans for entertaining the distinguished visitors went forward apace.

For the three weeks of the state visit the London streets were brightly illuminated every evening. In addition to the Prince's festivities there were balls, banquets, special theatrical performances, and entertainments given by the guilds and Lords Liverpool and Castlereagh, leading members of the government. The tsar also accepted the hospitality of the Duke of Devonshire and Lord Grey in defiance of the Prince Regent, who could not possibly be present at affairs given by members of the Whig opposition. The bad feeling between the two rulers increased, and each descended to juvenile tactics to publicly humiliate the other, with the gossips and newspapers having a glorious time in reporting and speculating on each new incident.

At the start of the visit, Tsar Alexander's attractive person and affability toward the British public made him a great favorite with the crowds. He and his sister toured London and nearby points of interest during the daytime, watched by an adoring public ever ready to give them a good-natured cheer.

Mrs. Taylor, in her widowed state, was not well enough connected with the governing families to be able to secure an invitation for her charges to meet the distinguished visitors, much to the young ladies' chagrin, for they were caught up in the fever that had overspread the metropolis.

It was well-known that the tsar and his sister often went walking in Hyde Park before breakfast, and the girls formed a resolution to put themselves in a position where they might at least catch a glimpse of the royal personages from a discreet distance. Mrs. Taylor had no strong objections to offer to this plan, only stipulating that they must take one of the maids with them for propriety's sake.

It was less than a mile to the Cumberland Gate from the Taylor house, but Hyde Park had any number of walks crisscrossing its three hundred fifty odd acres. The girls hopes went unrewarded on their first two sorties, though it was a pleasure to be outside so early in the day when the dew still spangled the grass and everything smelled fresh. Natasha, who missed the freedom of the countryside more than she was prepared to admit, was less disappointed than Lucretia and quite happy to continue their early-morning regimen for the sake of air and exercise.

Not so, Lizzie, however. Walking, other than to the shops, was not an activity that recommended itself to the young abigail who had been pressed into service as chaperon. On the third morning she presented herself in Natasha's bedchamber with a woebegone air, and upon being questioned as to the cause of her malaise, claimed to be suffering from a stomachache. She was ever so sorry but feared she would disgrace them by being sick if forced to walk for an hour. Suspecting mendacity but disinclined to make an issue of it with one who performed more than her share of work in the house, Natasha eyed the downcast maid sapiently, advised her to take a dose of the worst-tasting cure-all she could call to mind, and went off to apprise her cousin of the situation before she had completed her toilette.

Lucretia was tying a becoming straw bonnet decorated with pink ribbons and roses under her chin when Natasha knocked and was ill-pleased at her cousin's news.

"I'll go bail the girl is lying. She complained yesterday that her shoes pinched her feet and the sun gave her the headache. Today it is her stomach. Tell her she must come." She turned back to the mirror to make an adjustment to the angle of her bonnet.

Natasha hesitated, then said diffidently, "It just might be true; she looks a bit green about the gills."

"Oh, bother the girl! Well, she is more trouble than she's worth in any case. We'll do better without her."

"But your mother particularly desired us to take someone with us."

"Oh, Mama won't mind when we explain that it wasn't possible today. It's not as though there were any conceivable danger that could overtake us merely walking in the park in broad daylight. It was only for the look of the thing, and we are unlikely to meet any of the town's high sticklers abroad at this hour."

Never having become accustomed to the restrictions on her freedom of movement that prevailed in the town, Natasha allowed herself to be persuaded.

Today their luck was in, for they had scarcely entered the precincts of the park when they noticed a crowd of ordinary citizens, shopkeepers and artisans by their dress, hurrying along a path. With faith in the unerring instincts of the herd, they joined the throng, a decision eventually ratified when at the intersection of two paths they merged with a larger crowd surrounding a party of a half-dozen or so strollers. Their hunting instincts aroused, Mrs. Taylor's young ladies felt no ladylike hesitation in slipping in and out of the milling crowd to maneuver themselves into a more advantageous position to identify the members of the imperial party.

They had no difficulty in picking out the tsar from among an escort of his young Cossacks, though his height and breadth of shoulder certainly compared favorably with theirs. The pleasant open features and curling golden hair were as reported, and his amiability in the face of the curious mobs in constant attendance as he moved about London must be accounted to his credit.

The girls found their attention straying to the sole female of the party, a vivacious little lady somewhat past her first youth, who exchanged an occasional quip in English with their audience.

"Quite insignificant, one would almost say ugly, if it were not for the fine eyes," pronounced Miss Taylor judiciously. "That flattened nose must be considered a severe defect."

"Well, she is not precisely a regal figure, but her hair is beautiful, and she has such animation as must make her an interesting personality."

"You are overly generous. From what one hears, that animation you admire is too often employed in making rude and presumptuous remarks about her royal hosts."

Natasha did not feel able to combat this severity, so remained silent. Now that they had achieved their object she was becoming conscious of being in closer proximity to large numbers of hoi polloi than was quite comfortable. She indicated as much to Lucretia in an undertone, but they did not find it an easy matter to disengage themselves from the press of people. In the next few minutes it proved impossible to go against the direction of the flow of traffic. Though the mood of the crowd was friendly, the girls were jostled quite roughly in their attempts to break away, and Natasha read mounting panic in her cousin's eyes before she managed to extricate them both with some determined and well-timed elbowing of her own at another point where paths intersected. She kept a firm grip on Lucretia's arm as they were extruded from the moving mass of humanity and thus was able to prevent the younger girl from falling to her knees as she was spun about by a burly-shouldered man.

Lucretia gasped in pain and Natasha felt her sag. She bolstered her cousin's weight with an arm flung about her waist as they came to a halt just off to the side of the path.

For another minute or two the traffic flowed past on either side as a river flows around an island. Natasha took the buffeting on her own shoulders, encircling the taller girl with protective arms until the numbers dwindled as the imperial party pulled farther away. At last she raised her head, unconscious of her bonnet twisted wildly askew.

"Thank heavens the main crush is over. Are you much hurt, Lucretia?"

"I . . . I've wrenched my ankle."

Natasha saw with dismay her cousin's whitened cheeks and gritted teeth as she helped her to straighten up. "Can you put any weight on it?" She hovered anxiously while Lucretia attempted without success to do this. A swift mental review as she again took her cousin's weight on her arm revealed that their plight was indeed unenviable. They were on an interior walk without even a bench within easy distance. If they could reach the Ring, which encircled the perimeter, they might spot an acquaintance in a carriage, but with no Lizzie to assist her, it was going to be a slow, awkward, not to say painful progress.

"I fear there is nothing for it except to lean on me and take it slowly," she said in bracing tones, thankful that Lucretia was not the type to go off in hysterics. The injured girl did not attempt a reply, girding herself for a grueling physical effort.

She was ashen-faced and Natasha was trembling with the strain of the extra weight when a shocked voice hailed them.

"Miss Phillips, Miss Taylor, what has happened?"

Major Talbot, urging his horse into the footpath, pulled up before the exhausted pair, dismounted, and sprang to Miss Taylor's side. "I've got her, Miss Phillips. What happened?"

Natasha, recovering quickly once she was relieved of her cousin's weight, smiled a welcome and gave him a concise explanation.

"But is there no one with you? Your maid?"

"No," she replied briefly. "If you will be so good as to

take my cousin up before you, sir, I will follow as quickly as possible."

"I shall be happy to assist Miss Taylor, of course, but I cannot leave you here unattended."

"Nonsense, I am in no danger, and Lucretia is in great discomfort. I'll hold your horse while you lift her on."

Major Talbot looked disposed to argue with this high-handed attitude, but Natasha had already moved to the horse's head. His frown cleared as he gently lifted the trembling girl up onto the saddle. She moaned as the injured foot dangled off the ground and promptly fainted away.

"This isn't going to work. We'll need someone to hand her up to you, or I'll have to ride and hold her," Natasha decided as he caught the falling girl in his arms again. "Oh, Captain Standish, how wonderful to see you! Please—"

There was no need for further explanation. The captain took in the situation at a glance and was off his own horse as she spoke. The exchange was made expeditiously.

"Do not try to revive her," advised the practical Natasha as Major Talbot shifted the unconscious girl to a comfortable position and accepted his reins from Captain Standish.

"We had best walk along together," Major Talbot said carefully, "to prevent giving a singular appearance."

Natasha's irrepressible chuckle burst forth. "I can scarcely think of anything more singular than the appearance this odd procession presents, but," she added under his minatory look, "you may require Captain Standish's assistance at the other end, so let us be off."

Natasha and the captain followed in Major Talbot's wake, walking beside the well-behaved chestnut hack. She whiled away the slowly paced trip with a description of the events leading to the present predicament into the receptive ear of Captain Standish, who was interested in their impressions of the imperial personages. Major Talbot, going on slightly ahead, had nothing to contribute, but Natasha sensed the usual disapproval of her conduct in his silence. When eventually he mentioned the unwisdom of their unattended state, she passed it off with a quick account of their maid's sudden indisposition. Let him attribute their lack of chaperonage to her own lack of decorum if it pleased him to do so. She had no intention of telling tales and, in any case, had willingly acquiesced in her cousin's decision to go out alone.

Lucretia roused from her swoon before they arrived in Manchester Square, and bore the discomfort of being transported into the house with praiseworthy fortitude, remembering to thank her rescuers sweetly before they left.

Both gentlemen called the next day to see how she did and were received by all three ladies in the saloon, though Miss Taylor was confined to a daybed brought into the room so that she might not be deprived of all society during her recuperation. Natasha wore her customary smile and appeared not to be aware that Mrs. Taylor's half-playful remarks on the rashness of young ladies these days were directed mainly to her account. She did acknowledge the smiling commiseration in Captain Standish's eyes with a rueful twinkle in her own that vanished when she encountered Major Talbot's grave stare. She was therefore surprised to hear her own presence of mind and care for her cousin praised by that gentleman, but since Cousin Edwina managed to imply that practicality and a proper feminine sensibility were incompatible qualities, she could not be said to have benefited by his support.

It was a full week before Lucretia was able to get out and about, and during that interval Natasha elected to eschew evening engagements rather than leave her cousin alone by appropriating Mrs. Taylor's services as chaperon. During the daytime the house was full of company bent on keeping the invalid entertained, so Natasha was able to get out for air and to run errands, accompanied always by a chastened Lizzie. She looked forward to these simple outings, which constituted her only relief from the increasingly oppressive company of her relatives.

Matters improved substantially when they were at last able to resume their schedule of social engagements. Natasha, who loved to dance, was happily waltzing at

Almack's the next week when her partner whirled her past a trio chattering together on the edge of the dance floor. She flashed a general smile in the direction of Lady Frobisher and the Talbot cousins and promptly forgot their presence in the exhilaration of the dance. It would have surprised her to learn that she immediately became the subject of their conversation.

"Oh, how I wish I had the dressing of that girl," Charles Talbot sighed. His words were soft, almost as though spoken to himself, but Lady Frobisher, turning back to the major, paused and looked at him in some amusement.

"I am aware that your invaluable advice is sought by many hostesses when redecorating their reception rooms, Charles, but this is the first I've heard that you also aspire to become a couturier."

"In general I do not. I would never, for instance, dream of altering the smallest element of *your* appearance, my dear Priscilla," he drawled. "You know so well what becomes you best, but the little Phillips hasn't the least inkling of what she could become in the right hands."

"And you consider yours the right hands?" Lady Frobisher was intrigued. "How do you see Miss Phillips?"

"As the gloriously exotic creature nature meant her to be and that tedious cousin of hers takes great care she shall not be." Charles smiled a little at the expression of restrained disgust on his cousin's face, but addressed himself to Lady Frobisher, whose exquisite brows had escalated. "You do not agree with my evaluation?" he inquired in purring tones.

"She is a taking little thing, I grant you, and attractive in a way, but exotic? Really, Charles! She looks like all the rest of this year's crop of hopefuls."

Three pairs of eyes sought out the graceful figure of Miss Natasha Phillips swaying about the dance floor.

"But that is just it! With your usual discernment, fair lady, you come directly to my point. Natasha Phillips was not designed by nature to be one of the peas in that particular pod. Just look at that frightful dress she is wearing—expensive, in the current fashion, but completely wrong for her. What could be more unflattering against that glowing, rich coloring of hers than pale yellow? And it required rampant bad taste or positive genius—I'd give a monkey to know which—to find a style that could effectively disguise as perfectly proportioned a form as I've seen this year. And that glorious dark hair—totally wasted in a nondescript style that makes nothing of its abundance. It is a wonder they haven't shaved off the widow's peak to destroy the illusion that her face is heart-shaped."

"You speak as though there were some sort of conspiracy against Miss Phillips on the part of her own family," Major Talbot said sarcastically.

"You do talk a deal of nonsense, Charles," agreed Lady Frobisher.

"Do I?" Mr. Talbot's bright-blue eyes smiled knowingly at the lady and then shifted to his cousin's countenance, which was rigid with distaste at a conversation that dealt in personalities. "Perhaps I do, but if you have failed to observe Mrs. Taylor's none-too-subtle attempts to belittle her young cousin at every opportunity, I can only say that I have not, though I do my best to avoid the woman and her clever hypocrisy."

"Perhaps you should take the girl in hand, Charles." Lady Frobisher, speaking idly, noted the sudden tightening of Major Talbot's lips and went on deliberately, "You take a very . . . protective interest in Miss Phillips. Perhaps your armored heart has been pierced at last?"

Mr. Talbot was not the least disconcerted by this direct attack. "Who can say? It is a great pity, is it not, that my inadequate patrimony and expensive habits—I added that last, coz, to save you the trouble—have combined to make it imperative that I confine any matrimonial inclinations to heiresses. And now, although it grieves me to tear myself away from such scintillating company, I fear I really must circulate. It's a dead bore, but one must do one's duty at these affairs, after all. *Au revoir.*"

Mr. Talbot walked away, his mischievous nature mildly gratified by the knowledge that he had given both of his former companions a good deal to speculate upon.

6

Meanwhile Natasha, in happy ignorance of any speculation concerning herself, continued to mark time, often quite pleasurably, until she could return to her brother's home. The visit of the Allied sovereigns continued to provide grist for the gossip mills of the capital. There was a splendid dinner for seven hundred at the Guildhall on the eighteenth of the month. The young ladies had extracted a promise from Major Talbot, who was to attend the banquet, to call in Manchester Square the next morning to report on the affair.

All three were in the saloon, Mrs. and Miss Taylor occupied with pieces of fancywork and Natasha lost in a book, when the major was announced. After the forms of politeness had been observed, Lucretia got in the first question.

"Were you presented to the tsar?"

"Yes, as a matter of fact, only because I was with my uncle, *and*," he paused, with a rare twinkle in the clear green eyes, "to the grand duchess also."

"But I thought the banquet was to be a strictly masculine affair," Natasha exclaimed, laying aside her book.

"It was planned that way, but as the grand duchess insisted on accompanying her brother, as is her wont, Countess Lieven and the Duchess of York were also present."

"That woman is totally lacking in sensibility, as I have said all along," Mrs. Taylor declared tartly.

"I imagine everyone was most splendidly attired for the occasion," Lucretia put in.

"The tsar wore a scarlet-and-gold uniform, and the

other dignitaries were covered with honors too, but you will have to ask my cousin to describe the ladies' apparel. I fear I would make but a poor botch of it.''

Natasha blinked in surprise. She had never before suspected the major of possessing a sense of humor, but she didn't trust that bland expression. "Did the banquet go off well, as far as the atmosphere was concerned, I mean?''

Major Talbot hesitated. "The Regent provided the state coach driven by four creams for the tsar's transport, but there was no discernible increase in cordiality between the two, if I am any judge. When the honored party came into the Guildhall from an anteroom on their way to the dais through an aisle of guests, the tsar paused to say a few words to Lords Grey and Holland, which meant that the Regent was forced to stand and wait. In my opinion, it was not well done of a guest to put his host in such an invidious position. During the banquet Prinny seemed to avoid speaking to the tsar or his sister.''

"And how did the grand duchess comport herself at an event to which she had not been invited?'' inquired Lucretia.

The major laughed outright then, compounding Natasha's surprise at this new side to his personality. "You must have heard that she declares music gives her nausea?'' When all three ladies signified assent, he went on to say that a number of artists from the Italian Opera had been scheduled to sing special songs along with the many toasts, but the grand duchess had requested that they stop, giving her usual explanation. "It was only with difficulty that she was persuaded to accept the playing of 'God Save the King' after the royal toast.''

"Infamous! That woman wants all conduct,'' said Mrs. Taylor scathingly.

"Well I must agree with you, ma'am, that the negative attitude of the grand duchess has been in a large part responsible for the failure of this visit between the two rulers. Even the opposition leaders are embarrassed by the present situation, and the newspapers have begun to realize that an insult to the head of a state, however unpopular he may be, is an insult to the state itself. I would say that Field Marshal Blucher's geniality and willingness to be pleased has made him a more popular figure than Alexander by now."

The girls, demanding more details of the occasion, expressed satisfaction on hearing that the Guildhall's gold plate had been used and were agog at the sumptuous fare provided, which seemed to lend substance to the rumor that the banquet had cost upward of twenty thousand pounds.

At this point in the visit, Chudleigh announced the arrival of Lady Betancourt, one of Mrs. Taylor's cronies, and her two loquacious daughters. At any other time these pretty brunettes, whom Natasha considered the two silliest girls in London, would have hung on every word from Major Talbot's lips, but after declaring themselves enraptured to hear his account of the Guildhall banquet and clucking over the presence of the grand duchess, as reported by Lucretia, they ruthlessly interrupted his first sentence, unable any longer to contain their delight at having formed a party to visit Vauxhall Gardens the following week.

"And we plan to take sculls from Westminster across to the water gate, which will be so much more romantic than going by carriage across the bridge, do you not agree?" asked Miss Ramsey-Martin, turning her slightly protuberant blues eyes on Major Talbot.

He was spared a reply that would have had to reconcile veracity with civility when Miss Eleanor, barely waiting until her sister had paused for breath, rushed in. "Our brother Randolph will be down from Oxford by then with some of his friends, who will join us. Mama has rented a supper box, and we thought it would be so much more diverting if you were to come too." She beamed at the cousins, who turned hopeful faces toward Mrs. Taylor.

This lady had no very high opinion of the delights to be found in a public pleasure garden that admitted anyone with the price of a ticket, but she could not very well question her friend's want of propriety in allowing her daughters to attend such revels under the doubtful protection of very young men who might not be trusted to keep the line in the atmosphere of freedom prevailing at Vauxhall. Now she said, choosing her words carefully, "I fear I could not impose upon Mr. Randolph Ramsey-Martin's kindness to accept the added responsibility of escorting unknown young ladies as well as his sisters."

"Oh, Randolph will not object to such charming girls as Natasha and Lucretia, and he is to bring several friends along, you know, Edwina. The girls will have ample protection," blithely promised Lady Betancourt, apparently under the impression that the issue was numbers.

"I should not myself care to attend Vauxhall without a *mature* escort," Mrs. Taylor replied, accepting the necessity of plain speaking to a featherheaded creature like Arabella Ramsey-Martin.

"If you would accept my escort, ma'am," interposed Major Talbot, his gaze going from Lucretia's downcast face to Natasha's mobile mouth, which she was vainly trying to discipline after this last exchange, "I will endeavor to obtain the box next to Lady Betancourt's so the two parties might mingle."

Receiving an imploring look from her daughter, Mrs. Taylor, very much against her inclination, gave in at that point, forcing herself to a gracious acceptance while the young ladies somewhat shrilly expressed their pleasure at the outcome.

Lucretia's thank-you to Major Talbot for his great kindness was accompanied by a speaking glance that caused Lady Betancourt's birdlike black eyes to rove between the two with sudden interest.

"Quite stoical kindness," Natasha murmured dulcetly, and earned a quick look from the major which she received in studied innocence.

She repented a little of her teasing after he had gone, however. The invitation was indeed a kind gesture on the major's part. She could not suppose that he anticipated much pleasure in consorting with a party that included the hen-witted Ramsey-Martin sisters and a number of extremely young men just down from the university. If his sisters' artless revelations could be believed, Randolph Ramsey-Martin was one of the peep-o'day boys when let loose on the town. Of a certainty, his friends would be similar choice spirits, always ripe for a lark.

Before the evening was over, Major Talbot would no doubt be regretting the absence of Lady Frobisher with her elegance of appearance and manner, her calm measured conversation, which Natasha, after a number of meetings promoted by her guardian could only term dull and predictable. She would be the first to grant the woman's outstanding physical appeal and above-average musical accomplishments, but there was a want of any positive spirit about Lady Frobisher; in Natasha's eyes that lady seemed nearly characterless. That Major Talbot apparently found this beautiful vapid personality the epitome of feminine perfection filled her with contempt for his powers of discrimination and caused her to question his intellect.

When she reached this point in her ratiocinations, Natasha chided herself for intolerance. Throughout history men of brilliance and discernment had suffered from blindness with respect to one particular female. One must not pronounce harshly against those persons laboring under the restrictions that love imposed on judgment. Who was she, who had never felt the pangs of love, to condemn another's poor judgment? Perhaps the benefits of that state extolled by poets through the ages outweighed the drawbacks. Personally, she was not at all certain she wished to discover the answer to the enigma. It was a grave matter to surrender one's very intellect to such an unreasonable state, compared with which, surrendering one's person and fortune to the object of desire seemed a small matter.

The evening of their excursion to the famous pleasure gardens might have been ordered by the gods for the enjoyment of their favorites. The cloud cover of the morning had dissipated by midafternoon along with the damp little breeze that had made the day uncomfortable. A late-afternoon sun warmed the air, and a chorus of grateful bird song greeted the major's party as their craft approached the entrance to the gardens on the river's south shore.

Lucretia expelled a soulful breath and smiled at their host. "How glad I am that you decided to take the water route, sir. The approach is so lovely."

"Yes," declared Natasha prosaically, "and all the water traffic is most exciting and interesting. Look, there is a boat approaching with an escort boat of musicians, and those two sculls are racing."

"It is to be hoped their unfortunate passengers do not find themselves thrown into the water as a consequence of such irresponsibility."

Since the passengers in question, all young men, were enthusiastically urging on their respective rowers, nobody took much note of Mrs. Taylor's gloomy prediction. In the short period of time before they disembarked at the landing nothing untoward occurred.

The young ladies were enchanted with the mature land-scaping of the twelve-acre gardens, which had opened in its present form in the first half of the previous century. They strolled the lovely tree-lined walks and exclaimed over the realistic effect at the end of the South Walk of a painted Temple of Neptune seen through the existing three arches. The landscaping lent itself to such perspective effects, but there was plenty to see that was tangible, including fountains, simulated ruins, and little summerhouses tucked away down curving alleys that invited that dalliance between the sexes, which was part of Mrs. Taylor's objection to the place.

They did not return to the central area until after dark so the girls might enjoy the full effect of the thousands of globe lanterns giving their shimmering golden light to the walks. The sense of enchantment evaporated once they were among the numbers of fashionably dressed people milling about the boxes. There were about fifty of these small enclosures arranged in two wide semicircles around an open area where an orchestra was playing. The booths were quite attractive, each with its original painting on the back wall, presenting the overall appearance of a festive art gallery.

Major Talbot had been successful in reserving the booth next to Lady Betancourt's, a coup for which Mrs. Taylor thanked him with something less than convincing sincerity. They didn't have far to look for their neighbors. Sounds of merriment led them unerringly to the Ramsey-Martin party.

Randolph Ramsey-Martin was everything that Natasha would have expected of his sisters' brother, open-faced, good-natured, garrulous, and bacon-brained. His two friends, Mr. Dansin and Mr. Trevor, seemed to be cut from the same cloth, but as they were hovering about their friend's sisters, she had little conversation with them. Lucretia glued herself to Major Talbot's side, leaving Natasha to be entertained by Mr. Ramsey-Martin. This he was more than willing to do, launching immediately into a description of some famous tricks he had played on fellow students at his college. Since these tended to feature noxious substances dropped into the drinks of unsuspecting persons, Natasha formed an instant resolve not to eat or drink anything in Mr. Ramsey-Martin's company.

The sounding of a bell at nine o'clock announcing the spectacle known facetiously as the "Tin Cascade" was greeted with relief by Natasha, who in the general movement toward the north side of the gardens contrived to attach herself to the major's other side. The gentlemen were warned to watch their pockets as hundreds of people streamed down the walk to where the illuminated mechanical illusion was performed. When the curtain rose on a scene that had changed over the years but always featured a realistic waterfall turning a mill wheel, Major Talbot was in a position to observe the surprised delight that spread over Miss Phillips' expressive countenance.

"Oh, what a splendid sight! How is it done, I wonder?" In her excitement she had gripped his forearm lightly.

Suddenly an excited feminine voice near at hand squealed out, "Can it really be? *Tasha*, is it really you?"

The hand on his arm tightened for an instant, then released itself as Natasha turned swiftly toward the voice. "Susan!"

The next instant Natasha was exchanging an exuberant embrace with a tiny young woman with a vibrant face and red-gold curls. Both were talking at once, but Major Talbot had noted with some curiosity that in that first moment of deep emotion the animated Miss Phillips had become strangely still. There had been a shimmer of unshed tears in her eyes, and her voice had scarcely risen above a whisper. The impression was nearly erased as she turned eagerly to Mrs. Taylor, her face radiant with happiness and excitement.

"Cousin Edwina, may I present my oldest friend, Susan Blakeney . . . Oh, I'm sorry . . . Lady Flint? We have not met since her marriage, so I am unused to the sound of her wedded name."

The ladies bowed and expressed their pleasure, somewhat inaudibly under the circumstances of the spectacle still drawing much comment from the sizable crowd of viewers. Natasha presented her friend to Lucretia and Major Talbot in turn but made no effort to attract the attention of Lady Betancourt's party, which had pressed forward in the last few minutes.

After greeting Lucretia, Lady Flint leaned closer to the major and raised her voice to be heard above the spectators. "Did Natasha say Major Talbot? Of Krestonwood? I believe we are your closest neighbors, sir, though Krestonwood has been leased during the whole of my residence at Flint Abbey."

"Is Harry Flint your husband?"

"Yes indeed."

Major Talbot's slow smile embraced the diminutive Lady Flint, who sparkled up at him responsively. "Harry and I were at Eton and Oxford together. It will be wonderful to see him again." He glanced around. "Is he. . . ?"

"No." Lady Flint laughed. "Harry is at our booth with his mother. Richard, my brother-in-law, brought me here because I was desirous of seeing the waterfall again. Not that I *have* seen it tonight. Tasha's voice drove everything else from my mind. Ah, here is Richard looking like a thundercloud because he warned me to stick close to his side in this crowd," she added sunnily.

"So this is where you got to, Sue. You are the worst girl for wandering away." The chunky young man addressing Lady Flint in scolding accents glanced questioningly at her companions and drew up short at sight of Major Talbot. "Cam! When did you return?" He stuck out a hand that was gripped heartily by the major.

Their greeting, though less emotional than that of Natasha and Lady Flint, clearly afforded both men real pleasure, and one that was shared by the two ladies looking on with the proprietary smiles of mothers whose offspring had made friends.

When she could edge in a word, Lady Flint presented her brother-in-law to the ladies of the Taylor party, bubbling over with enthusiasm when she reached Natasha, whom she had saved for last, as she told him of her great good fortune in accidentally meeting her dearest friend.

Natasha sustained a penetrating look from Mr. Flint's shrewd brown eyes with her customary friendly composure, taking due notice of that gentleman's high complexion, pugnacious chin, and stocky build. The mechanical spectacle had run its course by now, but the large numbers of people drifting back toward the center of the gardens made conversation nearly impossible. Even keeping together became a chore. Natasha, arm in arm with a determined Lady Flint, soon found herself distanced from her own party. This was not to be wondered at in view of her cousins' somewhat formal reception of the Flints. Lucretia had not liked sharing the major's attention with his old friend if her bored expression had told the true story.

By now Natasha was familiar with her cousin's skill at maneuvering herself into the place beside Major Talbot, and she dismissed them from her thoughts, turning back to Lady Flint to inquire, "But why have we not met before this, Susan? We are out almost every night and it seems that we see the same people everywhere."

"We just arrived in town three days ago." The petite redhead, looking a little conscious, hesitated, then rushed on, "You must know that I am in the family way at long last and was feeling so wretched until about a fortnight ago that I could not face the journey."

"Susan, how marvelous! You must be so happy!"

"Oh, I am, now that I am feeling more the thing. But you must tell me all about your Season. I assume you are staying with your cousins. And what of Peter?"

Questions came tumbling out of Lady Flint, but they were already approaching the supper boxes. She groaned in frustration. "I positively cannot let you go at this point, dearest Tasha. I shall expire of curiosity before the morning. Tell me, did you meet the tsar when the sovereigns were here?"

Natasha's laughter bubbled up at this cheering evidence that marriage had not changed her old friend. Susan was still the same outgoing impetuous creature she had been as a girl, as she demonstrated in the next moment by accosting Major Talbot, who was coming toward them after having settled his other guests in their box.

"Please, Major Talbot, will you forgive my presumption and be a darling and lend Tasha to me for a little while? She has not even met Harry yet. I must warn you that I am increasing and must be granted every indulgence in my delicate state," she added with a disarming frankness that drove the color up above the major's moderate collar points.

"Hah, Cam, do not try to bring reason to bear with this minx," warned Richard Flint, who had accompanied the girls. "She keeps us all under her thumb with her wheedling ways." An affectionate smile directed at his now studiously demure sister-in-law robbed the words of offense.

Major Talbot had recovered his countenance sufficiently to accede to Lady Flint's request. "Tell Harry if I do not see him tonight I will call tomorrow," he added, bowing with great charm over the hand she extended to him.

"Mmmnn, he is the handsomest creature," murmured Susan approvingly as they were steered toward the Flint booth by Richard. "Is he engaged to your cousin?"

Natasha looked startled. "Why, no! At least, I have not heard . . ." She broke off in some confusion as Susan laughed.

"Well, that's a relief. She was doing her best to leave

78

that impression. Wouldn't it be wonderful if *you* were to marry him?" she proposed ingenuously. "Then we would be neighbors."

"Susan, there is absolutely no question of such a thing."

"Why not?" Mischievous hazel eyes swept over Natasha's shocked face.

"Why, for one thing he doesn't like me above half."

Indignation replaced mischief. "What can you mean, doesn't like you? Everybody likes you!"

"I don't mean that he has taken me in irremediable dislike precisely. It is more that he cannot quite approve of me."

Susan's eyes grew round. "Why? What have you done?"

"Nothing, you goose." Natasha's laugh was slightly forced. "I believe that Major Talbot prefers a more conventional type of female, one whose conversation and conduct are always distinguished by rationality of intellect, evenness of spirits, good taste, and moderation in all things."

"In short, a dead bore. Lud, if he prefers a pattern card of missishness, he's not going to deal well with me either."

"Nonsense, he isn't immune to charm, of which you have more than your fair share."

Susan ignored the blatant partiality of her friend's light disclaimer. Her brows were knitted as she digested what had gone before. "But you are his guests tonight, are you not? Why should he bother to distinguish someone he doesn't really like with special attention? Or is it your cousin, after all?"

"No, at least perhaps, but I should have explained that Major Talbot is a good friend of Peter's, and Peter has desired him to act in his stead as a sort of pseudo-guardian while I am in London. When you know the major better, you'll see that he is very kind and, above all, conscientious in his duty. He is our frequent escort and has been most considerate always and—"

"How dreadful for you, to be the object of grudging charity!"

"Not at all, Sue. I would not have you judge Major

Talbot harshly. His behavior toward us is always everything that is gentlemanly and considerate. It is not his fault that he cannot quite approve of someone like me. Have I made things clear now?"

"Clear as the Thames," came the cheerful reply.

Natasha shot her a doubtful look but was forced to turn her attention to Susan's family, for they had arrived at the back of the Flint box, where they entered.

Lord Flint was a refined version of his younger brother, taller, less stocky, and less rocky-jawed, though they had the same intelligent brown eyes, passed on by their maternal parent obviously. Natasha rather took to the dowager baroness with her plain, no-nonsense appearance and stout matronly figure. She made a welcome change from Cousin Edwina's friends, most of whom labored to present the most youthful image possible, occasionally going beyond the line of appropriateness in makeup and dress in this pursuit.

Everyone pressed Natasha to remain and share their supper, which she was most happy to do, partaking contentedly of a lavish spread that featured cold chicken and the paper-thin slices of ham and rack punch for which Vauxhall was known. For the next hour she relaxed completely in the undemanding company of the sort of close-knit family she had not thought existed in London, listening with patent enjoyment to Susan's descriptions, amplified, corrected, and embroidered by all the rest, of life at Flint Abbey. Her own eager questions received the consideration of all the Flints, and they replied in kind by demanding an account of the recently departed foreign visitors from one presumed by her recent life-style to have been in a position to hear all the things not reported in the newspapers.

The time flew by while the orchestra continued to play, and surprised friends strolling by the front of the box stopped to issue warm welcomes. Natasha's conscience was beginning to prick her for the length of time she had remained away from her own party, though she knew her cousins would be happier without her company, when Mr. Charles Talbot stopped at the box to say hello. She was firmly reiterating her intention of leaving at the time and apologizing for the necessity of dragging Mr. Richard Flint away as escort when Charles interposed, "It would be my great pleasure to escort Natasha back to her party, Dick. I believe I see Cedric Langley approaching to speak with you."

Since Susan had related the circumstances of Natasha's connection with Cameron Talbot, none of the Flints made anything of Charles Talbot's offer to conduct her back to his cousin, though Susan's arched brows escalated at the apparent intimacy between her friend and Mr. Talbot implied by their easy use of Christian names. Good-byes were said and Susan promised again to call on the morrow.

Natasha and Charles Talbot walked slowly around the outside perimeter of the boxes savoring the cooler air under the stars.

"This must be my lucky day. I had no idea you were acquainted with the Flints."

"I just met them tonight, but Susan, Lady Flint, and I grew up together in Devon. I haven't seen her since her marriage. I'll have to differ with you—it is *my* lucky day. It was such a joy to see her again, and especially to know she will be spending some time in town."

"Lady Flint is indeed a charming little widgeon. She was one of the successes of her Season, as I recall."

"Susan is not a widgeon," retorted Natasha, rounding on him. "She has plenty of sense and a very good understanding also."

"I cry quits." Charles threw up his hands in laughing surrender. "I'll take your word for it that the lady is well-furnished with intellect, even more than you have indicated, since she was clever enough to play the widgeon to capture Harry Flint, who certainly did not aspire to acquire a bluestocking for a wife."

"You sound very cynical," Natasha muttered, more nearly out of charity with her good friend than since the night of their first meeting when he had spoken caustically of his cousin. "Susan does not pretend to be anything. She *is* charming, kind, impulsive, and fun-loving, none of which precludes having a good understanding. And I am persuaded that Lord Flint would not change a thing about her." Her voice lost its hint of asperity as she went on softly, "She told me tonight that she is increasing, though that may not be public knowledge at present, so I know you will not speak of it yet. Just now the others treated her as though she were a fragile piece of Venetian glass. It must be wonderful to be so cherished."

Natasha was lost in her own thoughts and did not immediately perceive that they had left the area of the boxes and wandered down one of the lesser alleys until a curve hid the brightly lighted central area behind them. She stopped and peered about her, seeing only one lantern far ahead. "Goodness, Charles, where are we? This path is quite deserted and I cannot even hear the music any longer."

"Is that what you would like, Natasha, to be treated like a fragile object?"

"Heavens, no! I'm far from fragile, and neither is Susan." Her rich warm chuckle erupted, and Charles moved closer, reducing the distance between them to a few inches. His voice in her ear had a curious thrum to it.

"Is it that you wish to be cherished, then?"

She laughed a trifle uncertainly and confessed, "I am persuaded most women would like that. And now, Charles, we had best retrace our steps and rejoin the others. I have been away an unconscionable time."

"Must we go back when the stars are so much brighter here in the dark? It seems I never get to see you lately, at least not for more than a minute or two. Beggar's rations for a starving man."

"Now that is utterly false and you know it," she retorted bracingly. "There is no friend that I see as often as I see you."

"*Friend!* Do you really believe I wish to be your friend, my enchanting Natasha? Oh, why could you not have been a real heiress?"

Before she could make any sense of these astonishing remarks, Natasha found herself enclosed in a fierce embrace. She raised her head to protest and was promptly and thoroughly kissed. It was a new experience, and not one she enjoyed, since her lips were being pressed tightly against her teeth and a suffocating sensation was creeping over her. She conquered an instinctive need to release herself, remaining limp and unresponsive by a supreme act of will. She sensed a desperation about Charles that was confined by the glitter in his eyes as he pulled away and stared wordlessly down into her bewildered face.

Neither reacted to a footfall coming from the direction of the central area, but a cold voice brought both heads around sharply.

"The classic remark for this situation is, I believe, 'I trust I don't intrude', but I fear I plan to intrude very thoroughly."

The dim light in the alley did not quite conceal the surge of dark color that rose into Charles' cheeks as he whirled to confront his cousin, fists clenching.

"You!" he ejaculated with loathing.

"Yes, I, and we are going to break this up before there are others behind me. You may consider yourselves fortunate that you were not discovered by someone who would delight in spreading a little scandal broth about the town. I'll see you tomorrow," he said warningly as Charles sprang forward. He offered his arm to the silent girl, who automatically placed trembling fingers on his dark sleeve.

"Natasha, my dear," implored Charles, turning a shoulder on Major Talbot, "I will take you back to Mrs. Taylor. You need not suffer my officious cousin's company or listen to his sarcasm."

"It's all right, really Charles," she said in a soothing tone. "I prefer to go back with Major Talbot. I have been away from my cousins for hours; it was most uncivil of me."

Major Talbot shot his cousin one enigmatic look and walked away with Natasha on his arm.

7

For quite five minutes the only sounds in the still night air were those of the major's footsteps on the gravel path. Charles had stormed off in the opposite direction, and Natasha was prey to a number of unhappy but silent thoughts.

"He won't marry you, you know. My cousin's inflated opinion of his worth demands a greater heiress than you are."

The studied offensiveness of this observation reduced Natasha to incoherent distress. "I . . . It was not . . . I mean, I did not . . . I have no thought of marrying Charles!" she choked out, pulling her fingers from his rigid forearm as though she had been burned.

"It merely amuses you to have him kiss you?"

"It did *not* amuse me, and that was the first time it ever happened," she cried, whirling on her accuser. "He caught me by surprise."

"It has always puzzled me that young women who invite unwanted embraces by going off alone with men invariably declare themselves astonished to receive these embraces, but then I never claimed to comprehend the myriad mysteries of the female psyche."

A black rage such as she had never experienced before engulfed Natasha's whole body and propelled the hand that lashed out at him.

Major Talbot's reflexive dodging action averted the full force of the openhanded blow aimed at his cheek, which was indeed fortunate, he informed his quivering antagonist in a silky voice, since they would not otherwise have been able to return to their box until the mark had faded. "Which might have given rise to yet more unwelcome speculation, something I am persuaded you are as eager as I to avoid.''

Natasha turned on her heel, not trusting herself to reply to this latest taunt.

Not another word was exchanged between the pair until they reentered their booth, when Major Talbot offered a cheerful apology for being gone so long.

"I have not seen Harry Flint for over four years," he said, smiling with great charm and little truth at a rather stiff Lucretia and Mrs. Taylor, "and I fear I was unable to tear myself away as quickly as I should have done." He devoted himself to thawing the reserve that had arisen during his prolonged absence, to such good effect that their box was soon echoing with soft feminine laughter.

For Natasha the remainder of the evening was sheer nightmare, and to a bruised spirit craving solitude it passed at the same crawling pace as the most tormenting of dreams. She had been looking forward to witnessing her first fireworks display, but when the two parties had again joined forces and strolled over to the enclosure, she was too engrossed in the explosions going off in her own head to appreciate the artistic showers of brilliantly colored sparks produced for the entertainment of the Vauxhall patrons. It was a grueling experience in self-discipline to move through the final phase of the evening without betraying her disturbed spirits, a heroic feat she accomplished by not permitting her glance to cross Major Talbot's for the smallest fraction of a second.

By the time Natasha eventually gained the privacy of her bedchamber she had used up all her reserves of strength, both physical and emotional. For a full half-hour by the clock she sat on the side of her bed in too great a lethargy to contemplate undressing, the same plaint repeating itself endlessly in her head. How could he have been so cruel and unjust? And in such a suave, offensive style too!

There was no more acceptable answer at two in the morning than there had been three hours earlier. A burning sense of injustice makes a poor soporific, and Natasha rose from her bed the next morning less refreshed than when she had lain down upon it. Her mood was not lightened at breakfast by an improving lecture directed at her by Cousin Edwina on the lack of consideration on the part of a guest that forced a host to absent himself from his other guests to retrieve her from her own private entertainment. To set the seal on her misery, Lucretia went about wearing a smug, contented air that did not endear her to her ill-used cousin.

Natasha pleaded a slight indisposition to excuse herself from accompanying her relatives on the usual round of morning calls. She was moping about in the small back chamber the ladies used as a morning room when Chudleigh announced that Lady Flint had called.

"I have conducted her to the saloon, Miss Phillips."

"Oh, thank you, Chudleigh. Would you send along refreshments later? And, Chudleigh, if anyone else should call this morning, I am not receiving."

"Very good, miss."

Natasha bounded out of her chair, casting aside her unread periodical. She hurried upstairs to the saloon, ashamed that she could have been so wrapped up in her own misery as to forget Susan's expected visit.

"Good morning, Susan. I'm so glad you were able to come."

"Well, you don't look it," Lady Flint said frankly, eyeing her friend's wan complexion. "Are you unwell today? Shall I come back another time?"

"No, no, I am perfectly well, I thank you. You look very blooming this morning."

And indeed Lady Flint presented a charming picture in her crisp leaf-green walking dress filled in at the neckline with finely pleated white muslin that ended in a delicate little frill under her chin. A flat-crowned, narrow-brimmed hat of chip straw was perched at a jaunty angle atop her red-gold curls, its only ornament a dyed green feather wound around the crown.

"If you are not ill, then what has happened? You are a far cry from the vibrant girl I met last night." Lady Flint was removing a pair of straw-colored string gloves as she spoke, but the evasive look on Natasha's face was not lost upon her.

"Nothing has happened . . . nothing of a serious nature, that is." Natasha forced a laugh. "Merely a little minor unpleasantness with my cousin this morning over my behavior in staying away too long last night. I assure you I do not regard it."

"Hmmnn," said Lady Flint, her bright gaze never leaving Natasha's face. To the latter's relief she changed the subject. "I was surprised last night to find you so well-acquainted with Charles Talbot."

"Oh, yes, Charles and I are quite good friends," Natasha answered brightly before the conviction swept over her that last night's incident had irrevocably altered her friendship with Charles. Something of her distress must have appeared in her face, for Susan's eyes narrowed, but she pursued her own train of thought.

"You told me Major Talbot disapproved of you, but we were interrupted before I could ask your opinion of him. Do you like him?"

"I detest him!" The words were out before her brain could exercise any control, then she gasped and pressed her lips together . . . too late.

It would have been difficult to say which girl looked more surprised as the passionate words hung in the air for an awkward moment.

"I . . . Please, Sue, do not regard what I just said. It was terribly ungrateful of me and . . . and untrue besides, but I—"

"I *knew* something happened last night!" Lady Flint ruthlessly overrode her friend's frantic denials. "Out with it!"

After some initial resistance, Natasha broke down and related the events that had occurred after she had left the Flint box.

Susan listened with sympathetic attention that was yet tinged with amusement. "My poor Tasha! You certainly had a wretched time of it."

"I fail to see what aspect of the situation you can

possibly find humourous," complained Natasha, affronted.

"Forgive me, dearest, but I cannot help thinking that Charles Talbot came by his just deserts."

"Well, I did not come by mine!"

"No, no," Lady Flint agreed soothingly. "It was abominable of Charles to make up to an innocent girl when everybody knows he's been hanging out for a rich wife these three years past."

"But he has not been making up to me, as you put it. We have been good friends, that's all. That is why I was caught off my guard last night."

"Charles knows of your connection with his cousin, of course?"

"He knows the major is a friend of Peter's and our frequent escort."

"Harry told me that Charles has always resented his cousin's financial independence and his own father's fondness for Cam, who shares Sir Humphrey's interest in government and politics. Charles seems to go out of his way to present a frivolous image, and he is terribly expensive. He might find it amusing to annoy his cousin by ostentatiously dangling after the girl he has promised to protect."

"You are implying that Charles has cultivated my friendship merely to annoy his cousin? Not very complimentary to me."

"No, dearest Tasha, except that I am persuaded from what you have told me that Charles has been caught in his own snare. He has fallen in love with you."

"Oh, no, this is even worse than I thought," cried Natasha, jumping up from her chair and starting a rapid pacing of the room. "It is all the fault of Major Talbot!"

"How do you arrive at this conclusion?" Lady Flint asked with real interest.

Natasha paused in her stalking. "There is something so daunting and offputting about such expectations of perfection from others that one feels almost compelled to act in a contrary manner."

"Is that how you feel?"

"You may smile, but your whole family thinks you are perfect. You cannot conceive how it lowers one's spirits to deal constantly with people who disapprove of one. It has an insidious effect that wears one down."

"Poor Tasha. I am so glad that I braved that uncomfortable coach ride to come to town. You will do much better now that you have me to support your spirits." Lady Flint paused and glanced away for a second. "I have been asking Harry about Cam Talbot this morning. It might help you to understand him better if I explain that his mother was tremendously important in his life. Harry says she was very lovely to look at and a gentle, good woman. Cam almost worshiped her. Harry and Richard adored her too. Harry says that she was a rather serious-minded person of the highest principles and that her manners were always formal. She died shortly before he met Priscilla Fanshawe. Do you know about her?"

Natasha nodded. "I have met Lady Frobisher on several occasions."

"Have you?" Susan's eyes widened. "I know her from past Seasons, but Harry just told me this morning of her connection with Cam and what she did to him. It strikes me that he idealized his mother and measures all females he encounters against her multiple perfections. He made the mistake of believing Priscilla was like his mother because she is beautiful and projects a sort of regal dignity, which in her case has nothing to do with high standards of personal conduct." She shrugged expressively. "It is excessively tiresome and stupid of him to be so narrow-minded, but I find many men are stupid in their judgments of women. They all possess, for example, an ineradicable prejudice in favor of physical beauty that causes them to overlook major flaws such as a want of intellect or character, or a grasping nature or a shrewish temper. Similarly, they are much inclined not to recognize sterling worth if it is not paired with an eye-catching exterior."

Natasha was smiling by the time Lady Flint came to the end of her catalog of masculine foibles. She had half-forgotten Susan's incisive tongue and penetrating observation, and was deeply grateful that marriage and the years of separation had not loosened the ties between them. The companionship she had sought in vain from Lucretia was available to her once more.

Susan's friendship was the one bright spot in Natasha's existence in the next sennight. These days her cousins took less trouble to conceal their lack of regard for her, and though Major Talbot's public attitude was exactly what it had always been, her own burning sense of pique at being misjudged prevented her from behaving in a natural fashion when in his company. She knew she was being petty and uncharitable, but despite Susan's revelations about his background, she could not relinquish her grievance.

The London social whirl continued unabated. The Allied sovereigns had departed, but England's own hero, the newly created Duke of Wellington, was back on British soil for the first time in five years, and a grateful country was delighted to pay homage to its savior. In his honor, White's club was hosting a grand *bal masqué* at Burlington House, to which the Taylor ménage had received invitations.

The ladies devoted some considerable thought to their costumes, the end result of which was that Lucretia decided to assume the persona of a French shepherdess as depicted in romantic paintings, and Natasha, with a view to wearing her lovely *mantilla*, planned to go as a Spanish lady, equally romanticized in layers of white silk ruffles edged in lace. Mrs. Taylor, who planned to do no more than wear a domino over fancy dress, had protested at the cost of Natasha's finery. However, this young lady had celebrated her twenty-first birthday the previous week and was not so amenable to her cousin's direction of her purchases as she had been at the beginning of her stay in London. With the attainment of her majority came control of the substantial inheritance left her by her grandmother, and she coolly informed her cousin that, having handled the household finances of her brother's estate since her father's death, she felt quite competent to manage her own modest expenditures.

Persevering against Mrs. Taylor's reservations, the young women had elected to travel to Burlington House without a masculine escort in order to preserve their anonymity. They were not so preoccupied with thoughts of the evening's promises as to be entirely indifferent to what lay beyond the high screen wall and the imposing gateway, always shut in their experience. After they swept through the great wooden doors on Piccadilly they gazed back in appreciation at James Gibbs' fairy-tale semicircular colonnades that had been linked by Campbell's magnificent gatehouse. Ahead of them the graceful mansion with its Italianate facade and balustraded roof was ablaze with lights for this gayest affair of the Season.

With the prospect of a whole night of dancing upon them, intelligent females had spent the day quietly. Even before the dancing began, there was entertainment for the arriving guests. An entire ballet was being performed in one of the apartments, while jugglers, rope dancers, acrobats, and singers could be seen and heard throughout the public rooms. Each female guest received a ticket for a prize in a lottery of bijoux to be drawn after midnight.

As she wandered from room to room, each more magnificently decorated than the last, Natasha was gripped by a rising excitement, and the heavy sense of oppression and resentment under which she had struggled lately lifted from her spirit. Her eyes gleamed behind the dainty white lace half-mask as she prepared to enjoy the delights of the evening, secure in her anonymity from the censorious eyes of her guardian and the importunities of her friends. Lizzie's clever fingers had brushed her heavy hair into a soft rolled mass at the back of her head, firmly anchoring the beautiful tortoiseshell comb in the arrangement. The maid agreed that the *mantilla* draped over the comb altered her appearance out of recognition. For the first time she took a naive pleasure in her looks, preening under Lizzie's spontaneous approval and more or less confirmed in her opinion by the silent appraisal of her cousins.

If additional confirmation had been needed, it was provided by the steady parade of costumed gentlemen seeking a dance or a light flirtation with her over the next few hours. Most made concerted efforts to guess her identity and were quite satisfyingly reluctant to relinquish her into another man's keeping at the end of their dance together.

Natasha's customary vitality, in abeyance just lately, came surging back, fueled by her enjoyment. She was not immune to the rising temperatures guaranteed by more than two thousand persons circulating in an enclosed area, but her light clothing was an advantage. By midnight many of the gentlemen had discarded masks, heavy cloaks, and various accoutrements of their period costumes. With a silent giggle she recognized in one of her most persistent pursuers a rather stuffy young man in the dress of a cavalier, who had been all Season the most determined suitor of a girl whose personal attractions needed every inducement provided by her reputed fifty-thousand-pound dowry. Some of her friends she knew by their voices, but she refrained from identifying them and refused to confirm or deny any of their attempts to unmask her.

Though she would certainly be called to account for her dereliction on the morrow, Natasha had carefully avoided the company of her relatives all evening. She went into supper after one o'clock on the arm of a black-clad Puritan and joined a gay party at one of the crowded tables provided for the guests still present. A court jester with whom she had danced earlier slipped into the last empty place at the next table. Natasha smiled a recognition, having encountered his colorful but uncommunicative presence on several occasions already. He bowed in return, his gaze sweeping across the occupants of her table before taking his own seat.

There were only two other women at Natasha's table, a well-endowed Columbine in clinging draperies and a somewhat less-than-regal Queen Bess whose red wig was slipping toward one ear. The ladies gleefully exhibited their prizes from the raffle and demanded to see what Natasha had won. She held out her arm to display the bracelet containing a miniature portrait of the Duke of Wellington, which was duly admired. The gifts, though varying in value, were all decorated with the duke's image, and the ladies all vowed they would treasure them forever.

Supper was a boisterous affair. The company was somewhat less genteel than Natasha was accustomed to meet about town, and a substantial portion of the conversation was unintelligible to her since she was totally ignorant of the activities carried on at boxing matches or gaming hells. She had heard of Harriette Wilson, however, and she listened avidly as the Columbine claimed to have spotted her tonight, describing in some detail the costume the notorious courtesan was wearing. Natasha's eyes rounded as she recalled having seen just such a red-and-black-clad peasant girl earlier. She had been noticeable both for the revealing brevity of her costume and for the number of men clustered about her, seemingly captivated by her animated conversation.

By this time Natasha's escort was becoming annoyingly attentive, leaning closer than she could like as he paid lavish court to her charms. The man on the other side of her accidentally spilled wine on her arm, which he proceeded to mop up with a good-natured apology. The Puritan immediately voiced an objection to this familiarity, removing the serviette from the other's hand with a muttered imprecation against those too foxed to know how to treat a lady.

"No, no," Natasha protested, finishing the drying operation herself. "I am persuaded he meant no disrespect. At this point in the evening he is merely a trifle . . . jocose."

"Well, that is the first stage of drunkeness, after all," her partner argued.

"How many stages are there?" Natasha inquired idly, hoping to give his thoughts another direction while she signaled to the offender to make good his escape.

"Five. First comes jocose, then morose, bellicose, lachrymose, and finally—"

"Comatose?" guessed Natasha, laughing delightedly at her introduction to the old saw. Her laughter stilled when she noted the intensity of the Puritan's gaze on her mouth.

"Ah, clever as well as beautiful," he approved. "The noise in here is deafening, my dear *señorita*. Let us repair to one of the quieter rooms where we shall be safe from such buffoons as he who emptied his wine on you."

Natasha moistened her lips in a quick nervous gesture, unwilling to leave the noise and safety of the supper room in the company of an overardent swain.

"Unfortunately for your plans, March, the *señorita* is promised to me for the first dance after supper."

The quiet assured voice belonged to the jester, who had risen from the next table.

"You have the advantage in knowing my identity, sir, but I think we shall let the lady decide whose company she prefers."

"Ah, here is Lady March approaching. Perhaps she will help the *señorita* to reach her decision," drawled the jester.

"I must not keep you any longer, sir," Natasha said, summoning up a brilliant smile for the Puritan as she placed her fingers on the sleeve of her rescuer. "Thank you very much for the delicious supper."

The graceful figure clad all in white and the colorfully costumed jester headed for the main ballroom without speaking. Something about the controlled way the fool held himself, combined with an intangible aura of censure, struck a chord in Natasha's memory, but she refused to pursue it. Obeying a sudden compulsion, she turned to her companion and said softly, "The noise in the dining room was a bit trying after a time. I would deem it a great favor, sir, if we might dance this next waltz without any of the customary attempts at polite conversation."

Light-colored eyes gleamed behind his black mask as the jester bowed. "Your wish is my command, *señorita*."

The next few moments represented a blissful interval in an evening of near-frenzied entertainment. Not a single word was exchanged, but the well-suited dancers achieved a lovely harmony of movement, their steps matching perfectly as they circled the floor. Natasha's initial stiffness dissolved after the first few bars and she remained responsive to his slightest change of direction thereafter. When he pulled her closer to avoid another couple, her pliant body accommodated itself to his, and she did not protest when he made no effort to reestablish the conventional distance between waltz partners for the rest of the dance. She felt she would always remember the mingled odors of burning candles, floor wax, and the sweet scent of the rose trees and orange trees that had been brought in to decorate the room. She suppressed a pang of regret as the music ended, and her smile for her partner held a tinge of wistfulness.

His eyes too were intent on the naturally red lips that parted to reveal perfect teeth, but they caused no alarm such as she had felt in the Puritan's company, though she was aware of a rapidly beating heart and a shortness of breath—aware too of a strong desire to prolong this moment of enchantment.

"Thank you, *señorita*. I cannot recall when I have enjoyed a dance more. May I return you to your party?"

"If you please, sir, I think I shall go along to the suite reserved for the ladies' use."

The jester signified his acquiescence with a nod and left her at the entrance with a formal bow.

Natasha lingered awhile in the ladies' retiring room after she had removed the stickiness of wine from her forearm, weary suddenly of an excess of gaiety. It had been a wonderful evening, but now she was longing for her bed. Sooner or later she must present herself to her cousins and accept a well-deserved scold for avoiding proper chaperonage all evening.

In the event, Natasha was pleasantly surprised to receive only a cursory set-down from Mrs. Taylor. She had timed her meeting well, for the carriage had been sent for and her cousins were anxious to depart. She sensed a controlled displeasure about them and was grateful that the cause did not seem to lay at her door.

There was little conversation on the drive home, and

what there was consisted of questions to Natasha about people she had recognized. At last Lucretia came out into the open and asked if she had seen Major Talbot.

"Major Talbot did not identify himself to me," replied Natasha with perfect truth. "Did you not meet him tonight?"

Lucretia hunched a shoulder in pretended unconcern. "If I did, he remained in character. Of course, I did not remove my mask until supper, and we did not stay much beyond two-thirty."

As the carriage rolled over the cobbles, Natasha was conscious of a cautious little bubble of happiness somewhere deep inside her. Major Talbot had not sought out Lucretia all evening, or if he had danced with her, he had not given away his identity. Strictly speaking, he had not identified himself to her either, but she had been aware of the jester's unobtrusive presence most of the evening, and he had certainly constituted himself her protector in the supper room. She hugged the knowledge to herself as the carriage drew near the Taylor residence.

8

Nothing was verbally acknowledged by either party about their dances at the *bal masqué* at Burlington House, but relations between Major Talbot and Natasha improved perceptibly after this event. The lady stopped going out of her way to avoid the gentleman when he called in Manchester Square, and sometimes her captivating smile was turned in his direction. For his part there were occasions when he was actually beguiled into abandoning his determinedly superficial conversation to speak seriously to her about the current situation in Europe awaiting the upcoming meetings in Vienna. At such times he seemed to forget her age and gender and meet on equal terms, one intellect speaking to another.

This agreeable state of affairs lasted for nearly a fortnight before coming to an abrupt end at a select musical evening given by the Frobishers. The beautiful Priscilla had a lovely clear soprano that she used well. Natasha acknowledged the quality of her voice, but secretly considered her singing to be like everything else about Lady Frobisher—passionless perfection, a contradiction in terms perhaps, but an apt description of her looks, manners, and musical style.

There were two reasons why Natasha looked forwrd to the musicale with more than tepid interest. Susan was scheduled to sing that evening and she would at last meet Lord Frobisher. Lady Frobisher, one of the leading lights of society, was everywhere to be seen in fashionable circles, but her lord evidently failed to share her interests, for only once had he been pointed out to Natasha, disappearing into a card room during the early hours of a ball.

Contrary to her expectations, Natasha liked Lord

Frobisher on sight as he received their guests beside his lady. He was much older than his wife, nearer forty than thirty, and a large man in every sense, physically tall and wide, with a broad brow, large features, and bush brown eyebrows. When he welcomed Natasha an enormous hand engulfed hers as gently as if she were a newborn kitten. It was patently obvious from his expression of pride and wonder whenever he looked at her that he adored his lovely wife and existed only to please her. He put Natasha strongly in mind of a big friendly bear as he lumbered about, attentive to his guests' comfort. His wife's attitude toward him seemed to be a blend of absentminded affection and impatience that erupted once into sharpness when Lord Frobisher knocked over a chair in an over-zealous movement to assist in seating an elderly guest.

"The servants will attend to that, my lord; it is their job."

Pity for the vulnerability of one who loved so completely became an added element in Natasha's assessment as she averted her eyes from Lord Frobisher's subdued countenance and saw Major Talbot's glance flicker between his host and hostess.

Susan performed early in the program, accompanying herself on the pianoforte. Her sweet husky voice lacked the range for most operatic arias, but she sang with great taste and feeling. The ballads she selected were well-suited to her talents and very well-received by an appreciative audience. Natasha relaxed after the anxious interval of watching a close friend put herself in a sort of jeopardy. She listened enraptured to a fine baritone who had a way with Italian love songs and suffered through a mediocre violin performance from which the audience rose in thankfulness to seek refreshments.

Natasha drifted away from her cousins to join the admiring throng clustered around Lady Flint, listening to a flood of compliments, wearing what Susan laughingly termed her "proud mama" look.

"I do not know why it is, but I always find myself prodigiously hungry after performing in public. Come, let us storm the buffet table," she proposed, linking her arm with Natasha's. "The refreshments are always superb in this house."

They helped themselves liberally from a table loaded with beautifully presented food that was indeed more elaborate than the usual party offerings. Delicate peach-colored ices stood beside brilliant raspberry tarts, but there was plenty of substantial fare to tempt the masculine palate too, including ham and chicken in various guises.

"Don't miss the lobster patties," advised Susan, popping one into her mouth on the spot.

"I won't, and just look at the size of those strawberries! Thank you, yes." This last was to the waiter who invited her to accept a glass of sparkling wine. "Everything I have seen in this house is beautiful and costly," Natasha murmured as they brought their laden plates to a little table. "Lord Frobisher must be very wealthy."

"On the contrary, Harry says there is talk that he is quite done up. His wife's extravagance is a byword about town, and his lordship has been playing deep lately and losing more often than he can afford to."

About the time the two ladies had satisfied their unlady-like appetites, they were joined by their smiling hostess on Major Talbot's arm and by their host with Lord Flint.

Lord Frobisher smiled benevolently at Susan. "I understand from Flint that you are awaiting a happy event, Lady Flint. May I wish you continued good health and as happy an outcome as Lady Frobisher and I enjoyed."

"Thank you, sir; you are most kind. How old is your little boy now—four?"

"No, William was just three in January, but he is a lively scamp, isn't he, my love?"

"He is a bumptious child," amended his love.

"I must admit that he takes more after me than his beautiful mother," Lord Frobisher said with a rueful smile.

"As it should be with a boy, my lord," Susan replied. "It is enough if your daughters resemble their mother."

"That is my dearest wish."

Natasha didn't quite know what to make of the glance that passed between Lord Frobisher and his silent wife, but she had noted the curious stillness that came over Major Talbot and the quick look he had flashed Lady Frobisher when the age of her son was announced. After some rapid mental calculation, she guessed that he had not before realized how very soon after his departure for Portugal his fiancée must have married to have a child so old.

At Lady Frobisher's instigation the conversation took a different turn in the time remaining before the second half of the program. The guests had begun a general exodus from the dining room when Charles Talbot entered and made his way to his hostess. Natasha, who was standing close by, overheard his profuse apologies for his late arrival. She would have returned to the drawing room after a smiling greeting had Charles not detained her by a touch on her arm.

"Please, Natasha, I must speak to you."

"Of course. Come sit with me upstairs."

"We cannot converse during a performance, and what I have to say requries privacy. It is impossible to be private with you in your cousin's house. Please won't you stay behind for a few moments? No one will notice our absence."

That wasn't quite true, Natasha reflected silently as Major Talbot's eyes met hers for a pregnant second before he left the room at his hostess's heels. However, if merely speaking to his cousin was going to evoke her guardian's censure, then she would have to resign herself to remaining in his black books forever because she could not refuse to give Charles a hearing, especially when he was so desperately in earnest. She nodded and allowed him to lead her back to one of the small tables.

Charles was frowning to himself and drumming his fingers on the table, his manner a far cry from his usual urbanity. "God knows I owe you an apology, Natasha, and an explanation, but I haven't been able to get near you since that night at Vauxhall. I was away with my father for almost a fortnight, and when we've met since, it has been in company." Burning blue eyes met sympathetic brown ones as he seized her hand.

"Of course I shouldn't have kissed you, but you looked so dreamy-eyed and appealing that night that I simply lost my head. I didn't need my straitlaced cousin to remind me that my behavior was contemptible. But for the rest of it, I hope you know that I would not play fast and loose with a girl of your quality. We have been real friends, have we not, and I have flattered myself that you understood me a little."

"Yes, Charles, of course we are friends, and I have understood that the rather free manner you have adopted toward me at times was calculated to annoy your cousin."

He winced, and she looked contrite. "Only in the beginning, my dear, and never to mislead you. Please believe that. I would never hurt you, Natasha; I am more drawn to you than I have ever been to any woman, and if things were different—"

She leaned over and placed her fingers against his lips. "No, don't say it, Charles. Friends are what we have been and what we shall remain—good friends. There is no one in London except Susan with whom I feel so comfortable and with whom I am able to be myself, instead of a dressed-up doll with two topics of conversation and no opinions other than those approved for young ladies. And now let us return to the drawing room before our absence is remarked and we really find ourselves the subject of gossip."

Natasha thought Charles sighed as she rose and headed for the staircase, but for herself she was perfectly satisfied with the outcome of their talk. She had realized from her reaction to his kiss that friendship was all she could ever feel for Charles, and she was simply grateful that she would not have to forfeit this friendship in the future.

That she had again forfeited the major's regard was evident from the flinty expression that greeted their late entrance. The tardy pair slipped into the back row of seats during Lady Frobisher's performance, nearly unobserved except that Natasha, having just vowed she would not deign to glance in the major's direction, was instantly pinned by his nail-hard gaze. She could feel her cheeks burning and turned away, furious with herself. She must look the picture of guilt.

For the rest of the program she sat fuming about the maliciousness of a fate that had her always on the defensive. If the music reached her ears at all, it was powerless to charm her heart or engage her mind. Even Charles' amusingly libelous remarks failed to elicit more than a perfunctory smile or two from her.

By the end of the program Natasha had accepted the loss of the tentative new rapport with the major, but the evening was not to finish with mere passive misfortune. The guests rose from their chairs and began to mingle. She had started to make her way toward her cousins when she felt her arm taken in a grip that was firm to the point of discomfort. She was steered over to the relative shelter of a window embrasure where she was more or less obscured from the view of those in the room by the broad-shouldered figure planted squarely in front of her.

Natasha steeled herself to face cold disdain and looked instead into twin green flames.

"I have been made aware, of course, of your complete disregard for the rules governing the conduct of young ladies in their first Season, but I never thought you would carry it to the extent of offering an insult to your hostess."

The healthy color faded from Natasha's cheeks, but she held herself erect and raised her chin to meet his eyes unflinchingly. "I think you must know that I would not willingly insult Lady Frobisher."

"Then what do you call deliberately remaining away when she is about to perform and then compounding the offense by making an entrance in the middle of her performance?"

"Must you make a major crime of what was surely a minor offense? Charles needed to speak to me privately, we were away no more than ten minutes, and our late entrance was most unobtrusive."

"Would you have put yourself in such a delicate

position for anyone else? What kind of power has my cousin over you?"

"The power of friendship, and, yes, if another friend needed me, I would again venture outside the stupid rules governing female behavior."

Major Talbot brushed aside this radical declaration and went right to the heart of the matter. "Friendship! Is it friendship then that has you always sitting in his pocket so that everyone must remark your predilection for his society?"

The unfairness of this accusation crystallized Natasha's resentment into an urgent need for retaliation. "Yes, friendship," she insisted with a haughty toss of her head and a challenging gleam in her eyes. "Can you offer the same explanation for sitting always in Lady Frobisher's pocket?"

He looked thunderstruck at this attack but quickly found his voice. "How dare you compare my association with Lady Frobisher to your flagrant—"

"That's right, there is no real comparison, is there? *My* indiscretions are not committed with *married* men. I withdraw the comparison, and now, sir, if you will be so good as to let me pass, I should hate to have people remark the length of time I have spent hiding in a corner with you, my fragile reputation being what it is."

With this final outrageous retort uttered in the same low tones in which the entire argument had been conducted, Natasha sidestepped swiftly and walked away, leaving Major Talbot to master his spleen before showing his face to his fellow guests.

It was indeed a rare occasion when Cameron Talbot's self-control proved inadequate. In the first few minutes after Natasha spun away from him, his thoughts defied description, but along with anger at her flaunting of convention and defiance in the face of his reprimand was an infuriating recognition that his own reaction to the situation tonight had been overly severe. Equally infuriating was the knowledge that Natasha's accusation had gotten under his skin and she was well aware of the fact.

In a short span of time Cam was able to rejoin the Frobishers' guests for what remained of the evening without betraying his mental agitation. He did not trust himself to call at the Taylor residence for over a sennight, however. For one thing, he had no desire to be in the company of Miss Natasha Phillips at present, and for another, in view of his own reactions at the Frobisher musicale, he was not altogether certain he could restrain a compulsion to deliver some unpalatable home truths to that young lady about the extreme undesirability of an unbridled tongue in a gently bred female. Some deft footwork on social occasions where the Taylor ménage was present enabled him to avoid Natasha and yet spend enough time with Mrs. and Miss Taylor to allay any suspicions that he was deliberately staying away from Manchester Square.

He was less successful in avoiding his own thoughts. Granted that Natasha Phillips had leveled her accusation in a spirit of retaliation, there was just enough truth in it to make him examine his own behavior after his initial anger had died down. The result of this self-questioning was a grudging and surprised admission that he did spend more time in Priscilla's company than in anyone else's—at least in any feminine company, including that of his unofficial ward. The possibility that Natasha might feel neglected and therefore resentful of his attention to Lady Frobisher crossed his mind to be instantly dismissed. There was not a shred of evidence to support a theory that the popular Miss Phillips desired any more of his society than she was accustomed to receiving. He was forced to regard her observation as disinterestedly accurate, which led to the further question of why he had allowed himself to spend so much time with his former fiancée that it had been remarked. He shied away from the unpleasant corollary that, if the inexperienced Natasha had questioned the amount of time he spent in Priscilla's company, the town's gossips must be speculating wildly and scandalously on the nature of their relationship by now.

It didn't help that he had only himself to blame for this

mortifying situation, but he put aside his chagrin in favor of a thorough examination of his recent behavior. In the beginning he had been struck anew by Priscilla's beauty, unprepared in his own mind to find her appeal undiminished by the passage of time and the history between them. At first he had blindly flown at the light of her radiant beauty, instinctively seeking some kind of gratification of his senses in her presence. Looking back, he could see that he had fallen into the habit of seeking out his former love everywhere he went, initially with unquestioning acceptance of pleasure in her society. At some point, he realized with a growing sense of shock, his mind must have begun to function again because just lately he had found her company less satisfying. He had discovered himself committing the apostasy of thinking she would be improved by a little more animation. Her conversation struck him as a bit repetitive and limited in its range, and, worst of all, he had begun to suspect that her nature might be rather cold. Her demeanor toward her husband and cool dismissal of her child as a topic of conversation on that fateful night had fueled his latent suspicions.

When he compared his present analytical state of mind with what, in retrospect, he could only call the mindless adoration of four years ago, he wondered in some perplexity which of them had changed, he or Priscilla. An additional period of concentrated soul-searching produced the tentative conclusion that perhaps neither personality had altered substantially, that the crucial factor was the existence or absence of love. He was inclinced to agree with those who say that love is blind, and he experienced a rush of gratitude at being free of such an incapacitating emotion.

Thank heavens he had never viewed Natasha Phillips through a disfiguring emotional haze. He needed all his wits about him to deal with Peter's mercurial sister.

Cam tried to bring a dispassionate intelligence to bear on the continuing problem of Natasha, but found that her essential nature eluded him. *She* certainly did not lack spirit or warmth—that much must be obvious to the meanest intelligence—but her true character remained shrouded. He had thought her forward at first because she didn't conform to the pattern he had been taught to admire in women, but at this point in their acquaintance he conceded that the behavior he criticized sprang from an eager interest in life around her rather than any unbecoming desire to push herself onto the center stage. She had exhibited admirable restraint in refraining from criticism of her chaperon, who did indeed (he had noted since Charles had raised the issue) avail herself of every opportunity to paint her young cousin in a poor light. Natasha was a thought too impulsive, but often this was another consequence of her loyalty to her friends if his somewhat revised estimation of her conduct with respect to his cousin was correct. Far from actively encouraging the sentimental advances of the men who paid court to her, she seemed to treat them all as platonic friends, to be unaware of the significance of their behavior toward herself.

The more he considered Natasha's actions, the more Cam inclined to the belief that it was innocence and immaturity that prompted her careless seeming behavior with regard to her masculine admirers. He did not confuse this with a basic lack of intelligence. His own conversations with her had shown her to be exceedingly quick to grasp the essentials of any situation. He did not admire her volatile temper or too free tongue—neither trait became a lady of quality—but as the days went by, the conviction grew that he had treated her harshly. When he intercepted a wistful look in his direction one night at an assembly when she thought herself unobserved, his conscience smited him mightily.

The next day he called in Manchester Square, but when he left a half-hour later, it was with no sense of having mended matters between himself and the girl he was pledged to befriend. Natasha had been polite but remote, volunteering no unsolicited conversation at all. In contrast, Mrs. and Miss Taylor had seemed a bit too eager to make him welcome; in fact, it had struck him of a sudden that there had been just a hint of the proprietary in

Mrs. Taylor's manner when she had assumed he would escort them all to a private ball later that week. He had agreed but had allowed his surprise to show. This was an unlooked-for complication he could well do without.

On the evening of the ball Cam was pleased to see Natasha in blooming looks and better spirits than of late. After a covert but thorough appraisal in the carriage, he decided white was definitely her best color. Against pure white her skin glowed with a rich color, highlighted by a deep rose at high cheekbones and lips, and everywhere possessing a sheen of satin just begging to be stroked. Beside her cousin, Miss Taylor's well-groomed fairness appeared insipid to the point of nonentity. It needed someone as strikingly beautiful as Priscilla Frobisher to provide a foil for the spectacular coloring of Natasha Phillips.

When the party was announced, the eyes of their hostess narrowed at sight of Miss Phillips, and her greeting was cool as she adopted a protective stance at the side of her pale and painfully shy daughter. Cam had noted that, unless their own girls were diamonds of the first water, mothers preferred not to expose them to comparisons with the vibrant Natasha. Tonight Mrs. Mortimer's efforts were nullified by her ingenuous daughter, who brightened as Natasha appeared and begged her parent's permission to take her friend aside to meet the visiting cousin whose praises she had been singing.

Cam kept an unobtrusive eye on his friend's sister, observing with heightened interest that as many females as males came up to speak to her. Such was certainly not the case with Lady Frobisher, who had collected a court of young bloods about her but did not seem to be on intimate terms with any of her feminine acquaintances. It was not until he had done his duty by dancing with several young ladies presented to him by Mrs. Mortimer that he eluded his efficient hostess and sought out his unofficial ward, who had been whisked away before he could write his name on her dance card. They were starting up a waltz, but he was too late. Before he drew within speaking range of the gaily chattering group of which she was a part, Captain Standish detached Natasha from it, leading her away.

But not onto the dance floor, Cam saw with barely suppressed annoyance as the pair disappeared into a small room obliquely across the hall from the ballroom. Would the chit never learn discretion? He stationed himself near the ballroom entrance with one eye on the closed door, willingly exchanging banter with passing friends but refusing to be drawn away from his vantage point.

It was fully fifteen minutes later when Captain Standish emerged from the apartment—alone. He was frowning as he made some minor adjustments to his neckcloth before striding in the direction of the card room.

Cam was entering the room he had quitted before the captain was out of sight. He closed the door behind him, leaning against it, arms akimbo, but the sarcasm trembling on his tongue was never uttered. Natasha had been facing the fireplace with her hands raised to her face when he came in, but she spun around, dropping her arms and fixing a smile to her lips at the sound of the closing door. Traces of hastily wiped tears still glistened on one cheek.

He took an impetuous step forward. "What has happened? Did he dare—"

"Please don't scold," Natasha begged, her smile wavering under his scowling scrutiny. "No one did anything. I . . . I was just thinking sad thoughts, that's all. I'm fine now, quite ready to return to the ballroom."

"What kind of sad thoughts? Stand still." Cam produced a handkerchief from an inner pocket and proceeded to take her chin in the fingers of one hand while he dried the remaining tears with the other.

His gentleness disarmed Natasha into relaxing the guard on her tongue. "It is sad that love doesn't always beget love in return, is it not?"

"Yes, but many things in this life are sad, little one. I do not believe Peter would have considered Standish an eligible *parti* in any case. He is a younger son with only modest expectations."

"What has that to say to anything? Had I returned his

108

feelings, material considerations would not have weighed with me."

The green eyes hardened as Cam's hands dropped to his side. "Are you suggesting you would defy your guardian's wishes on such an important matter?"

"Peter isn't my guardian. I am of age, but that is beside the—"

"You are of age? When?" he shot at her.

"Last month, but even if I were not, how could Peter, who is not here, be expected to exercise judgment on a man I might decide to marry?"

"You are saying then that you would set your will in opposition to your brother's if it came to that? Or against another who stood in his place as guardian?"

Natasha looked up at him in some perplexity. "Not at all. I am saying that Peter would expect *me* to choose a man with whom I could hope to achieve that complete mental communion that is necessary for a real marriage, but I digress and time passes. Let us return to the ballroom before our absence is noted." Her smile flickered and faded. "I don't really mean to make scandals, you know, Major."

Cam looked searchingly into brown velvet eyes, conscious that time was his enemy in this situation. He could think of nothing to say to one whose essential nature resisted his attempts at understanding. He responded instead, as he had before, to that wistful quality, taking her wordlessly into his arms as they joined the whirling throng on the dance floor.

9

The joyous festivities in the British capital continued apace as the summer advanced. The Duke of Wellington had taken his seat in the House of Lords in June and had been thanked for his services to his country in July by the speaker in a message to the House of Commons that ended with congratulations on his appointment as Britain's ambassador to France. After five hectic weeks in England, the new ambassador set out for his post early in August with the intention, on his way to Paris, of inspecting the military setup of the peace-keeping force stationed in Brussels.

Meanwhile, London's parks were being cleaned up in preparation for a grand celebration of one hundred years of Hanoverian rule and to commemorate the anniversary of the Battle of the Nile. A wooden bridge surmounted by a Chinese pagoda, all painted a vivid yellow with black lines, was built over the creek in St. James's Park while a huge canvas replica of an embattled Gothic castle was being erected in Green Park, which was to be the site of a spectacular display of fireworks. Hyde Park was being readied for a regatta, to be followed by a splendid neumachia on the Serpentine, depicting the destruction of the French fleet. Ornamental booths and galleries, and entertainments such as swings and roundabouts were also set up there.

The young ladies from Manchester Square were aware of all these preparations, of course. Their earlier experience of mixing with crowds in Hyde Park notwithstanding, they were as eager to participate in the celebrations as any ordinary citizen of London. Their persuasive arguments came to nothing this time, however. Mrs. Taylor was adamant in refusing to permit the girls to attend the public events even heavily escorted by willing males.

"I'd as soon turn them loose at Bartholomew Fair," she said flatly when Mr. Randolph Ramsey-Martin volunteered his and his friends' services as escort. "There won't be a halfpenny's worth of difference in the vulgar atmosphere of Hyde Park and Smithfield this week."

When Natasha ventured to suggest that it might be possible to witness the gigantic fireworks display from a location at some distance from the worst of the crowds, she was informed that Mrs. Taylor had committed them to attending a private ball on that evening, escorted by Lord Wembley. Denied any avenue of appeal, Natasha subsided, outwardly submissive but disgruntled. Cousin Edwina must always be considered to have good *ton*, but she was lamentably lacking in a spirit of adventure. As for Lord Wembley, a widowed contemporary of Mrs. Taylor, he was as fussy as an old woman and equally as addicted to gossip.

Despite her efforts at concealment, something of her feelings must have appeared on her face because Captain Standish, who had dropped in to return a book she had lent him, closed one eyelid in a solemn wink that nearly caused her to lose her countenance altogether.

On the evening in question, Natasha took even less interest than usual in her appearance, accepting the pale-pink gown Lizzie selected without even glancing up from the acrostic puzzle she was attempting to solve. Likewise, the abigail was able to exercise her creativity on a coiffure with no restrictions placed by an indifferent mistress. The resultant braided chignon secured at the nape emphasized the exoticism of a heart-shaped face dominated by a pair of extraordinary dark eyes set above high cheekbones with delicate hollows beneath. Natasha approved the final effect with a smiling thank-you, totally oblivious, in her haste to finish the ritual, of the artificial rose Lizzie had set into one side of the chignon. She remained in her room until it was time to join her cousins, when she caught up her lace *mantilla* to use as a shawl and slipped the matching fan and a beaded reticule over her wrist.

Lord Wembley, stout, balding, pink-faced, and perspiring above his high shirt points, enlivened the drive to the ball with a recapitulation of Princess Charlotte's broken engagement and the subsequent quarrel with her father that had culminated in her running away from Carlton House to her mother. The fact that the recalcitrant princess had been banished to Cranbourne Lodge at Windsor for an indefinite time and denied all contact with her mother or her friends seemed to afford Lord Wembley the greatest satisfaction.

"Perhaps they will be able to drum some manners and decorum into her there."

"I should sink into the ground if a daughter of mine ever displayed such a want of conduct," said Mrs. Taylor with a shudder. "I do not even speak of the tenor of her mind or the indelicacy of her conversation . . . if but half of what one hears of her is true."

"She is said to be very fast." This from Lucretia.

"Oh, but she is still so young, just eighteen," pleaded Natasha out of sympathy for a girl whose whole existence had been a bone of contention and a weapon in her parents' perpetual warfare. "Surely there must be some better method of improving her behavior than depriving her of all society."

"She is unfit for decent society," pronounced Lord Wembley.

By dint of biting her tongue, Natasha kept herself from pointing out that incarceration was scarcely likely to achieve the goal of fitting anyone for polite society, but her customary submissiveness to her elders was very delicately balanced at this point.

Within an hour of their arrival at the Penderly ball this balance had been overset. She had been one of a group of young people laughing at a comic reenactment of a spill taken by a would-be whip showing off in his new curricle when she had noticed Mrs. Taylor's beckoning finger. Obedient to the summons, she slipped away from her friends and went up to her chaperon, who began without preamble.

"My dear Natasha, I know you will not take it amiss if I venture to point out to you that a lady never indulges in excessive public merriment lest she be judged a sad romp. If you will just try to emulate your cousin, you will do very well at these affairs. Remember, my dear, moderation in all things."

Natasha stared at the pious arrangement of features that could not disguise her cousin's cold blue eyes, then past her to Lord Wembley, whose nod of agreement indicated that he had heard every word of the reprimand. Astonishment gave way to angry comprehension as she realized that it had been Edwina's intention to humiliate her in front of her friend, and suddenly she couldn't bear her situation another minute. Try as she would she could do nothing to please, unless one considered that it pleased Edwina to be displeased with her unwanted young relative. She turned on her heel and walked rapidly away before her tongue should betray her resolve to be conformable in all things.

Natasha headed blindly for the doorway, not knowing where she was going but desirous of putting as much distance as possible between herself and her cousin. She wished herself a thousand miles away from this city of coldhearted people. She wished she'd never come here in the first place, never left Devon . . .

"Whoa there, Natasha, where are you off to in such a hurry?"

The fleeing girl came to a halt and blinked up at the handsome face of her most persistent admirer. "Oh, Captain Standish, hello. I didn't see you. I did not expect to see you here tonight."

"I came solely for your sake."

"For my sake?" she echoed warily, alerted by a wicked gleam in the hazel eyes smiling down at her.

"I could not help seeing the other day that you would much rather be watching the fun in the parks tonight than stuck here at this tame ball, so I have come to take you away, if you are game."

Laughter leapt into Natasha's eyes and her lips smiled at the challenge in his, but she demurred. "Do not be foolish.

You must know that my cousin would never permit me to go off with you on such a spree."

"I do not propose to ask her permission. I have bribed the porter to tell no one of our escape and to let us back in long before Mrs. Taylor should desire to leave. All you have to do is fetch your wrap in case it gets colder—and your courage, of course. Well?"

She stood there, visibly tempted but undecided.

"Have you no taste for a little harmless fun after all? This house is practically next door to St. James's Park. We'll come back anytime you say."

A rush of reckless elation sped through Natasha's veins as she gazed into his amused face, daring her to defy authority. "I'll come," she decided, stomping on her conscience. "Wait for me downstairs while I get my cloak."

Taking a leaf from the captain's book, Natasha bribed the maid who fetched her silk cloak to deny any knowledge of her. She headed for the stairs with this garment, white, as luck would have it, folded as compactly as possible and placed over her forearm under the lace *mantilla*. Now that the fateful decision had been made, she was as collected as an actress in midperformance who knows she has the audience in the palm of her hand. No thought of painful consequences troubled her spirit as she sauntered away from the reception rooms. It wasn't confidence in the captain's skills as an intriguer so much as an uncaring state of mind that enabled her to pretend she had not seen Cameron Talbot's hand raised in greeting as she passed a jolly group without altering her casual pace. Once on the stairway, however, she fairly flew down to meet Captain Standish in the hall below.

The man she had affected not to see continued to devote most of his attention to his conversation during the next few minutes. A small corner of his mind was reserved for Natasha, however, and when she did not reappear in the next half-hour, the corner spread to include his thinking apparatus. He excused himself to begin an apparently aimless tour of the reception rooms that convinced him some fifteen minutes later that though Mrs. Taylor was sitting with some of her cronies in the designated ballroom, and Miss Taylor was part of a set performing a spirited country dance, his charge was nowhere on the premises.

Summoning up a mental picture of Miss Phillips as last seen, he grew thoughtful. There had been no indication of any indisposition that might have made it necessary for her to leave early; her color had been good, her expression composed, and the graceful glide that generally characterized her movements very much in evidence. She had been wearing a pale gown—pink, he thought—and carrying a lace shawl on one arm.

His brows drew together with the effort of reconstructing his memory picture. The shawl had not been set across her shoulders or draped above her elbows as was the fashion for long stoles; she had been carrying it. Now, why, if she did not wish to wear it, would she choose to carry it at a dance rather than leave it with her cloak? Cam's lips tightened as a disconcerting alternative presented itself for consideration. A female desirous of leaving a ball unnoticed might elect to carry her shawl over her arm to conceal a folded cloak. While possible destinations flashed into his head, Cam conducted another search of the rooms, this time looking for a tall military figure that he had glimpsed briefly earlier, but his search for Captain Standish was equally unsuccessful. He wasted no more time in speculation but collected his hat and gloves and approached one of the footmen at the entrance.

"Did you happen to notice a military-looking gentleman leaving within the hour with a dark-haired young lady in a pink gown?"

"I really can't say that I did, sir," replied the bewigged servant blandly as he opened the door for him.

"How much did he pay you to ensure such a faulty memory?" Dryness crept into the major's voice.

The man's eyes flickered once, but he maintained his unknowing expression. "Sorry not to be more helpful, sir. A very good night to you, sir."

Cam permitted himself a sardonic curl of his upper lip as he was bowed out the door. Once on the flagway, he drew his dark brows together again as he hesitated, then walked off in the direction of St. James's Street. If one ruled out an elopement, which seemed reasonable in the wake of Natasha's confidence to him following Standish's proposal the week before, and discounted a sudden indisposition, for which there was no evidence, one was left with an assignation of a temporary nature. He'd take his oath she wasn't in the habit of sneaking off with her swains, which brought him back to the question, Why begin tonight?

A shower of colored sparks bursting above the treetops overhead drew his eyes up and gave him an answer. Of course! The celebrations in the parks. That accounted for the increase in foot traffic through this quarter and the loud reports like isolated bursts of gunfire. Of a certainty he would find Natasha in the center of the activity. Obviously, Mrs. Taylor had forbidden the girls to go among the London crowds this week, and Natasha had chosen to defy the edict with the connivance of her besotted captain.

Cam was of two minds whether to continue his search. She should be safe enough with Standish, who would guard her with his life, and he was tired of figuring as an ogre in her estimation. At Pall Mall he hesitated, half-minded to return to the ball, but the staggering progress of two men a few yards ahead was a timely reminder that the city's population was celebrating in the usual fashion. It would cost nothing to head in the direction of the scheduled activities. If memory served, the fireworks were in Green Park, but there seemed to be a steady stream of people into St. James's.

Suddenly Cam's nostrils twitched and his head swiveled. *Smoke!* Coming from St. James's Park. His feet turned automatically in that direction.

As he neared the water, the crowd grew thicker and louder. Women were wailing and squealing, men were running around as people burst out of the central area heading in all directions.

"What has happened?" Cam demanded of a man in a rusty black coat and battered, low-crowned hat escorting a brightly clad, brassy-haired damsel whose dark eyes were dilated with pleasurable fear.

"That there pagoda thing over the bridge burst into flames."

"Was anyone injured?"

"Dozens of 'em, sir, shrieking and screaming to—"

"Hush, Amy. Don't pay her no heed, sir. There was a few got burnt, that's all. There's more danger they'll trample all over one another, if you was to ask me."

"Thank you." Cam tossed the acknowledgment over his shoulder, already running toward the water, dodging those streaming back toward the Mall. He was in time to see the blue-painted roof of the pagoda, engulfed in a crown of flames, sink slowly into the stream with a hissing sound as flame became steam. He was staring entranced at the firelit scene, vaguely conscious of dark faceless figures moving in and out of the bright areas as though performing grotesque dances to unheard music when a husky feminine voice penetrated his absorption.

"Cam, oh, Cam, thank heavens it *is* you! Captain Standish is injured, but he refuses to let me take him to a hospital."

The nagging worry that had accompanied Cam to this frenzied scene evaporated, to be replaced by exasperation as he contemplated the anxious face of Miss Natasha Phillips. For a basically sweet-natured girl, she had a singular propensity for attracting minor disasters. Before he could frame a remark expressive of his contradictory emotions, she seized his arm and tugged him over to a nearby lime tree, at the base of which sat Captain Standish with his eyes closed, one hand holding a bloodstained handkerchief to the side of his head.

"Good Lord, Standish, what happened? You are not burned, are you?"

"No," intervened Natasha. "It was by the sheerest bad luck that the captain's foot slipped just as a couple of people lurched against us, and he was sent crashing into this tree. He was a bit stunned and received a bad gash above his ear, but I have not been able to persuade him to go to a hospital."

As she spoke, Natasha removed the wadded handkerchief from under Captain Standish's fingers to display the still-bleeding gash to the man bending over him. Even in the poor light a quick glance confirmed that it required attention, but Cam was occupied with restraining the injured man's efforts to get to his feet.

"Must take Natasha back to the Penderlys' before she is missed."

"Yes, of course, but I will see to that, man, after someone attends to you."

"It's not serious," the captain insisted. "I was a bit groggy at first, but my head is much clearer now." This time his efforts to rise, assisted by Major Talbot's strong right arm, were successful, though he wavered a bit on his feet at first. "I'm all right now, don't need a doctor; my man is as good as any field surgeon. He'll attend to the cut after I've returned Natasha to her cousin."

"Nonsense, man, you cannot appear at the Penderlys' looking like a war casualty if your object is to avoid gossip. You can trust me to get Miss Phillips back to the ball after we see you to your rooms."

Captain Standish frowned and immediately put a hand up to his aching head. He could not fail to see the force of the major's argument but insisted stubbornly that the first priority was to return Natasha to the ball. It was finally agreed, over that young lady's protests, that the captain would go home alone in a hackney cab while Major Talbot escorted the truant back to her party. A few moments later they saw him off, still abjectly apologizing for placing Natasha at risk.

"I feel wretchedly guilty," she confessed in a small voice as the hack disappeared around the corner. "The captain planned this excursion, knowing how disappointed I was not to be allowed to witness the public festivities, and now he is hurt and worried, and it is all my fault."

"Whose brilliant idea was it to come here tonight, yours or Standish's?"

She hesitated briefly before electing to tell the truth, adding with characteristic candor, "Not that it required any persuasion on my part. I was annoyed with my cousin at the time and consequently ripe for mischief. My father always claimed my besetting sin was emotional impulsiveness. He said I would never be fully mature until I had conquered this tendency." She sighed and went on as though speaking to herself. "I really thought living in my cousin's house had taught me to subdue my temper and curb all impulsive behavior, but it seems not. Had I not allowed myself to become so angry tonight, none of this would have happened."

"Before you plunge into an orgy of self-castigation," her companion said dryly, "permit me to point out that by far the greater blame for this escapade belongs to Standish, who was certainly not demonstrating maturity by allowing his judgment to be overset by a pair of appealing dark eyes. He should be well past that stage at his age."

"I don't suppose you ever went through a stage where feminine eyes could influence you against your better judgment," she said coolly.

They had resumed walking back toward the Penderly house. Natasha's hand had been resting lightly on her escort's sleeve, but now, though she did not physically remove it, there ceased to be any pressure on his arm at all. Glancing sideways at the charming profile, he was aware by her absolute stillness that she had distanced herself from him mentally. He ignored the pang of regret that resulted but couldn't prevent some harshness from coloring his own voice.

"Then you suppose wrong, but one profits from the experience if one is ever to achieve that maturity extolled by your father." With an effort he lightened his tones as he pulled out a watch from his pocket and glanced at it. "To return to tonight's little adventure, it is barely eleven-thirty now. With a little luck we shall be able to slip back into the ballroom during supper with no one the wiser."

As though to remind a presumptuous humanity that luck was a quality dispensed at the whim of the gods, the comparative quiet of the summer evening was shattered at that precise moment. Afterward, Cam and Natasha agreed that the shout came first, followed by a confused medley of carriage wheels, a horse snorting and rearing, an impact, and a steady stream of fluent cursing. What they saw was an unsuccessful attempt on the part of a hackney jarvey to avoid hitting a man dashing across the street. Natasha closed her eyes in horror at the impact, but she was right behind Major Talbot when he raced to the aid of the accident victim.

The man, dressed in the tattered remnants of a military uniform, was lying facedown on the cobblestones, one leg crumpled under him and one sprawled at an unnatural angle.

Ignoring the driver's vociferous attempts at self-exculpation from his position at the horse's head, where he was calming the beast, Cam gently turned the victim over, straightening the left leg carefully.

"This is definitely broken," he said to Natasha, who was squatting by his side. "I wanted to get it into position before he regained consciousness."

"I think he is coming around now." Natasha wiped away a trickle of blood from a cut over the man's eyebrow, using a handkerchief she had taken from her reticule.

"Beechy!"

"What?" An inquiring glance at her companion revealed a man rigid with shock and concern as Major Talbot stared at the face of the injured man. "Do you know him?"

"He was a sergeant in my brigade, Sergeant Beecham. Beechy, can you hear me? Wake up, Beechy!"

The man on the ground groaned and his eyelids fluttered, then lifted. His unfocused gaze passed over Natasha and lighted on the man at her side. Slack lips in a colorless face grimaced, half in pain, half in greeting.

"I knew it was you across the street, sir. Damn-fool thing to do, dashing across like that." He stirred a little, biting back an exclamation of pain.

"It would have been more prudent, certainly, to wait until the street was clear of traffic, just as it would have been more prudent to wait until the firing had stopped before you pulled me back behind that embankment at

Salamanca. But don't try to talk now, Beechy. We'll take you to a hospital and get that leg set first. Any other injuries?''

"My head feels like someone is hammering on it, but my arms seem to be functioning," said the victim, moving the aforementioned limbs gingerly.

"Don't move your head, Sergeant Beecham," Natasha said softly. "It makes the cut over your eye bleed more." She was now using the hem of her petticoat to wipe the blood away from his eye, having already saturated the tiny square of embroidered lawn. The major's handkerchief had been donated to Captain Standish earlier.

Major Talbot sprang into action, dispersing the gawkers who had gathered at the scene and propitiating and absolving the irate driver from all blame for the accident. He dispensed immediate largesse and promised more, ordering the jarvey to knock some of the interior roof slats of the hackney loose to use as splints before they attempted to move the injured man to a hospital. This done, Natasha stepped into the vehicle momentarily to remove her petticoat, which she proceeded to tear into strips for tying the makeshift splints to the leg. Knowing they could not all crowd into the hack, she hailed the next one to come down the street and held the horse while the driver assisted Major Talbot in lifting his comrade inside, a difficult maneuver that sorely tried the sergeant's fortitude.

Up to this point Major Talbot had accepted her practical help unquestioningly, but now he looked at her with compunction.

"I should have sent you back to the Penderlys' in a hack before attending to Beechy, but that's impossible now. There is blood and dirt on your gown and cloak. I'm terribly sorry, my dear girl, but I fear there's nothing for it now except to keep you with me until I can deliver you to your cousin personally."

Natasha nodded. "First things first. You ride with the sergeant. I'll take this other hack and wait in it while you see him safely in hospital." She climbed inside without another word, and the strange procession set off for St. George's.

Fortunately for Natasha the night was balmy. She was only just beginning to feel a bit chilled an hour later when Major Talbot returned from settling his comrade. His face as he entered was so set and stern that a thrill of apprehension feathered down her spine.

"What's wrong? Is Sergeant Beecham—?"

"He's exhausted, but he'll do, now that the leg is set." Cam eased into the seat, dropping his head against the inadequately padded backrest momentarily as the hack jerked into motion.

He looked exhausted himself, Natasha thought, and for the first time, with his eyes closed, vulnerable somehow. Those grooves at the sides of his mouth were new.

"Now we must concentrate on your problem," he said briskly, sitting upright once more, his expression controlled, though Natasha suspected it had embarrassed him to detect sympathy in her gaze. Or perhaps he simply regarded her concern as an invasion of his privacy. His inner self remained a mystery to her.

"Well, I have been thinking about that while you were in the hospital," she said, determinedly cheerful, "and it does not seem so very bad to me. Naturally, my cousin is bound to be a trifle cross," she added when his eyebrows shot up, "but she is a rational person and she will appreciate, when we explain the unfortunate circumstances, that there was really nothing else to be done. The merest decency dictated that Sergeant Beecham must be attended to first. We could not leave him there in the street."

Cam did not even bother to respond to this hopeful piece of naiveté, and Natasha subsided with a sigh after a long look at his uncompromising countenance. The rest of the drive home was accomplished in total silence, grim on his part and uncertain on hers. Surprisingly, there was still considerable pedestrian traffic on the streets at this late hour, and theirs was by no means the only vehicle clopping along the cobblestones. Natasha concentrated her gaze on the passing scene, refusing to think of the moment when she would have to confront her cousin's displeasure.

The eventual pulling up of the hackney outside the Taylor house caught her unprepared, giving the lie to her apparent interest in their surroundings. A trifle shaken, she turned hastily to her escort.

"Thank you, sir, for seeing me safely home. I shall be fine now."

For a second a rare spark of humor lit the fine eyes of the man preparing to descend. "You do not imagine, do you, that I would allow you to face Mrs. Taylor's wrath unsupported?"

"No, truly, sir, it might be better if I explained everything to her myself. Besides, it is very late and she may have retired for the night."

"Do you know, I find that extremely unlikely. Come!"

He held out an imperative hand, and Natasha, secretly grateful, put hers into it without further expostulation.

10

"Whether or not I believe this extraordinary account of your actions tonight doesn't signify in the least." Mrs. Taylor bent a glance of cold distaste on her young cousin. "What does signify is that you disappeared from a house where you were a guest, with no word to anyone, and could not be found when it came time for your party to depart, leaving a gap of several hours unaccounted for."

"But we *have* accounted for them," cried Natasha. "And of course it matters that you believe me! It would be terrible to think one had been harboring a liar in one's home."

"Are you implying, ma'am, that you doubt the veracity of our explanation?" Major Talbot's voice was quiet, but there was that in it that gave Mrs. Taylor pause, for she retreated quickly.

"Not at all. As a matter of fact, I am quite willing to accept that everything happened exactly as you described it, but that is beside the point, which is that Natasha is known to have been absent from the Penderlys' for most of the evening."

"Known to be absent by whom, ma'am?"

"Lord Wembley for one, naturally, and Mrs. Penderly and her son. She sent him to find Natasha when Lord Wembley called for his carriage at midnight. You may depend upon it, it will be all over town by tomorrow." She turned to Natasha and snapped, "I hope you are satisfied, miss, now that you have succeeded in ruining yourself by what I can only term a complete disregard for propriety, surpassing even your lack of consideration for those who offered you a home."

Natasha blanched under this attack but said disbelievingly, "There may be a little gossip at first, but surely it will die down once we explain what really happened."

"You cannot get around the fact that you went traipsing off alone with a man, something no gently reared female would dream of doing."

Major Talbot glanced from the shamefaced girl, drooping with fatigue in her stained and bedraggled gown, to the cold vindictive visage of the woman who had been awaiting her cousin's return in this little sitting room on the ground floor and made his decision. His voice deceptively mild, he said, "Oh, I am persuaded most people will regard a girl's jauntering off with her betrothed as no more than a minor peccadillo, do you not agree?"

"*Betrothed!*"

"But I refused Captain Standish!" Natasha's objection drowned out her cousin's exclamation.

"I think perhaps it would be as well to forget Captain Standish's part in this adventure, do you not?" Major Talbot smiled intimately at Natasha before addressing Mrs. Taylor in tones of amused conspiracy. "No one knows it was Captain Standish with whom Natasha left tonight, so we shall simply represent the affair as a case of a lovely lady using her wiles to persuade her new fiancé to take her to see the fireworks. That should answer reasonably well—they do say all the world loves a lover."

"But . . . you cannot . . ." began Natasha.

"This absurd quixotic gesture on your part is quite unnecessary, I assure you, Major Talbot." Mrs. Taylor, visibly shaken, regained command of her voice. "Matters are not so desperate as all that. I daresay we might contact Lord Wembley and the Penderlys in the morning to explain the situation and ask their cooperation in keeping it quiet."

"Unfortunately, it is much more likely that the juicy tale is already circulating in the clubs. Albert Penderly is not known for his discretion." Major Talbot shook his head. "No, all things considered, I believe my solution is best, and it is not a quixotic gesture, Mrs. Taylor, but rather a case of hastening the inevitable. I should have preferred to have written my intentions to Peter before any formal announcement appeared, but . . .'' He shrugged in resignation and seemed to become aware all at once of the pale, determined girl tugging at his sleeve.

"*No!*" she protested fiercely. "I will not have you sacrifice your freedom for the sake of my reputation. I will leave London, and that will be an end to it. I would have returned home soon in any case."

Major Talbot possessed himself of the grubby, blood-stained fingers whose clutch was wrinkling the sleeve of his newest evening coat and gently raised them to his lips. "You are nearly asleep on your feet, my dear. Go to bed now and we will talk in the morning. No one will try to coerce you into doing anything you do not wish to do, that I promise you. Now, will *you* promise *me* to put everything that has happened tonight out of your mind until tomorrow and try to get some rest?"

For a tense moment uncomprehending brown eyes stared into compelling green ones, then Natasha nodded, whispered a quick good-night, and left the room, her eyes downcast as she edged around her cousin, who stood stock-still in frozen resentment.

Not until the door clicked shut did the man and woman remaining in the room look at each other once more. Mrs. Taylor squared her shoulders and met the watchful glance of the man she had hoped to secure for her daughter.

"Am I to take it, then, that you intend to go through with this ludicrous betrothal scheme?"

"I would not myself so describe my intention to marry Natasha, but naturally I would be most interested to learn your reasons for terming it ludicrous."

Words and tone were exquisitely courteous, but Mrs. Taylor's lips thinned as she said shortly, "You two strike me as being singularly ill-suited to each other."

"Do we?" he asked, still with that marked degree of courtesy. "How curious. The hour being so late, I won't press you for specific examples of ways in which we are unsuited. Suffice it to say I have great hopes that we may become very well-suited in time. I'll take my leave of you now, ma'am, with a request for a private interview with your cousin in the morning." He waited for her acknowledging nod before adding, "You needn't trouble Chudleigh, I can show myself out."

"But I prefer to satisfy myself that all visitors are off the premises and the house is secured for the night before I retired," she replied, ringing the bell.

He bowed ironically. "As you wish. Cheer up, ma'am. Natasha may share your views as to our lack of compatibility. She may refuse my proposal."

Mrs. Taylor's lips curled in derision. "Fustian! The girl's not a complete fool!"

"Very true, but neither is she on the catch for a wealthy husband. If she does not feel we shall suit ultimately, she'll turn me down."

"You seem quite sanguine at the prospect of a refusal."

"Ah, but I intend to be very persuasive tomorrow."

"There is no guarantee that a convenient betrothal will restore the girl's reputation, you know," warned Mrs. Taylor, unwisely allowing spite to overcome prudence.

Chudleigh entered the sitting room just at the end of this speech, but Cam ignored his presence as he said, "I do trust you may be mistaken, for if that should prove to be the case, I shall know where to place the responsibility, *and so will Lord Phillips*. Your very obedient servant, ma'am." Neither the major's soft accents nor the deferential bow he swept his hostess in farewell detracted one whit from the menace in his parting remark.

As he passed the undoubtedly curious but still-impassive butler and went down the steps to the flagway, Cam experienced a grim satisfaction in having for once gotten the upper hand with the overbearing Mrs. Taylor. The satisfaction was transient, however, while the grimness increased with the distance he put between himself and Manchester Square. He was glad he'd dismissed the hackney on their arrival. Hopefully, the brisk night air would cool his fevered thoughts.

A sudden fever of the brain was as likely an explanation as any for what he had just done. Would a man in the full possession of his senses have saddled himself with a wife he didn't want by the kind of quixotic gesture he had just denied to Mrs. Taylor? On the other hand, what alternative course had he? If the girl's reputation was compromised, then he was the man who had compromised it. Even bleeding like a stuck pig, Standish would have escorted her back to that ball at a decent hour; he was the man who had blithely accepted her generosity in succoring one who was a stranger to her. And once that harpy had begun her attack on Natasha, the outcome had been inevitable. Right from the beginning of their acquaintance when he had not really liked his friend's little sister, he had found himself constrained by some inner force to go to her rescue at the least suggestion of difficulty. For one who strove always to project an image of good-humored competence, she had about her an air of vulnerability that evoked his protective instincts.

Perhaps this strange match might prosper despite Mrs. Taylor's ill-natured predictions of disaster. Apparently Priscilla had cured him of the folly of falling in love—certainly none of the interchangeable young women he'd met during this hideously social London interlude had quickened his pulses a jot. He preferred Natasha with her innate simplicity and intrinsic honesty to the lot of them. She wasn't in love with him, of course; in fact, he was not altogether sure she liked him above half. He could not deny that their relationship had had its fair share of acrimonious encounters to date, but there was something, if only their shared affection for Peter, that had forged a tie between them. Though she was far from ready for marriage, there had been one or two instances of late when he had been sharply aware of her as a desirable female. He would not like to swear that the recognition had been mutual, but he would have to chance that it could become so in time.

By the time he reached his lodgings, Cam had mastered his initial misgivings and was able to greet his man Walker in his usual calm manner. He arrived at the Taylor residence the next morning prepared to deal with the practicalities of the situation only to be met by a strangely intransigent Natasha. Gone was the disheveled, tired, and bewildered girl of the previous night, and in her place was a composed and resolute young woman with her own solution to propose.

She joined him in the saloon within two minutes of Chudleigh's showing him into it and wasted no time coming to the point. "I thought I would save you the trouble of making any pretty speeches, if that is what you planned to do, by telling you right off that no pretense of a betrothal will be necessary. I intend to return to my home immediately."

"Good morning, Natasha." He had risen on her entrance and now indicated a chair, which she approached after a slight hesitation. "I trust you slept well?"

"Good morning, Major Talbot. Yes, thank you, I slept very well. I—"

"Why am I Major Talbot again? Last night you called me Cam."

"I did?" Natasha didn't trust the wounded expression the major was attempting to portray. "When?"

"When you called out to me with such touching gratitude for being in St. James's at the critical moment, as it were."

"Oh. Well, that was, as you say, in the heat of a crisis. And why am I become Natasha suddenly when you have consistently refused to avail yourself of my permission to use my name?"

No quarter asked or given, he recognized with reluctant admiration as he elected not to respond to the implied accusation. "It would surely seem a trifle formal to continue to give one's betrothed her title?"

"But I have already explained that I do not intend to become engaged to you. Once I am gone, the talk will die down. After all, there will be no one to talk about."

"I think you cannot have considered the situation in all of its ramifications, my dear girl. Forgetting, but only for the sake of argument, your own damaged reputation, if you permit gossip to chase you out of town, it will be said of your cousin that she banished you, and of me that I allowed you to be ruined socially.''

"But that is manifestly unfair!" She glared at him. "And untrue!"

He shrugged in reply.

"You can explain, surely, that I leave by my own choice."

"Oh, yes, I can explain, and so can Mrs. Taylor, and also, no doubt, Captain Standish, who will certainly press his suit once more when the talk begins."

She was silent, considering the implications raised by the major's speech. He was content to sit and watch the interplay of emotions on her expressive countenance, only wishing the looks she darted at him were not so full of doubt. At last she said, "Very well, then, let there be a betrothal announcement. We can say we will set the wedding date when Peter returns. When I can decently go down to Devon, I shall do so, and the engagement may then be forgotten. Why are you shaking your head?"

"Because it won't answer, my dear. This betrothal must be followed in short order by a wedding."

"But I don't think I wish to be married!"

There was a certain rigidity about Cam's features as he said carefully, "Do you dislike me so much, then?"

"Of course not! I do not dislike you at all. Why should you think such a thing?"

"If you prefer scandal to marriage to me, how can I not think it?"

"It is not marriage to *you* that I object to, but the condition of marriage for a woman," she explained patiently, but apparently not lucidly because Cam's puzzlement remained.

"I would have said marriage was the object of every young woman here in London for the Season. Why else come?"

"That is true for a good many females, of course, for varying reasons—some cultural, some economic—but a married woman has no legal standing whatever. In these enlightened times she still becomes the property of her

130

husband, and what is more to the point, *her* property and fortune go to her husband on her marriage."

"But that was ever so."

"Granted, but I do not believe I wish to give up control of my fortune, which I now have under the terms of my father's and grandmother's wills."

"You do not wish . . ." He paused and began again. "Would you mind telling me, if I am not being indelicate, the extent of your fortune?"

"Upward of thirty-five thousand pounds invested in the funds, but it is more now because a ship in which I invested has just returned from India ahead of schedule with a rich cargo."

"Do you mean me to understand that you personally make financial investments?"

"Yes, with the advice of my man of business, naturally. My father was not much interested in money or investing, but my grandmother and I enjoyed reading the financial news, especially anything concerned with trade and shipping."

"And you have full control of assets of more than thirty-five thousand pounds?"

"Plus my grandmother's jewelry, which is fabulous. I should perhaps explain that, though my grandmother claimed to be the illegitimate daughter of a Russian nobleman, she was a ballerina when Grandfather married her. He seems not to have minded that much of her jewelry was given to her by other men. He died before I was born, but my father said Grandfather considered himself too fortunate to have won Grandmother at all to quibble about her trinkets. I believe not all men would feel that way."

"I believe you are correct," said Major Talbot without a blink. "Both your grandfather and father seem to have been something quite out of the common run of humanity, not to mention your grandmother."

"That is true. My own mother sometimes found them all a bit difficult to deal with, but since she was richly endowed with common sense, they left most of the running of the estate in her hands until she died, when I was fourteen. Then Father had to bestir himself. Peter was away by then, so he had to rely on me. But we are wandering from the point of this discussion, sir."

"Which was your disinclination to enter the estate of matrimony on financial grounds. Tell me, do you have other personal or ethical objections that would preclude your marrying me if I were to legally eschew all interest in your fortune, now and forever?"

"If my husband ever needed my money, he would be welcome to it," Natasha said with quiet dignity. "My objections are to an aspect of our society that I consider a social evil. In their youth my parents were friends with Mary Wollstonecroft and William Godwin and others of the Joseph Johnson set. They taught me that it is wrong to regard half the population as being intrinsically unable to benefit from education. Do you know there are still those who argue that women do not even possess a soul, let alone an intellect?"

"I will take your word for it that such ill-informed creatures exist somewhere, but may we now turn our attention back to the reason for this interview? I hereby renounce any claim to your assets in perpetuity. Do you have other objections to our marriage? If I know anything of the way Mrs. Taylor's mind works, she will be suspecting me of having ravished you by now."

Natasha did not respond to this attempt at jocularity. Her lovely face wore that cast of wistfulness he had noted on other occasions. "There ought to be more to marriage than convenience or an evasion of scandal," she said sadly.

"Our marriage will be much more than that, Natasha, I promise you. I want to take care of you, I wish to remove you from this house where you have not been appreciated. I know you do not love me, but if you can trust me, we will achieve a good marriage. Do you trust me, Natasha? Will you marry me?"

Her eyes, utterly serious and searching, probed his intent face for a long moment before a softening effect seemed to spread from the nerves in her tense jaw to the muscles in her neck and shoulders. "Yes," she breathed on a sigh of surrender.

Cam had not touched her at all except with his eyes, but now he seized the hands she had turned palms upward in a curious little gesture of surrender. He brought them to his lips, pulling her gently out of her chair at the same time. Their eyes still clung together. There was a strange light in the green depths as his head descended toward hers.

A sharp knock at the door brought both heads around as Mrs. Taylor entered the room.

"I see you have decided to proceed with a betrothal," she said somewhat dryly.

"We have decided to proceed with a wedding, Mrs. Taylor . . . Oh, merely a private ceremony by special license, following shortly on the heels of a formal betrothal announcement, which I trust you will issue as proxy for Natasha's brother."

"Surely there is no need for such unseemly haste," protested Mrs. Taylor. Her eyes darted between the two, but Natasha, with the warning pressure of Cam's hand on hers, which he still held, remained silent, though she looked dazed.

"In this kind of situation I feel the sooner people's attention is diverted to a new topic for speculation, the better. We'll give them a hasty marriage to chew on. Unfortunately, my estate is still let for another few weeks and I will need to set some renovations in order before taking Natasha there. My lodgings are totally unsuitable and inadequate for her occupation, so I plan to install her in a suite at the Clarendon Hotel during the interim. I would be exceedingly grateful to you, Mrs. Taylor, if you will permit Miss Taylor to stay there with Natasha as a companion, for much of my time in the next few weeks will be spent at Krestonwood."

Major Talbot had the undivided attention of both ladies. Mrs. Taylor was staring at him in fascination, and he felt Natasha's instinctive protest in the jerk of her arm, but again he pressed her hand for silence while he watched the rapid calculations cross the older woman's features.

"This is all most inconvenient, Major Talbot. Why should not Natasha remain here while your estate is being readied?"

"As a newly married woman she will have to be prepared for a flood of congratulatory calls. I would not think of putting such a strain on your establishment, nor would I dream of troubling you to provide occasional accommodation for me here. I really believe my solution is the only practical one."

"I realize that my daughter's presence would lend countenance to Natasha's stay at a hotel, but it would mean a severe interruption in her own and my plans."

"I am aware of the considerable sacrifice Miss Taylor would be making, ma'am, and I insist on making her a substantial gift to show my gratitude, though I know one of her generous nature will volunteer to perform this service for her cousin. I depend on your efforts to persuade her to accept my practical gratitude."

Natasha felt like she was at the theater watching two seasoned performers declaim their lines with a convincing show of belief. She had no doubts as to who would ultimately prevail. Last evening's escapade had turned the suave accommodating Major Talbot—her future husband, she must remember that—into a ruthless juggernaut crushing all opposition in his path. Her own presence did not seem to be at all necessary to the discussion going forward, and she had still not uttered a single syllable when Major Talbot took his leave a few moments later, having carried all before him. He kissed her hand again, deploring with charmingly articulated apologies the press of pre-wedding details that would keep him from her side more than he could like in the next few days.

"I quite understand," she said, a brave but untrue statement, since there wasn't much about this entire situation that seemed accessible to the process of logical thought.

The one clear fact was that she was about to sail into marriage with a man who was acting purely out of chivalry, and that the seas of matrimony were often studded with uncharted reefs. As if to prove her fears well-founded, she bumped into a minor reef in the person of her young cousin almost immediately.

Lucretia slipped into the room the instant Mrs. Taylor and Major Talbot quitted it together. She leaned back against the door, her arms behind her in a graceful attitude that seemed to Natasha's disordered fancy to be a deliberate blocking of the avenue of retreat. Her scornful eyes raked the figure still standing irresolute in the middle of the room.

"If you expect me to offer my felicitations on your upcoming marriage, I fear you will be disappointed, but I do congratulate you on contriving the neatest piece of entrapment since the Trojan Horse."

11

Exactly one week later, Natasha was again standing irresolute in the middle of a drawing room, this one her own, at least temporarily. Her state of mind as she surveyed the room's more than adequate furnishings was not much improved over that on the day her future had been summarily settled. The intervening days had been crammed with activities and a number of unavoidable social events where she had had perforce to endure the cross questioning of a few stiff-rumped matrons and certain sly innuendos from several young sparks whom she had resolved to avoid in future. It didn't help to realize there would have been a great deal more in the same vein to bear except for Cam's attentive presence at her side during evening engagements.

Her eyes fell on her hand, and she held it away from her body, testing the unfamiliar weight of the gold band on her finger, the outward symbol of her new status. She was no longer Natasha Phillips but Mrs. Cameron Talbot. The brief ceremony that had joined their lives had been performed privately at St. Peter's in Cavendish Square with only her cousins and Cam's uncle present to represent their sadly attenuated families. Susan and Harry Flint had acted as witnesses, and Mr. Richard Flint and the dowager Lady Flint had kindly demonstrated their support by their presence.

Susan had been all atwinkle, seeing in Natasha's marriage to her neighbor a continuation of their childhood relationship. Despite her friend's pleasure and optimism, Natasha had not felt she was actually present at a wedding, nor did she feel like a married woman once the small bridal luncheon given by Sir Humphrey Talbot was finally ended. Thanks to the geniune friendliness of the Flint family and the well-bred graciousness Cousin Edwina had adopted once she had accepted defeat, this ostensibly social occasion had passed off more smoothly than she could have hoped, given a group of ill-assorted persons, not all of whom were convinced there was cause for celebration.

If Cousin Edwina had put a good face on the situation and lent her considerable skill for organization to the diverse preparations necessary to a hasty wedding, the same could not be said of Lucretia. Though Natasha could not see that Cam had ever given her cousin the least encouragement to hope for an eventual declaration from him, disappointment had bitten Lucretia sharply. Coerced by her mercenary parent, she had agreed to stay at the Clarendon with Natasha, but unless others were present, she made but small pretense at civility. Thank goodness she was not scheduled to arrive here until tomorrow after Cam should have departed for Krestonwood. Tonight promised to be awkward enough without the addition of her cousin's quietly fulminating presence.

A sound from the hall door brought her head around. Cam stood there smiling at her, but she had the impression that initially there had been surprise on his face, swiftly transformed.

"I don't believe you've moved an inch since I left you here almost a half-hour ago," he said with a slightly inquiring inflection. When she didn't reply immediately, he went on, "Have you looked over your temporary domain yet? Will it suit?"

"No . . . I . . . Not yet. Did you complete your arrangements for tomorrow?"

"Yes, Walker will have the horses brought 'round by eight. He has found a reliable groom to take care of the carriage and horses I have recently purchased, who will drive for you whenever you desire. You have only to send a message to the stables. His name is Jonathan Bascombe."

"I . . . thank you."

There was another pause, which Cam broke by holding out an imperative hand. "Come, since you have not yet explored the suite, I will do the honors."

Natasha responded with a shy smile and allowed herself to be conducted around a substantial set of rooms, the gracious size and appointments of which soon had her goggling. She turned impulsively to the man awaiting her approval.

"Surely all this cannot be necessary for a mere fortnight or so? I have been told that this hotel is outrageously expensive."

"It is not more than we need or I can afford," he replied with smiling dismissal of her qualms. "There are three bedchambers, all quite necessary, you will agree, with your cousin in residence." He went smoothly on, though he was now presented with a splendid view of thick curling black lashes that had fluttered down to lie on flushed cheeks. "Then the small room is for your maid, whom you will wish to have within earshot, though I have arranged that the butler will stay on the floor beneath us."

"Butler?" The lashes sprang back as her eyes opened roundly.

"Certainly. You may desire to do some little entertaining, and most assuredly there will be a stream of callers once it is known that you are 'at home,' so the dining room is essential, you see. Naturally you will not wish to plan anything as elaborate as a dinner party without a host, but you may like to have the Flints to an informal meal one evening."

While Cam was speaking, they were standing in the doorway to the large dining room furnished with an oval table surrounded by a veritable forest of shield back chairs —Natasha counted twelve of them. "You have accomplished a great deal this past sennight," she said, speaking her thoughts as the extent of his preparations was revealed to her, "a carriage and groom, this enormous and elegant set of rooms, a butler—"

"It wasn't by my choice that I could be with you only in the evenings," he said, giving her hand a friendly squeeze. "There was much to be accomplished if you were to be moderately comfortable during this difficult period of time when we will be essentially homeless. The butler, by the way, is called Dawson. I engaged him through the registry, but I interviewed several candidates before I was satisfied that I had found a trustworthy individual, and I checked his references thoroughly. You may place your entire confidence in his ability to keep things running smoothly here while I am away. The hotel will supply anything you might want, food and drink, fresh flowers, additional or different furniture, even a pianoforte. Simply relay your requests through Dawson; he'll see to everything.''

Natasha had been vaguely aware of muted sounds in the background during their inspection of the dining room, but her attention had been riveted to her husband's conversation. Now, as they reentered the drawing room, she stopped in surprise to see a completely appointed small table, right down to lighted candles and a lovely white floral centerpiece, placed in front of a merry little fire in the grate. Beside the table, giving a finishing touch to the silverware arrangement, was surely the tallest and thinnest individual she had ever seen outside of a fair. He was dark-complexioned, with hair more gray than brown, and looked at the world out of a pair of alert brown eyes under straight brows in a long, sharply angled face. This rather forbidding collection of features was transformed, however, by the benevolent smile he gave Natasha on being presented. She beamed back at him in relief as she slid into the chair he indicated.

Over the next hour or so, Natasha gradually relaxed under the influence of well-chosen food and wine and the undemanding company of the one person, apart from the Flint family, who did not appear to be sitting in judgment on her. She could not have faced a groaning table in her simmering state of suppressed tension, but the clear soup, followed by a cold salmon in a marvelous dilled cucumber sauce, proved just the menu to revive and tempt an appetite that had been almost entirely lacking of late. To encourage the process of relaxation, Cam dismissed Dawson when the salmon had been served, thereafter seeing to her wants himself.

The conversation was one-sided of necessity, for

Natasha was full of questions about her husband's home. He warned her not to expect more than a neat plain house, built of the gray limestone that was indigenous to that part of the country. It was not, he said, one of those historic old piles that had been in one family for a dozen generations and was continually being added to or demolished as fashion, dry rot, and unpredictable fluctuations in family fortunes dictated. On the other hand, having been built less than fifty years ago by his grandfather and a very competent architect who did not despise functional considerations, Krestonwood could boast that none of the chimneys smoked and the kitchen was sizable, well-lighted, and well-equipped, within easy reach of both family and formal dining rooms. He preferred, he added, to let her form her own impressions of her future home without too much description on his part, and Natasha was content to leave it at that, having already formed a firm impression of her husband's deep attachment to his boyhood home.

Cam removed her plate to the wheeled trolley conveniently placed for self-service and presented her with small dishes of sweet meats and maids of honor to nibble on, as well as a Stilton cheese. He refilled her glass with champagne before seating himself again.

"I'm glad you wore white today," he said with an admiring glance.

She had removed her bonnet on entering and now sat opposite him in her simple gown, with the candlelight casting a radiance over arms and shoulders whose smoothness always invited a man's touch. He pulled his straying hand back and filled his own glass. "To a successful partnership," he offered, and bit back any additional wishes as she raised her glass but not her glance to his. Her hand, he noted, was not quite steady.

"Shall we also drink to our next meeting with Peter?" He refused to let any awkward pauses develop and was rewarded by a flash of that spectacular smile that was the only feature brother and sister shared.

"May it be soon," she added fervently.

"There's no need to ask whether you have received any further communication."

She shook her head. "Just the one letter written at the end of May while they were waiting to sail out of the Garonne. He didn't even know their ultimate destination."

"That was to be expected, of course. It's barely possible that the fleet may have arrived in American waters by now. There might be news in a few weeks from the intermediate stop, Bermuda, or perhaps Jamaica. Do not worry about him, my dear, he'll be back."

She managed a brief smile, but Cam was aware yet again of that strange half-wistful stillness he had observed before. There was about it something of sadness and more of acceptance, and as always, he was conscious of a strong desire to make things right for her. It struck him for the first time that perhaps the worst thing about being a woman must be that so much of importance in life was beyond her control. For most women material existence and comfort depended entirely on the goodwill and fortune of first father then husband. Women neither started wars nor fought them, but theirs might be considered the greater portion of war's evil in having to live with constant fear for the safety of the men they loved.

And here was Natasha sitting at a table making polite conversation with a near stranger who happened, by no choice of her own, to be her husband. Scarcely a week ago she had boasted of having control of her own money; today the control of her future, even her person, had passed to him. A wave of revulsion swept over him that he should be the instrument of depriving her of choice and curtailing her cherished independence, illusory though it had been.

Cam stared intently across at the lovely young face with its high cheekbones and delicate hollows beneath, shadowed and accentuated now by the flickering candlelight. She should not be deprived of all control over her own life. In this fait accompli of a marriage she must at least be allowed to dictate the pace of increasing intimacy. He owed her a breathing space in which to subdue any rebellious feelings and accustom herself to the idea of being his wife. His own desire, confounding him by its suddenness and intensity, to seize those shapely shoulders and kiss those enticing lips until she begged for breath, must be relegated to the background for the present. Perhaps this irksome but necessary trip to Krestonwood might be regarded in the light of what his mother would have called a blessing in disguise, after all.

Natasha, reaching across the table for a sugared walnut, risked a peek at her silent husband and froze, her fingers outstretched above the dish, huge eyes on his face. She comprehended the violence of his expression but not the emotion that inspired it, and questions instantly ricocheted around in her head. What had happened, what could have happened to turn her charming attentive companion into this grim-faced stranger? Had she done or said something to irritate him?

Cam espied her wary bewilderment before long lashes dropped in protection. He threw off the weight of his own thoughts and said with a coaxing smile, "I beg your pardon for going off in a reverie for a moment. I was thinking of all the work necessary to put Krestonwood into shape to receive a new mistress. Am I forgiven?"

"Of . . . of course, but I would not mind being there during the alterations, you know, Cam. Perhaps I could be useful."

She always hesitated before pronouncing his name, he realized with a little pang of remorse—his own stupid fault for trying to keep her at a distance in the beginning. One more reason to go slowly now.

"You're doing it again."

He blinked. "What?"

"Going off in a reverie." Natasha's smile was a better effort this time as she watched him with her head a trifle angled so that her pointed chin was elevated.

He chuckled. "You look like an inquisitive blackbird. I was considering your suggestion, but, you see, my tenants won't be out for another three weeks. They have kindly consented to my beginning some repairs during their tenancy, but I'll be bedding down at a local inn that is barely adequate for a male guest. I would not subject you to such a degree of discomfort."

wo men had asked her to marry them, and Charles
bot had hinted at romantic feelings for her. With no
bts in her own mind that she regarded these men as
nds only, she had blithely assumed herself impregnable
Cupid's arrows. Obviously love had crept up on her
wares.
sheer intellectual satisfaction at solving the enigma gave
y all too quickly, however, to increasing dismay as the
plications of such an irrational emotion forced
emselves on her attention.
Chief among these was the recognition and acceptance
f the fact that Cam was obviously not in love with her.
ot being susceptible to comfortable self-deception,
Natasha succeeded in facing this truth, though not without
onsiderable pain. This did not take the form of tears, a
source of emotional release to which she never resorted
except in extremis. Mitigating against this normal feminine
reaction was a basically optimistic nature enhanced by a
trait of character she thought of as perseverance and her
fond brother termed obstinacy. Thanks to her slowness in
recognizing her own feelings for Cam, it was now too late
to avoid an awkward situation by escaping, so she bent her
mental energies toward devising ways and means of
making her husband fall in love with her.

The first step, dictated by her character, was to refuse to
concede that there were very few actions of a positive
nature available to a gently bred young lady. But surely
there were steps she could take to improve her appearance
now that she was out from under Cousin Edwina's
ultifying thumb. Susan would help her.

As the long night ticked past, one minute at a time,
atasha sat among her pillows in the one small pool of
ht in the large dark room, weaving her toils until sheer
haustion overcame her at last. This occurred at so late an
ur that she never stirred the next morning when her
sband, dressed for travel, looked in to take his leave of
. After a long study of the dusky hair spread over the
ows and the dark crescents her lashes made on her
eks, he tiptoed out again.

"I don't wish to appear to plague you, but I should be willing to do it."

"Thank you, my dear, but things will go along faster this way." He cleared his throat. "I understood from Mrs. Taylor that your maid will be arriving with your cousin tomorrow, so I have made arrangements through the hotel to supply you with a maid for tonight. By now she will be in your bedchamber awaiting instructions."

Natasha sat as immobile as a painted portrait, though her heart had started a rapid heavy pounding that threatened to become visible. What did he mean by this abrupt introduction of a maid into the conversation? She cast a furtive glance at the French clock on the mantelpiece, a glance that he intercepted.

"I know it is early yet, but I expect today has been long and rather arduous for you. You must be exhausted."

"And you have an early departure planned for tomorrow morning." She slid smoothly into the breach, rising to her feet as she spoke, a smile pinned to her lips.

Cam rose too, taking her hand and leading her into the hall. He paused outside her bedchamber and stood staring at their clasped hands. His grip tightened momentarily, then she was released as he stepped back. "Good night, my dear. Sleep well."

He had already turned away before a reply, nearly inaudible, succeeded in passing Natasha's lips. Her confusion was plain to be seen, but there was no one to witness it as Cam disappeared into the drawing room once more. It took another minute or two to recompose her features and prepare herself for an unanticipated encounter with an unknown abigail.

In the event, the maid proved to be a thin, tired-looking individual who performed her duties with a minimum of fuss and a welcome lack of conversation. She ascertained that Mrs. Talbot would like hot water in the morning, accepted the money pressed on her with a fleeting smile that underlined the gray look of weariness, and removed herself silently.

Natasha, attired in a diaphanous nightrail of white silk, so sheer its bulk easily passed through the circle of a wedding ring, gazed at the closed door through which the maid had disappeared for a few seconds longer, then allowed her glance to drift around the room, past the handsome mahogany armoire where the clothes she had brought with her for tomorrow morning now reposed in solitary state, past the fireplace with marble surround to the large window, shrouded at this hour in heavy brocade of an aggressively pink shade. Her eyes lingered briefly on the great bed with its massive canopy from which matching pink hangings descended. The maid had turned down both sides of the bed, but Natasha knew now not to expect a connubial visit from her new husband. Cam's eagerness to see her safely retired for the night could not have been mistaken for that of a bridegroom anxious to consummate his marriage.

Her brow puckered with the effort to summon up his face as it had looked when he left her at the door. He had been ill-at-ease, and the warmth that she had seen in his eyes earlier in the evening had cooled to mere formal courtesy. She had not the slightest guess as to the reason. If she had done or said something that had displeased or alienated him, she could not think what it might be.

Her eyes passed on to the dressing table, its top unsullied as yet by her few cosmetics and creams, then fixed on the small writing desk before swinging to a wing chair and ottoman nearby. There were several lamps casting a soft glow about the large room. That chair looked comfortable and was served by a candle stand, but there were no books to read. How foolish of her not to have brought a selection of reading materials with her. The hotel had thoughtfully supplied the desk with writing paper, pens, and sealing wax, she found on opening a drawer, but to whom could she write on her wedding night?

She drifted over to the dressing table and contemplated her image in the mirror hung above it, her head a little on one side. He had said she looked like a blackbird with her head in that position. He had said he was glad she had worn white on her wedding day. She was wearing white now, although, as her skin gleamed beneath the rail with every movement of her body, she decided "wear" was not

quite the precise term for a garment so nearly [...] Her critical eye continued to survey the figure [...] Nothing was going to change the fact that she [...] and willowy, though her form was dee[...] proportioned by Cousin Edwina's dressmaker, [...] of some slight comfort, she supposed. Her legs [...] long and shapely, her ankles neat, her feet small [...] all this would please her husband. One day.

Or perhaps not.

Impatiently she turned away from the mirror, [...] fied with her reflected attributes. If only she kne[...] was in his mind, she would know how to act, [...] present herself in the most flattering light withou[...] untrue to her basic nature. Wounded pride notwith[...] ing, Natasha realized and acknowledged that it had [...] been an object with her to please Cameron Talbot, ev[...] the beginning when she had been so disappointed in her brother's friend. For Peter's sake at first.

And later?

Her brown furrowed in thought, Natasha wandered around the strange room extinguishing all the lamps excep[...] the one on the bedside table. She pulled back the curtain[...] and opened the window, undaunted by the purporte[...] perils of night air. Though far from sleepy—her brain wa[...] ticking over like a runaway clock—she climbed into th[...] huge bed, wrapped her arms around her knees, and prepare[...] to subject the entire history of her acquaintance with th[...] who was, unbelievably, her husband to the minutest s[...] of her intelligence in the pursuit of an answer to the ri[...] why she had always wished to please him.

In due course she discovered the reason in the fu[...] of its inexplicable simplicity: *she was in love with C[...] Talbot.* Though itself proving impossible of expl[...] by her probing intellect, love's existence explaine[...] thing else. She now knew why the happiest momen[...] entire stay in London had occurred during certai[...] with Cam, knew too the cause of the exultation[...] experienced while helping him with Sergeant [...] Also explained were many of her angriest mom[...] most of her unhappy ones.

12

Natasha opened her eyes slowly, then came fully awake, nudged by an interior knowledge of things to be done. There were no rays of sun coming in the window on this gray day and no clock visible to tell her the hour. A sense of urgency jerked her spine upright just as a knock sounded on the door.

"Come in," she called, frantically combing her fingers through her unruly mane of hair and tossing it behind her shoulders. The eagerness faded from her face as the hotel maid entered carrying towels and a can of hot water.

"Good morning, Mrs. Talbot."

"Oh . . . I thought . . . good morning. Do you know what time it is?"

"Just after nine, madam."

"*Nine!* Oh, no!" Natasha halted with her legs swung partway over the side of the bed. "Was Major Talbot in the dining room as you came in?"

"No one was in the dining room when the butler let me in a few minutes ago. He asked me to ascertain what you would like for breakfast."

"Breakfast?" echoed Natasha as though she had never heard the word before.

"Yes, ma'am."

Natasha was grateful for the absence of curiosity on the maid's patient, weary face. She would have enough of that to cope with when Lucretia arrived. The thought of her cousin's prying eyes helped her to gather her wits and put her disappointment behind her as she put her feet firmly on the floor and prepared to face whatever the day had in store.

A substantial breakfast in her room, shared with the nervously protesting but ultimately grateful maid, helped replenish the neglected bride's usual stock of optimism and energy. By the time Miss Taylor and Lizzie arrived with numerous trunks and cases, Natasha had her immediate plans all worked out in her mind. She introduced Dawson, conducted them on a tour of the rooms, and then set the excited Lizzie to work on the chore of unpacking and settling all three of them into their quarters.

Lucretia had been openly studying her hostess's animated face during this initial business. Now, as she followed her into the drawing room, she said in the slightly acerbic tones she had adopted toward her since the announcement of the betrothal, "You are looking very bright-eyed for a woman whose husband has deserted her the day after the wedding."

"I do not think I would use the term 'desertion' actually to describe Cam's trip to set the renovations in motion at Krestonwood," Natasha replied mildly as she waved Lucretia to a chair and selected a corner of the settee for herself.

"And did you find . . . Cam . . . eager to depart on his mission this morning or reluctant to leave his new bride?"

"Those emotions cover the situation nicely." Natasha smiled at her cousin, refusing to be riled by the thinly veiled spite. "I have ordered coffee to be served in here while I acquaint you with our schedule for the next few weeks."

Light eyebrows flew upward in a fair imitation of her parent's supercilious attitude as Miss Taylor tossed her head. "I assume our schedule, as you call it, will continue as it has all Season, and my mother will acquaint you with the details as it becomes necessary."

"Not for the next two or three weeks," Natasha rebutted quite gently. "You see, I plan to take up my dancing again, and that will mean a curtailment of some of our social activities, since you will naturally play for my daily practice session. I have already arranged to have a pianoforte moved into the dining room, which will serve the purpose very well once the table and chairs have been removed."

"Take up dancing! What on earth can you mean?"

"You know, of course, that I have been trained in ballet by my grandmother. No? Well, no matter." Natasha smiled in a kindly fashion at her cousin, who looked utterly taken aback. "The thing is that I have become terribly rusty since she died, and I desire to get back into the habit of daily practice again."

Lucretia had recovered from her surprise by now. "You may do as you wish, but I do not choose to commit myself to a dreary daily routine of piano playing for dancing. May I remind you that I am here solely as a favor at the request of your husband."

"A very well-compensated favor in actual fact. I am persuaded neither Cam nor your mother would care to learn that I was forced to hire a professional musician because you were so disobliging as to refuse to play my accompaniment." Her dark eyes opaque and unreadable, Natasha watched the angry color flare into her cousin's cheeks. "I shan't practice for more than two hours a day, so you won't find it terribly fatiguing."

Lucretia opened her lips, then thought better of a hasty reply, and pinched them together again. It was she who looked away first.

"That's settled, then," Natasha declared cheerfully. "Ah, here is Dawson with refreshments. And I believe I hear the door knocker."

The caller was Lady Flint, who entered on Dawson's heels. "I came to cheer you up, knowing you'll be missing Cam already," she explained after hugging her friend exuberantly. "Good morning, Miss Taylor, how do you do? I recall now that Tasha mentioned you would be staying here with her." As Lucretia acknowledged the greeting with some stiffness of manner, Lady Flint's eyes toured the tasteful drawing room unabashedly. "Quite impressive. Cam has done you proud, dearest."

Natasha laughed aloud, more grateful than she could admit for the timely intervention of Susan's cheerful presence. "Sit down, Sue. We were just about to have coffee, so your visit is well-timed."

Lady Flint obeyed, joining Natasha on the settee. When the cups had been handed around, she addressed her friend with the air of an expectant child. "What will you do with yourself for the next few weeks?"

"I've just been telling Lucretia that I'd like to get back to my dancing. She has consented to play for me while I practice."

"Marvelous!" The diminutive redhead in her daffodil silk bonnet turned to Lucretia. "Tasha's a wonderful ballerina, good enough to go on the stage, should Cam ever lose his fortune." She giggled at her own joke, seemingly unaware of the cold reception her words were receiving in one quarter.

"Indeed?"

"Yes, she's very talented," she assured the unsmiling Lucretia.

"I'd like to do some shopping soon, Susan," Natasha interjected, thinking it time to change the subject. "I'll need a new wardrobe for the autumn in the country. Will you come with me?"

"Of course!" Lady Flint's eyes gleamed in anticipation. "Frankly, I've been itching to take a hand in outfitting you properly." She rolled her eyes heavenward. "Those dreary pastels will have to go—give them to your maid. I'll see that you select the rich shades you need to compliment your wonderful coloring."

"If Lady Flint is to accompany you on these shopping excursions, I beg you will hold me excused, cousin," Lucretia said. "I do not like to desert my mother entirely, and since these dance practices will take up a good portion of our time, I feel I should bear her company at other times."

"Yes, of course you must not neglect your mother," agreed Natasha cordially. "I should never forgive myself if Cousin Edwina were to find me so ungrateful as to deprive her of all your society during the next weeks."

"Thank you." Lucretia rose to her feet. "If you will pardon me now, Lady Flint, I would like to see that my maid has put things away properly. Cousin?"

Both ladies assenting, Lucretia retired to her room to go

over the events of the last hour in her mind before reporting them to her parent.

The women in the drawing room refrained from looking at each other until they heard a door close in the background. Lady Flint then said thoughtfully, "I must admit I'm not ill-pleased that your cousin does not wish to join our shopping expeditions. I always feel she is radiating silent disapproval in my direction. We shall do better without her."

"Much better," Natasha agreed readily.

"Still, it was nice of her to offer to play for your dancing practice. I would not have expected her to be quite so obliging."

"It all depends on how one approaches Lucretia," Natasha explained. "The next few weeks won't be boring, at all events."

No truer words were ever spoken in prediction. Natasha embarked on her self-improvement regimen the very next day when the hotel delivered a pianoforte to the suite and removed the dining-room furniture until it should be required. She did not begin dancing right away but eased into a routine of exercising and stretching all the muscles in her body; she gradually increased the exercises in duration and intensity as the days went by. She suffered some initial stiffness that she did her best to conceal from her Friday-faced cousin, who did indeed radiate indiscriminate disapproval. It was fortunate for the success of Natasha's program that she no longer felt any necessity to concern herself with Lucretia's goodwill, being content with a grudging but adequate assist on the pianoforte. The increasing suppleness of her disciplined body, the sheer joy of movement, and the knowledge that her skill and technique were returning rendered any negative contributions from her cousin negligible. In the beginning she had offered to teach Lucretia some basic stretches to limber up her body, but her overtures were spurned, thus liberating her conscience from future reproach.

Dancing increased her vitality and brought her intensely alive, a change that was soon reflected in her appearance. Susan brought her to her own modiste, whose flair for enhancing a client's assets and concealing her imperfections was vastly more to be prized than mere proficiency with a needle. Mrs. Simmons, delighted to have a supple young figure worthy of her talents to clothe, devoted her considerable skills to creating a wardrobe for one who, as she put it without roundaboutation, "might as well aim to feature as an original since she was downright hopeless as one of the crowd." She would have preferred that Natasha's exciting coloring be allied to a few additional inches, but conceded that it was rare indeed to find every desirable quality united in one person. They would, she decreed, do away with any extraneous trimming around the bodice and waistline and stay with a single color in her designs to present an unbroken line for the eye to travel, thus giving an illusion of extra height. The sleeves and the hemline would remain the areas for embellishments.

Like a magician she produced a length of coral-orange silk and another the exact color of spring violets. All pastel shades would henceforth be eliminated, she declared with a minatory air and a look of contempt for Natasha's pale-pink muslin gown. If pink she must have, then let it be the deep rich pink of the rose. Also scarlet and perhaps gold, she promised with the air of one offering palliatives to a disappointed child. Natasha hid a smile and promised solemnly to follow all Mrs. Simmons' dictums as if they were the Ten Commandments.

The meekness of this response was accepted by the dressmaker as no more than was necessary for a good working partnership, which translated to having everything proceed on her own terms. Not taking more than a mild interest in fashion under any circumstances, Natasha was quite content to place her purse and her person in Mrs. Simmons' undoubtedly capable hands, with Susan to oversee the contiguous purchase of hats, shoes, gloves, and all the accompanying impedimenta necessary to turning out a young lady of fashion.

Susan's only regret was that the greater portion of society was not to be accorded the privilege of being dazzled by the new Natasha since it was already mid-

August and the ranks of the *Ton* still in London were thinning daily. Cam too had the intention of repairing to Krestonwood as soon as practicable, and the Flints would be leaving town before the end of the month, too soon to gauge the full impact of Natasha's conversion into a possible trend-setter. Still, there was no sense in crying for the moon, especially since any little twinges of disappointment Susan suffered because of the unfortunate depletion of the natural audience for what she referred to in her own family as "the blossoming of Natasha" was amply compensated one memorable evening when she was privileged to witness the reaction of Lady Frobisher to her protégée's new glamour.

The circumstances surrounding the Talbots' newsworthy marriage were well-known around town concerning the indiscretions that had taken place on the night of the fire in St. James's Park. Equally well-documented was the fact that Cameron Talbot had been seen consistently in the company of Natasha Phillips almost from the moment of his return from the war. This lent credence to the theory, popular among persons of a romantic or charitable nature, that, *au fond*, the impetuous marriage was indeed a love match. Susan was at great pains to aid in the dissemination of this version by providing subtle embellishments to the story whenever an opportunity arose; in fact, she was not above creating an opportunity whenever possible.

Among those skeptics unlikely to be convinced by this tale of sweet romance was Lady Frobisher, who considered, not without some justification, that if any female was entitled to figure as the object of Cameron Talbot's affections during the past Season, *she* was that female, at least until quite recently. Add to this the natural reluctance of someone of her all-pervading vanity and jealous temperament to acknowledge another lady's charms as equal to her own, even privately, and no one could be surprised to find her ranged on the side of those who looked for explanations less creditable to the parties involved in the hasty marriage.

Since her ladyship hadn't scrupled to reiterate her theory

on more than one occasion, Susan was aware that Lady Frobisher held buckle and thong to the notion that Cam had offered marriage in a spirit of pure chivalry to rescue his friend's sister from the consequences of an act of calculated indiscretion rather than the innocent folly to which more generous souls ascribed Natasha's behavior. It was therefore a vindication of sorts to know that Lady Frobisher, from the vantage point of a box directly opposite the Flints' at the Theatre Royal Haymarket, could not fail to witness the tremendous popularity of their guest one evening about a fortnight into Cam's absence from town. It would not be an exercise in hyperbole to declare that Natasha, radiant in the deep-orange costume created by Mrs. Simmons, held court throughout the evening. The box was jammed with callers during each interval, most of whom displayed a flattering reluctance to give way to others in their turn.

Susan was able, by the discreet use of opera glasses, to satisfy herself that Lady Frobisher's own glasses were trained on Natasha too often to be dismissed as casual interest. A diabolical little smile flitted across Susan's lips as she pictured the probable reaction the lovely Priscilla would evoke the next time she tried to expound on her chivalry theory, at least if her audience should happen to be masculine.

The first weeks following Natasha's wedding constituted a period of enormous change in several aspects of her life, though it wasn't until months later, when she had leisure for reflection, that she was able to appreciate the extent of this. Since coming to London she had chafed occasionally under the restrictions imposed on unmarried young women, and it had not been easy to subordinate her own personality and preferences to conform with her cousin's expectations. For someone reared in an atmosphere that encouraged independence of thought, stern self-discipline had been required to achieve the necessary conformity, a discipline that often placed a strain on her temper. Her marriage and the subsequent establishment of her own domain, however temporary, removed at once the necessity for future conformity to Cousin Edwina's domination and the concomitant strain on her disposition. She had recognized this fundamental change during the meditations of her strange wedding night and had heartily thanked Cam mentally for his thoughtfulness in setting her up at the Clarendon as her own mistress.

It had not taken her long to establish the new relationship with her cousins; all that was required was a degree of resolution Natasha had been confident she possessed. The lack of affection on either side was lamentable but unalterable at this late date. She must settle for mutual understanding and respect. Interestingly, it was Lucretia who proved the more difficult to deal with. There was a certain hardheadedness in Mrs. Taylor's makeup that enabled her to recognize when she had not been dealt the winning hand and, further, to play those cards she possessed to best advantage. Lucretia, younger and more at the mercy of her passions and ambitions, could not subdue her resentment at what she perceived as Natasha's unfair ascension to the married state at her own expense. She repulsed each and every tentative advance her cousin made toward a better understanding to the point that every moment spent in her company was a penance, and only a grim determination not to be worsted kept Natasha to her program of exercise and dance despite its multiple benefits.

Not the least of these benefits was the elimination of a number of hours each day that might otherwise have been appropriated by her cousins in paying and receiving calls. Most of the people Natasha saw with great regularity were, naturally enough, her relatives' friends of long standing, many of whom were indifferent at best and unsympathetic at worst to herself. It was manifestly true that her marriage rendered her of greater interest to them, but not in any sense that was likely to be of satisfaction to the new bride.

Under the circumstances of her marriage, even the society of those she sincerely regarded as friends was not an unmixed blessing just then. Her female acquaintances generally looked upon her exploits on the fateful night with awe mixed with disapproval and pegged away at her motives and emotions—"however did you *dare*?" et cetera—until she heartily wished them, or herself, gone.

There could be no doubt that she now enjoyed an enhanced standing among her male friends, though "enjoy" was perhaps a misnomer, since she did not at all wish to figure as a dasher in anyone's estimation. And the situation vis-à-vis her two favorite men friends was even less enviable.

Despite the formal betrothal announcement in the *Times*, Captain Standish had importuned Natasha to marry him on two separate occasions during the week before her wedding. He had railed against a fate that had placed Major Talbot by her side at the crucial hours, pledged his undying devotion, implied without actually putting it into words that Talbot's feelings were not engaged to the same degree as his own, and had finally gone away wounded by her perisistent refusal to entertain his suit. Those unavoidable meetings since her marriage had been conducted in an atmosphere of awkwardness that tweaked her conscience and aroused her pity.

Charles Talbot, on the other hand, had been visiting in the country when his cousin's betrothal was announced. He had paid a formal call shortly after his return, saying all that was correct to the occasion and bringing with him as a wedding gift a painting of a vase of flowers that she had once admired when they had toured an exhibition together. Natasha had been moved almost to the point of tears by his thoughtfulness and extravagance, but there was something new in his attitude toward her, an element she refused to recognize as pity, that made her uneasy in his company. She wanted desperately to reject it, to tell him he was wrong in his assessment of his cousin's coldness, that she knew Cam did not love her yet but that she was determined to win his love in time. She was aware that she chatted too much in an effort to seem perfectly at ease, detailing for him all the improvements her husband had mentioned in his infrequent and businesslike communications from Wiltshire, but she couldn't seem to stop herself. Nor could she make that expression vanish from his eyes. With the exception of the Flints, however, Charles was the closest personal friend she had made in London, and now she was part of his family. She certainly had no intention of avoiding him despite a cowardly wish to become invisible whenever he approached.

In truth, for all her frenzied activity, Natasha was simply marking time until her husband should return and they could take up a united life. She filled her days with activities designed to improve her health and appearance to the ultimate benefit of her marriage, and she accepted the evening engagements that offered because anywhere was preferable to an evening spent alone under the same roof with Lucretia.

On returning from an assembly one night, they were escorted to the door of their suite by Charles Talbot after leaving Mrs. Taylor at her residence. Dawson opened the door to them as usual, but it was a greatly altered Dawson. His gaunt features were drawn with pain in an ashen complexion, perspiration stood out on his forehead, and he was shaking like a leaf in a breeze.

"Good heavens, man, what ails you?" Charles exclaimed.

"Dawson, what has happened? Are you ill?"

"I cannot be sure, madam, but I believe it was some fish I ate earlier."

"You should have gone directly to your bed when you first felt ill. Lizzie could have let us in. Charles, would you see that he gets safely to his room while I ask someone to send for a doctor?"

"Yes, of course. I'll report back later. Come along, man, lean on me if you feel shaky."

After warning Lucretia to listen for her return, Natasha sped down to the ground floor to request that a doctor be sent for.

It was nearly an hour later when Charles came back with an encouraging report. The doctor had called and administered an emetic that had done its job. Dawson was now on the verge of sleep and should be fully restored to strength in a day or two.

"Well, that is good news indeed," said Natasha, much relieved. "Thank you so much for your time and help, Charles. I am going to pour you a glass of brandy before you go." She had led him into the drawing room while he

157

spoke so that Lucretia too might hear the news, but now that young woman stood up and declared she couldn't keep her eyes open another minute. Natasha had barely handed Charles the brandy glass before she had bidden them a short good-night and vanished.

"I am aware I am not your cousin's favorite caller, but she must have known I would not be here above a minute or two. Why should she disappear like that?"

Natasha shrugged. "She has been complaining since we got back that there was no need for both of us to stay up to hear a report on a servant."

Charles had been on the point of sitting down, but now he rose again, a thoughtful expression on his good-humored face. "In that case, my dear girl, I think I shall be on my way too. You may tell your cousin in the morning that I had one sip of the brandy and didn't even sit down. Good night, Cousin Natasha."

She was handed the glass without more ado and treated to a wicked grin and a formal bow, then Charles was gone. She bolted the door behind him, still a trifle bemused by the swiftness of events in the last few moments. Lucretia's behavior just now was easily explained: she didn't like Charles and resented having her rest postponed to await a medical report on a servant. Her abrupt departure had been the result of irritation, not scheming, but it was sweet of Charles to be so concerned for her reputation. She extinguished the lamps in the drawing room and carried her candle to her bedchamber, her mouth twisting at the wry reflection that if she had had more of a care for her reputation a few weeks ago, Charles would not have found it imperative to curtail his visit tonight.

Natasha was not to know that Charles' precautions included making sure that the clerk at the desk noted his departure by reporting to him the result of the doctor's visit to Mr. Dawson on his way out while he waited for a hackney to be called.

Dawson reported to work the following afternoon, pale but resolute, and the incident was forgotten.

13

Cam returned to London three days later in the waning hours of a warm afternoon. Natasha had gone to Mrs. Simmons that morning for final fittings on several items of her new wardrobe, including two new riding habits, one severely plain in black gabardine, the other a daring creation in brown velvet. Because of this obligation, the usual dance session had been postponed until afternoon. She and a bored Lucretia had been hard at work for over an hour when Cam was welcomed at the entrance door to the suite by Dawson.

Piano music reached his ears immediately, and he glanced involuntarily at his dusty leathers and travel-stained top boots.

"Company, Dawson?"

"No, sir. That is just madam at her practice."

"I didn't know my wife played the pianoforte," he said in some surprise.

"No, sir. Miss Taylor is playing while Mrs. Talbot dances."

Mystified, Cam handed over hat, gloves, and crop to the waiting butler. "By the way, Dawson, we leave for Wiltshire tomorrow, so my man will stay at my old lodgings tonight to pack up. Someone will be 'round soon with a change of clothes, and I'd like hot water sent up for a bath."

"Very good, sir. Shall I announce you?"

"No, don't bother. I'll announce myself. How have things gone here? Any problems?"

"No, sir. The hotel is very good about supplying us promptly."

At a guinea a bottle for champagne or claret and upward of three pounds for a full dinner in the dining room downstairs, the Clarendon should be overjoyed to supply all its guests' wants, the major reflected ironically. He said, "Fine. That'll be all, Dawson."

Neither girl noticed when Cam slipped into the erstwhile dining room and glanced around. His first thought on taking in the lack of furniture was, "Where do they eat?" but then a moving figure entered his field of vision and all thought ceased. He was vaguely aware of Miss Taylor's presence at the instrument somewhere to his left, but his glance was riveted on Natasha as she spun past in a series of beautifully executed pirouettes. She was wearing something white that was short and floating, and her hair hung down her back in a great dark cloud, tied at the nape by a white ribbon. For power, speed and grace she was the equal of any ballerina he had ever seen on an opera-house stage. His fascinated eyes clung to the flying figure, roving up over strong beautiful legs, supple torso and outflung arms to her rapt face. She was in another world, he guessed, where no one existed, just the music and the movement.

Suddenly the music ended with a crash of chords. Cam didn't take his eyes from Natasha as she came to a halt, her filmy skirts and flying hair drifting back into place.

"What's wrong?" she demanded of her cousin with a frown, then following the direction of Lucretia's glance, her eyes encountered her husband's and her face lit up, breaking into the characteristic smile. "Cam!"

Instinctively she started toward him with swift grace, and he moved to meet her, but remembering their audience, contented himself with gripping her hands, which he raised to his lips. He smiled down into eyes sparkling like black diamonds in a glowing face flushed with exertion, the rich color on high cheekbones contrasting with shadowed hollows beneath that had surely deepened of late.

"Have you just arrived? I was not expecting you. Why did you not let me know?" She was breathless, excited, and completely enchanting.

"Yes, had we known you were coming today, Natasha

would have been properly dressed to greet you," said a cool voice behind them.

"Oh, pish, Cam has seen dancers before," retorted her cousin, sweeping a damp curling strand of hair back behind her ear with impatient fingers.

"None more talented, I vow," said Cam, smiling, "but I fear you will become chilled after all that exertion if you do not take care."

"I'll change quickly," she promised. "Don't go away."

"Won't you come into the drawing room?" invited Lucretia, assuming the role of hostess. "I'll ring for some tea."

Cam turned to her with a pleasant smile as Natasha's door closed. "What I would really like is a large mug of ale to clear my throat of the dust of the road. Please forgive my deplorable manners, Miss Taylor. How do you do? I hope I find you well?"

Dawson had reappeared in the hall in time to hear his master's request, so the other two proceeded into the drawing room. Until the butler returned with refreshments they discussed the sultry weather and Major Talbot's journey from Wiltshire, which, though tedious, had produced no problems. He took a long gulp of the cool ale before settling back in his chair in a relaxed attitude.

"Have you and Natasha been getting about socially these past weeks?" he inquired with civil intent.

"Indeed yes, we were out every evening and are promised tonight to the Ramsey-Martins." She produced a light laugh. "It is amazing how a hasty marriage will increase one's popularity. Natasha is the current rage of London, I promise you."

"To my knowledge she never languished among the wallflowers before her marriage," Cam returned in dry accents. He swigged another long drink of the ale with deep appreciation.

"No, of course not, but her former admirers find it difficult to get near her these days what with the likes of Lord Brandywine, Sir Archie Nesbitt, and Lord March, among others, elbowing the younger men aside." Her laughter trilled again.

Cam's eyes narrowed slightly, but there was no other reaction to hearing that three of the most notorious rakehells in the empire were members of his wife's court. "Have any of these gentlemen called on you here?"

"Lord March called once, but I prevailed upon Natasha not to receive him again. The style of his conversation is not quite what one is used to."

"I see I am in your debt, Miss Taylor. Your larger experience of town life has no doubt been of great benefit to your cousin."

"Well, I have tried to guide her, but you know how impulsive and headstrong Natasha can be. Her own openness of temperament, which no doubt is a virtue in a restricted country society, leads her sometimes into errors of judgment where so-called men of the world are concerned. In her innocence she accepts them at their own valuation."

"Well, deficiencies of experience are soon overcome."

"Yes, of course. I am persuaded you are correct, and I daresay there hasn't been much talk around town yet." Lucretia hesitated, then leaned forward a little, her face a study in sweet earnestness. "It goes against the grain with me to mention this at all, but no doubt a hint from you will serve to warn her that it will not do to let Mr. Charles Talbot run tame here. I am persuaded she believes the family connection makes all proper, but I confess I could not like it when he was still here one night at nearly two. That was when Natasha sent me off to bed at all events, and he was settling down to drink brandy at that point."

There was a pinched look about Cam's nostrils, but his voice was coolly controlled. "I make no doubt Dawson saw him off the premises shortly thereafter."

"But Dawson wasn't here that night. He had taken ill earlier, and my cousin insisted that he go down to his bed. Pray do not imagine I mean to suggest that anything of an improper nature occurred. Indeed, knowing Natasha, you will not, but I believe it is always wiser to avoid the appearance of impropriety, do not you agree?"

Natasha came back into the room at that moment, relieving Cam of the necessity of producing a response, which was just as well because his first reaction was an urge to wring the wretched girl's neck. As she poured tea for her cousin, he studied the demure face of Miss Lucretia Taylor, unable to credit his ears. She could not be implying what the same words coming from a more experienced person would have connoted.

His attention shifted to his wife, who was thirstily drinking her first cup of tea. Against his will he acknowledged that there was something different about Natasha today. She looked different to begin with, sitting there in a simple muslin dress the color of a red rose, her cheeks still flushed and her curling hair still hanging down her back—younger in a way but, as her eyes met his over the teacup, fully mature and intensely alive.

"I wonder that you should join us with your hair still undone, cousin," commented Lucretia as she refilled the cup being held out to her.

"It's a bit damp so I didn't want to braid it yet, and I was perishing for my tea." She turned eagerly to her husband, but he forestalled the questions hovering on her lips.

"Miss Taylor tells me you are to go to the Ramsey-Martin assembly tonight."

"Oh, but we do not have to go if you are fatigued from your journey. Lucretia must, of course, because Cousin Edwina will be there, but I can send our regrets."

"I am not at all tired, just travel-stained, and I believe I will like to come with you. Since we are leaving for Wiltshire tomorrow, it will afford us an opportunity to say our farewells."

"Tomorrow! Goodness, I shall have to set Lizzie to packing at once, and there are all those new clothes I have ordered and—" In her agitation Natasha had half-risen.

Her husband interposed soothingly, "Do not be in a pucker, my dear. Drink your tea and relax. There is ample time for packing, and you may leave a letter for your dressmaker directing her where to send the completed garments

163

and the accounting. The wedding gifts are already prepared for shipping by carrier."

"Under the circumstances, I think I had best begin my
packing now," said Lucretia, setting down her cup. "If
you have no objections, cousin, I'll have Lizzie get my
things together first. She can pack for you after we leave
tonight." She turned to Cam. "If someone can drive her to
Manchester Square this evening with my baggage, I may go
directly home with my mother tonight."

Cam promised to make the necessary arrangements and
delivered himself of a graceful speech of appreciation for
Miss Taylor's services to his wife in his absence, to which
Natasha added her mite but, decided her husband with his
critical faculties on the stretch, in a more dutiful than
spontaneous fashion.

As soon as Lucretia left the room, the talk veered to the
improvements at Krestonwood. Throughout the ensuing
discussion of the practicalities of their upcoming journey,
Cam's intellect was operating on two levels, one concerned
with the actual subject and the other with a study of
Natasha in the light of what he had just learned from her
cousin. On reflection he found himself unable to dismiss
Miss Taylor's comments as exaggerations to be expected
from one inculcated with her mother's overnice sense of
propriety. The change in Natasha could not be accounted
for by a different hair arrangement and style of dress, nor
even attributed to the fined-down appearance of a body
trained in a pursuit as athletic as ballet. The beautiful
sculpturing of her face was more prominent, but there was
also a look about her, a new awareness that excited and
dismayed him in equal proportions. He was no stranger to
that look of invitation in a woman's eyes. It had not been
in Natasha's the last time he had seen her. What—or who
—had put it there in his absence?

As Natasha sat opposite her husband, chattering on
about all the things she would have to attend to at the
beginning of her reign at Krestonwood, she was enveloped
in a minor rapture composed in part by heightened
physical well-being and eager anticipation of a new life full
of interest that was about to commence, but the main con-

tributing factor was the powerful rush of joy like an elixir through her entire system that had welled up and filled her at the first sight of Cam in her practice room watching her with a light in his eyes that she had glimpsed briefly on other occasions. In the past this light had been as evanescent as that of a firefly—pray God this time it would endure.

Natasha's innocent prayer was doomed on her lips. The solid chair in which her husband sat apparently at his ease might have been the fastest chariot ever crafted, poled up behind a team of the fleetest horses in the world, to account for the emotional distance Cam had traveled since his first sight of his dancing bride less than an hour earlier.

She soon sensed his withdrawal despite the unfailing courtesy that was natural to him, but such was her optimism at the moment that she attributed it to delayed weariness from traveling and dared hope that a hot bath and a good meal would work wonders.

By the time the Talbots entered their suite together shortly after midnight, having already delivered the Taylor ladies to their home, optimism had had its day and Natasha's recent hopes were in temporary eclipse. Clearly, absence had not made her husband's heart grow fonder. Cam had accorded her no more attention tonight than their status as a newlywedded couple on their first public appearance demanded, and his compliments on her appearance in the wood violet gown she loved had been perfunctory at best, negating the extra time she had spent achieving an elaborate high coiffure that drew raves from a number of other gentlemen present at the Ramsey-Martins'. He had danced with her only once, and despite the best will in the world to reexperience the nameless magic that had occurred during former waltzes with Cam, Natasha had been aware instead of his muscular rigidity and an emanation of what she would be tempted to call inimical feeling if that had not been so patently absurd.

She could not know that Cam, wallowing in an uncomfortable state of mixed desire and jealousy that he could never have envisioned a month ago, had seen in the goings-on at the Ramsey-Martin assemblage confirmation of the doubts planted in his mind by Lucretia Taylor about his wife's innocence. Natasha had certainly been surrounded by a flock of admirers tonight, among them a few who should never be allowed within hailing distance of innocent young maidens if those whose duty it was to protect these damsels were on their toes. Obviously Mrs. Taylor had relaxed her vigilance since the wedding or Natasha had turned a deaf ear to her remonstrations.

However, his irritation at witnessing his wife encouraging a set of debauches—an exaggeration he refused to question in his present state of mind—wasn't a patch on his feelings when she vanished in the company of his cousin Charles for a full half-hour. He exerted admirable control over the homicidal impulse this generated, according Charles his usual cool greeting and forcing himself to accept his cousin's congratulations with a decent grace, though the penetrating look he bent on him would have caused most men to search their consciences and memories for past offenses. It was a few minutes after this meeting that he proposed cutting the evening short on the grounds of the next days' travel plans.

Natasha had been more than willing to leave early, though the bubbling fountain of expectation that something wonderful was imminent had long since dried up. During the silent carriage ride she took herself sternly to task for harboring unrealistic expectations. What did she think could have changed about their situation while Cam was away from her? First he must get used to her presence and, in time, hopefully, learn to value her companionship.

By the time she bade her husband a quiet good-night at her bedroom door, Natasha had her dreams well under restraint, but she didn't immediately prepare for bed. There was a restlessness and tension in her body that she sought to relieve and subdue with a few easy stretching exercises. After ten minutes or so she was much more relaxed and ready for repose. She was seated at the dressing table pulling the anchoring pins from her complicated coiffure when the pile of trunks and boxes in the corner impinged on her consciousness, bringing with it the dismayed realization that Lizzie was gone and, in the confusion of Cam's arrival, she had forgotten to make arrangements with the hotel for the services of a maid. With her hair tumbling down her back she twisted around, staring doubtfully in the mirror at the row of buttons down the back of her gown.

Ten minutes later, Natasha gave up, her cheeks flushed with exertion and frustration. The buttons below the waistline were undone, and she had managed those almost up to her shoulder blades, but though her arms ached with the effort, she could not reach the top few. Even the regrettable use of some words learned from her brother had no positive effect, so she sighed in defeat and headed toward her husband's room, knocking smartly on the door. The sight of Cam, resplendent in a blue brocaded dressing gown with a forbidding look in his eyes, did nothing to alleviate her embarrassment, but she gritted her teeth and spoke as lightly as possible.

"I'm sorry to disturb you, Cam, but I forgot that Lizzie wasn't going to be here and neglected to engage the hotel's maid. Will you please undo these last few buttons for me?" She turned her back immediately, relieved not to have to look at him anymore.

"Is it my turn now?"

"Your turn?" As she looked back over her shoulder, Natasha's puzzled expression cleared. "As my maid, do you mean? Well, there's no one else, is there? If I had remembered about Lizzie earlier, I might have had Lucretia undo the top buttons in the carriage."

"I was inquiring whether it was now my turn to enjoy your charms."

"What did you say?" The words made no initial impact on Natasha, who, with her hair dragged over one shoulder out of his way, was concentrating on remaining still under the touch of his fingers on her back. Those fingers grasped her upper arms all of a sudden and whirled her ungently around to face him. His anger increased at the sight of her bewilderment, but he had it under rigid control.

"Must I repeat it again? Is it my turn to enjoy your

charms? Is that why you are here in your enticing *déshabillé*? It would have been more effective if you'd loosened your stays also."

Natasha had whitened and grown very still under the lash of contempt in his voice. Her eyes alone moved, searching his face in vain for some sign of relenting. Her stillness seemed to enflame his temper further.

"Well, have you no defense to offer? Aren't you at least going to quote me your mentor, Mary Wollstonecraft, who, I believe, had one child out of wedlock and married Godwin just in time to give a name to another?"

"How could you marry me, thinking of me as you do?" whispered an anguished Natasha.

"I've been asking myself that question since my return today. I would have sworn to your innocence when I left for Krestonwood, but a blind man could see the change in you since then. I thought your cousin was exaggerating the case, but tonight I saw for myself the type of men you have collected around you in my absence—"

"My cousin! So Lucretia is responsible for this idiocy," blazed Natasha, rallying fast. "You are the stupidest man I have ever met when it comes to a knowledge of females. You placed that utterly spurious Priscilla Frobisher on a pedestal, you cannot recognize Lucretia for the jealous vindictive cat she is, and yet you have always believed the worst of *me* in every situation, have seemed to wish to believe the worst. I'll have nothing more to do with you."

She tried to wrench away from him, but managed to release only one arm in her struggles.

Cam, still icily controlled, demanded, "Are you telling me there is an innocent explanation for Charles' presence in this suite at two in the morning?"

"Of course there is! But I couldn't corroborate my story at this moment, and since you never accept my word without proof, I wouldn't demean myself by offering an explanation."

"Oh, I could prove your innocence or guilt tonight if I chose, but I'd be a fool not to wait until the possibility that you might be carrying another man's child was past."

"If you think I'd ever let you lay a hand on me after that

168

insult, you are mightily mistaken," cried Natasha, her temper incensed beyond caring what she said. "I'll start annulment proceedings tomorrow."

This time she succeeded in freeing her arm with a swift savage twist, indifferent to the pain the movement sent down her nerves. She spun away from him and dashed into her room.

The door would have reverberated off its hinges with the force she applied in slamming it had not her husband caught it in flight. Standing with his back to it, arms akimbo, he surveyed his flashing-eyed termagant of a wife, her small slim body drawn up in an aggressive posture, uncaring that her unfastened gown had slipped entirely off one sholder and her amazing wealth of hair was rippling down her back and over one breast.

"There will be no annulment. You may forget about that."

Natasha was beyond reason by now, for she ignored the menace in cold green eyes. "You cannot stop me," she defied. "This marriage was a mistake. I didn't wish for it in the first place, and I—"

"You may not have wished for it, but you've got it and *me*, and I am going to lay more than a hand on you." When she would have fled, finally aware of he danger, he sprang away from the door and grabbed her by one wrist. "There will be no more talk of annulment after tonight."

"You can't do that; it's no better than rape," she panted, trying to squirm out of the encircling arms that were dealing efficiently with her stays. She clawed at his hands and succeeded in drawing blood but didn't halt the unlacing process.

"There is no question of rape, but the more you struggle, the worse it will go for you."

"Cam, you are a reasonable man. Don't do this, I beg you! You know you'll be sorry afterward." Natasha ceased her struggles and tried to look her husband in the eye, but he avoided her glance.

"I'll be sorrier if I don't. I do not intend to travel with a wife who is talking about annulment. Who knows when you may take it into your head to disappear? You've seen to it that you have control of your fortune. I don't see that you've left me any choice."

Natasha shivered, and not because Cam had divested her of all her clothing by now. The cold reasonableness of his logic while discussing the unspeakable had chilled her to the marrow. It wasn't fear but a sense of degradation she experienced when he swept her into his arms with scarcely a glance at the slim perfection of her naked body and dumped her on the bed. She didn't try to escape while he disrobed quickly, but as he slid between the sheets and pulled her to him, she shrank into herself in an instinctive attempt to protect the integrity of her person from the ultimate humiliation of a possession inspired by punitive motives.

It might not have been rape, but what followed was a painful loss of her virginity unaccompanied by any redeeming aspect of goodwill or tenderness. Cam neither kissed nor caressed her. Completely unprepared for the pain of a quick penetration, Natasha gasped and cried out—just once. She scarcely heard his muttered apology when he withdrew at last. Free of his smothering weight, she drew up her legs and curled into herself as if to lessen the misery by exposing less of herself to whatever unseen forces were operating on her. Cam was speaking, but the words didn't register in her mind, still encased in a protective numbness. Not until the door closed some little time later, signaling a blessed privacy, did she stir even one muscle.

Bitter indeed were the hours before sleep claimed her violated body and erased the frenzied products of a mind disordered by the bleak circumstances surrounding the episode. The few moments following Cam's unexpected appearance during her dancing session today had been the most tumultuously joyous in her life, bursting with the promise of imminent fulfillment of her romantic dreams. A few short hours had seen fulfillment of a sort, but one that mocked and scattered her dreams beyond recall. She had thought herself in love with Cam and longed in her innocence to become his wife in fact. Tonight Cam had obliged her in a manner so brutal and callous as to destroy even the memories of her budding desire. She would never forgive him for so wanton an act of desecration—*never*!

Lying there in the big bed that had seen the death blow to her hopes, Natasha felt like something left for dead on a battlefield, but she wasn't dead, worse luck, and the battle would recommence tomorrow. The last thing in the world she wanted now was to accompany Cam to Wiltshire; she didn't ever want to look upon that cold perfect face again.

There had been a number of occasions since her arrival in London when she had yearned to be back in Devon, but never more so than now. How she would love to sit once more beneath the cool green umbrella of her favorite willow tree and mindlessly track the placid progress of the stream sparkling in the sunshine filtering through the trees on the opposite bank. Instead, she would be confined in a closed carriage with a man who despised her but refused to rid himself of her because of some strange sense of duty beyond her comprehension. How tragically stupid Cam had been just now to allow his anger at her perceived treachery to make him throw away the one avenue of escape from this doomed marriage!

She had been angry beyond description herself at his attitude, but hers was the righteous anger of the unjustly accused. Still, as the hours ticked by, she couldn't suppress a nagging suspicion that her own fury might have goaded him into losing his control. She had called him stupid about women, but what did *she* know of a man's passions and pride except from her reading? The discipline of a lifetime of looking at all sides of an issue could not be disregarded for long, even if in exercising it she destroyed the small comfort she might have taken in knowing right was on her side in this debacle of a deflowering.

14

Natasha caught sight of her bridegroom's straight back as
he rode ahead of the carriage, and she pulled her head back
from the open window, settling deeper into the thickly
cushioned interior of the well-sprung carriage that smelled
of newness, mingling the heady scents of varnished and
painted wood and new leather with a rich earthiness, for
they were traveling now through the Savernake Forest. The
beauty and majesty of the oaks and beeches on either side
could not fail to stir even the most oppressed spirits.
Natasha's had begun a slow ascension yesterday morning
from the moment it became clear that Cam did not intend
to ride inside the coach with her. The sight of his man
Walker, mounted and holding the reins of a saddled horse,
had signaled the start of a relaxation of the knot of tension
that had formed in her stomach on the instant of
awakening. This had enlarged moment by moment while
she went through the motions of a sketchy unassisted toilet
in preparation for a day of travel, her ears straining for
any sounds that would indicate Cam's approach. A knock
on the door had brought her heart into her throat,
strangling her first attempts at speech. The person who had
entered when she succeeded in giving voice to a reluctant
permission had been merely a hotel messenger bearing
written instructions from her husband to meet him downstairs on the Albermarle Street side at her earliest
convenience, leaving her baggage in her room to be
collected. She had scuttled out of the suite shortly thereafter, only delaying long enough to assure herself that
Dawson, unaccountably, was not present to receive her
thanks for excellent service.

Without looking directly at Cam, busy issuing orders to various hotel employees about the deployment of their baggage, she had ascertained that his features seemed a trifle more austere and fine-drawn than usual, a discovery that resulted in an admittedly mean-spirited little squiggle of satisfaction that she had not been the only one to arise from her bed unrefreshed. She had not been able to prevent an instinctive recoil when he had held out his hand to assist her into the carriage. Her hesitation had been brief, but the line of his mouth had tightened still farther. He had announced that they would breakfast on the road at the first change of horses, the only words he had addressed to her before closing the carriage door and going about the vital business of distributing vails to an inordinate number of flunkies who had contrived to be present at the early-morning departure.

Natasha had spent the entire day in splendidly cushioned isolation, untroubled by her husband's company at the posting inns where they stopped for breakfast and lunch. Cam made every arrangement for her comfort, even hiring a private room, while telling her on both occasions not to wait for him as he would be "seeing to the horses." They had spent the night at Reading, but any little increase in apprehension as they entered the inn together was quickly dissipated when she was shown to her room by the innkeeper, who casually indicated which of the doors led to her husband's room. She had already spotted the key in the lock, and she made use of it the second she was alone, a precaution that later appeared ridiculous. Cam had dined with her but had nothing to say beyond the merest commonplaces that would occur between chance-met strangers, and that only while the waiter was actually in the private dining room with them. For the rest of the time he was absent in spirit, preoccupied with his own thoughts, which, judging by his closed-up visage, were morose in nature. Natasha's healthy appetite hadn't been adversely affected by her unhappiness, and she succeeded in making a good meal once she sensed that Cam was as anxious to dispense with her company as she was his. To that end she excused herself at the earliest opportunity, feigning a yawn that brought a brief spark of wry amusement to his dour face. She fought against a betraying rise of color as he bowed and wished her a formal good-night.

Once safely in her own room, Natasha gave way to an irrepressible ripple of silent laughter as she contemplated the polite circling she and Cam had been indulging in that day, for all the world like two mutually antagonistic chldren whose mothers had brought them together with instructions to make friends. The momentary mirth faded, however, replaced by a sobering consideration of a polite circling marriage that soon crowded out unseemly amusement. After an essentially sleepless night, followed by a day of confinement, alone with unhappy thoughts she couldn't escape, Natasha was too emotionally drained to dwell long on her problems. She had been careful that morning to select a gown that was easy to get into, having already sufficient cause to regret not having engaged a permanent lady's maid during her last weeks in London. The potential humiliation of having to approach Cam for assistance a second time was inducement enough to complete all her preparations for bed in record time. She had slept within minutes of laying her head on the pillow.

As the carriage emerged into a more open area she glanced around with interest. The last time her husband had addressed her had been during the changeover at Hungerford, where she had enjoyed a light lunch. He had told her they would be leaving the turnpike before Marlborough and that the last leg of the journey should take no more than an hour or so. They seemed to be coming out of the forest, so the end was in sight now.

It had not been a difficult journey physically; the new traveling carriage was most comfortable and a recent rain had done away with much of the dust that generally plagued summer travelers, allowing her the relief of open windows. On balance, she was grateful for the respite traveling had afforded her from the necessity of maintaining social interaction in London while trying to keep up of facade of normality. Granted, it had been impossible to escape her misery, but Natasha's was a basically optimistic nature and she now found herself looking ahead. It would be a rare female indeed who did not look forward to becoming mistress of her own establishment, and Natasha had the additional blessing of knowing her dearest friend was to be her near neighbor, easing her path into local society. There would be much about her new life for which to be thankful, even though her relations with her husband were strained and difficult.

Cautious optimism was on the ascendancy when the pace of the team slowed gradually to a halt. They had left the turnpike about a half-hour before and begun a gradual climb on a lane undulating through lush green countryside. Natasha was staring about her with heightened interest when the door opened and her husband climbed inside.

"Are we arrived already?" she asked in some surprise, not having seen any sign of habitation yet save an occasional farmhouse.

"No, we have three or four miles to go." Cam rested his broad shoulders against the light-brown corduroy backrest and regarded his wife soberly as the coachman set the horses moving once more. She sat composedly under his stare, her dark eyes unflinching.

"I know you are not feeling particularly well-disposed toward me at present, Natasha—understandably so, though I still hold that there was ample cause for my doubts—but this is not the time or place to go into that," he added hastily when she would have spoken. "I am here to ask for your cooperation. Some of the servants at Krestonwood have been there since I was in short coats. Naturally they have a certain affection for me, and I would not like them to take it into their heads that our marriage is not . . . is anything but an ordinary one, not just for their sakes, but for yours too. I'm not putting this very well," he half-apologized, falling silent.

"I understand you perfectly," Natasha said quietly. "Do not be in a pucker. I would not give the servants cause to speculate on the nature of our marriage in any case, and of course I realize that at first I shall be on trial with them too, so to speak."

"Natasha, please! There is no question of your being on trial with anyone!"

"Isn't there?"

"No!"

"I'm glad." Seeing him looking lordly and impatient but unhappy too, Natasha's tender heart was touched despite her deep-seated anger at him. "Tell me who has been at Krestonwood since your boyhood."

"The housekeeper, Mrs. Hazeltine, for one," Cam said readily, relieved to be safely back on impersonal territory. "She was a young widow when she came to us when I was still in leading strings. She isn't a very jolly person, I fear, but is most loyal and efficient and very good at keeping the young maids from the village in order. They tend to come and go after a few years when they marry, but the cook has been with us for about fifteen years. She stayed on when the place was leased, as did my father's head groom."

He went on in this vein, giving a brief sketch of each old retainer whle the horses steadily diminished the remaining distance.

Natasha maintained an attitude of polite attention while wondering privately if it was possible to go on living in the same house with someone for an extended period without ever coming into close mental contact. She was roused from the state of incipient despair induced by this line of thought when she heard the note of controlled excitement in Cam's voice.

"Here are the gates coming up on your right. The drive is almost straight and lined by beeches."

Natasha's first impression of Krestonwood was inextricably bound up in her husband's joy at returning to his home, but she'd have felt the pull of the mellow stone dwelling with its gracious symmetrical facade under any circumstances.

"Oh, Cam, it's beautiful, but I did not expect it to be so large," she exclaimed, eyeing the short curving wings firmly embracing the three-storied central structure with its regular chimneys and high-hipped roof.

For the first time since their estrangement there was a slight thaw in iced green eyes as Cam demurred, "It really isn't all that large—only about twenty bedrooms. Except for the stables and outbuildings in the back, this is the extent of it; there are no meandering wings or crumbling original structures attached at odd angles. Flint Abbey is almost twice as big."

"Well, it cannot be any lovelier," declared his wife, her eyes on the beautiful Venetian window above the entrance in the shallowly projecting center bay.

Natasha's next surprise came when she stepped out of the carriage and recognized the tall bony figure at the head of a line of servants streaming out of the entrance. She paused on the top step, her mouth dropping open.

"*Dawson*! How did you get here? I looked for you the other morning. I . . . I did not expect you."

"No, madam, I know. Major Talbot was good enough to think that it might be a pleasant surprise for you to find me here to welcome you, as it were, on your arrival at your new home."

"Oh, it is!" she assured him fervently. "But how did you get here so quickly?"

"I traveled on the royal mail as far as Marlborough, where I was met at the master's instructions, ma'am."

"Oh, Cam, how very kind of you! Thank you so much." Natasha turned a sparkling face on her husband, who was smilingly aware that his coup had reaped unexpected dividends. The two young footmen flanking Dawson were staring at their new mistress in open admiration, the maids and the stout cook were beaming approval of Natasha's delighted reception of the surprise her husband had planned for her, and even Mrs. Hazeltine permitted herself a small smile on being introduced to her employer's wife.

"Welcome to Krestonwood, Mrs. Talbot."

"Thank you, Mrs. Hazeltine," Natasha responded in her frank manner. "My husband has promised me that I may rely on you to teach me how to go on smoothly in this big house."

"Certainly you may count on me for any asisstance you require, ma'am."

"Thank you," Natasha said again. She had a smile and

177

a friendly word for the curtsying domestics and remembered which of the blond footmen was Albert and which was Henry a few minutes later when one of them brought her jewel case to her in the ground-floor sitting room where a delicious tea awaited the travelers.

"Thank you, Henry, for bringing it to me so quickly," she said in smiling dismissal as the footman bowed himself out of the room.

"Well, you've succeeded in captivating my entire household within ten minutes," observed her husband as she handed him the cup she had been filling. "Was that a lucky guess just now?"

"Was what a lucky guess?" Natasha paused in filling her own cup.

"Albert and Henry are brothers and as alike as two peas in a pod. How did you tell them apart?"

"I thought they must be related. Albert is taller and Henry's hair has a slight curl. This is a pleasant room, so full of light." Natasha's eyes roamed about the cosy apartment with glazed doors in one wall that opened onto a garden that still rioted with color in late summer. All the stuffed furniture was covered in a gay floral chintz that brought the garden indoors.

"My mother used this as her morning room and for informal visiting, and she generally went over the day's schedule here with Mrs. Hazeltine. I haven't touched anything in here, but of course you are free to change anything that doesn't please you."

"Well, this room pleases me enormously. It is warm and welcoming and someone has a real talent for flower arranging."

Cam was eyeing her rather intently and Natasha raised her brows in silent query when her glance returned from admiring the flowers on mantelshelf and side table.

"My mother had a particular fondness for flowers; she trained Mrs. Hazeltine to make this type of airy casual arrangement." His scrutiny unwavering, Cam continued as though his words were being pulled from his grasp one at a time. "You have an uncanny knack of saying the one thing that would most please people."

"But you aren't pleased," Natasha pointed out when silence had again filled the space between them. Her bafflement was obvious as dark eyes challenged light.

Cam broke the contact by placing his cup on the handsome tea table with its pierced fretwork. He rose to his feet and held out a hand. "Come, let me take you to your room. The rest of the tour can wait until tomorrow. You'll wish to make sure your wardrobe is unpacked and arranged to your satisfaction, and I'd venture a guess that you'd relish a bath and a rest before it is time to dress for dinner."

Natasha lowered her eyes submissively and allowed herself to be led up a graceful curved staircase to the first floor. Perhaps Cam believed they could have a marriage without exploring each other's minds and personalities, perhaps he wasn't even interested in having a real marriage. Speculations of this nature could wait, however. At the moment a hot bath sounded like a promise of paradise.

It was a case of love at first sight when Cam opened the door to Natasha's bedchamber and stepped back for her to precede him. After an involuntary murmur of surprise and pleasure at the brightness of the large room with its delicately patterned plaster ceiling and wall paneling painted white, she indulged in a silent appraisal of the handsome mahogany furnishings in the style made popular by Mr. Hepplewhite. The only exception was an exquisite little French escritoire of marquetry work that drew her eyes like a magnet. The color in the room was provided by a glorious silken rug that was undoubtedly Persian, its lustrous colors enhanced by gold threads woven right into the design. The deep red in the rug had been repeated in the brocaded upholstery on a chaise longue and the canopy over the bed, but bed covering and hangings were of a beautiful white lace Natasha recognized as Venetian in origin because her grandmother had had a partiality for such work.

Her feet took her automatically over to the bay window, unexpected in a house whose hallmark had seemed to be symmetry. A charming painted and japanned window seat with shield-shaped ends facing each other across a caned seat beckoned her to sit and gaze her fill at the rose garden below. Natasha dropped onto it, noting in passing that the curtains were also of Venetian lace with red overdraperies pulled back. She smiled warmly at her husband, who had remained silent during her survey, letting the apartment speak for itself.

"Did you plan all this loveliness, Cam? The room is simply beautiful—everything in it contributes to its perfection."

"A white background seems to become you, and I recalled that my mother had some lace hangings she treasured. Mrs. Hazeltine unearthed them from the storerooms for me and assembled this suite, using some of the less ponderous furnishings in the house." He moved over to the bed wall and pulled a cord. "Whoever comes will see about getting a bath ready and unpacking for you." He frowned at the pile of baggage in the corner. "You should have taken on an abigail in London. None of the girls here is a trained lady's maid."

"I don't require a tonnish abigail," Natasha replied cheerfully, "just someone to help me in and out of dresses that button down the ba-back." She realized too late the infelicitous path down which her errant tongue was taking her, and she hurried on, hoping she had not betrayed any consciousness. "I am persuaded Mrs. Hazeltine will find a suitable girl in no time."

Cam's face was unreadable as he nodded to a door in the fireplace wall. "I'm through there. You will understand that I cannot very well hand you a key, but you have my word that you will have nothing to fear from me. We'll take things at your pace from now on. I hope you will be happy at Krestonwood, Natasha."

Under Natasha's bemused gaze, the stranger who was her husband bowed and took himself into his own room. She was still gazing thoughtfully at the closed door when a smiling young maidservant arrived to do her bidding.

Natasha was very nearly content during her first weeks at Krestonwood. Cam took her through the house the day after their arrival. The touch of reserve in his manner melted under the warmth of her enthusiasm during the hours they spent inspecting each and every chamber at his bride's insistence. The structure was in a high state of preservation, having been maintained throughout its short existence by careful owners. The fabrics in some of the sunnier apartments might show signs of fading, but everywhere the floors and furniture shone with polish, and no spinners of cobwebs had been permitted to take up residence in the unoccupied rooms. Everything sparkled with regular care and attention, including the maids' quarters in the spacious attics. Most of the male servants were housed in the stable block, which was currently being enlarged, Cam informed his interested bride.

She poked her charming little nose into every corner, patiently enduring a shelf-by-shelf tour of the still room and producing the required admiration for the new closed cooker that had recently been installed in the spacious kitchen presided over by Mrs. Smollett, the accommodating cook, whose brawny arms looked strong enough to handle unaided the sides of pork and beef hanging in the smokehouse.

Natasha's favorite room, not surprisingly, was the library. Her eyes passed over the fine paneling and comfortable leather chairs, not even pausing at the mammoth carved desk that was slightly incongruous in a modern house. Her feet followed her eyes to the rows of freestanding shelves set perpendicular to the long wall that was entirely given over to crammed shelves.

"My grandfather was an inveterate bibliophile whose passion for books finally outstripped the original space planned for his collection," Cam explained, "so these shelves were added later. They tend to divide the room into two separate areas, I fear."

"But I could read in here sometimes without disturbing you at your work if I stayed in the back section," Natasha suggested eagerly.

"My dear girl, what I have is yours. This is your house now. As its mistress, all doors are open to you."

The words were said almost impatiently and there was

no doubting their sincerity, but Natasha, though grateful, demurred.

"Everyone needs a certain amount of privacy, Cam, perhaps you more than most. It was excessively kind of you to lend us your escort so often during this past Season, especially so since I have observed that you are not so comfortable in feminine society as some men—your cousin Charles, for example. There will be times when you will not wish to be burdened with my company, and this room will be a natural retreat. As long as you make me free of the books," she finished with an impish grin, "I may read them anywhere."

Cam's eyes had iced over at the mention of his cousin, but he was piqued enough by her comments to try to explain himself. "I'm no misogynist, my dear, don't think it, but I confess that the female mind remains a mystery to me—yours for example, is a mystery to me."

"It is not my wish to add to your burdens," she replied somewhat dryly, "but I can assure you there is as much variation in the female mentality as in the masculine. If I am still a mystery to you, so too are you to me. We do not really know each other very well as yet."

"But you and Charles do know each other well." It was not a question but a flat statement.

Natasha accepted the challenge. "Yes, but then Charles is not so guarded as you." Her mouth twisted a trifle ruefully. "And perhaps he likes me better."

"Likes you! My God, Natasha, do you think I don't like you?"

At this crucial moment the couple was interrupted by a servant with a message that took Cam to the stables. Though Natasha would have welcomed a reopening of the subject, Cam didn't broach it again, and she was still too shy of him to bring it up herself.

With the arrival of Natasha's riding habits, bride and groom settled into a pleasant routine of starting the day with a ride before breakfast. On her first visit to the stables after their initial ride together Natasha was amazed to see a man with a crutch hobble out to meet them.

"Why, Sergeant Beecham, what are you doing here? I mean, I am most happy to see you but I did not know—"

The man's stolid features broke into a wide smile as he took the reins from her slack grasp. "Ye didn't know the major here had handed me a ticket for the stage with orders to present myself as soon as I could travel with this confounded leg? Begging your pardon, ma'am, but if that isn't just like him. It's over a fortnight I've been here by now, and right glad I am to be settled, let me tell ye, what with decent jobs being as scarce as hens' teeth these days."

"How is your leg, Sergeant?"

"The cast comes off tomorrow, I'm thankful to say, ma'am, and while I'm about it, I never had the chance yet to thank ye for what ye did for me that night."

"I did nothing, Sergeant, it was all the major's doing, but I am happy to see you almost restored."

"Come down off that horse before your muscles solidify," Cam commanded, appearing at her side. He lifted her down and steadied her as her knees, unaccustomed to riding for months, displayed a tendency to buckle. Clinging to her husband's arm, Natasha took leave of Sergeant Beecham, laughingly pointing out that her present gait was as unsteady as his.

She acknowledged the stiffness as they walked back to the house. "I should have listened to you when you first suggested I had had enough riding for the first day, but there was so much I wanted to see. Your property is lovely, Cam."

"There will be other rides. You should not try to do too much at once. You had better soak in a hot tub right away. And no ballet practice today."

"Yes, master . . . no, master," she chanted with mock humility, admitting, "I'd fall on my face if I tried to dance today. Mrs. Hazeltine is sweet to spare the time to play for me."

"She's a good soul, if rather joyless."

"It must have been heartbreaking to lose her husband so young. And she has no children at all?"

"To my knowledge there is only a married sister somewhere in Somerset. Mrs. Hazeltine spends a few weeks with her family every summer. I believe there are two or three nieces.''

"I'm glad she has someone at least. Has Sergeant Beecham any family?''

"No. There was a wife once, but she went off with another man when he was sent to Portugal. He's not heard from her since.''

"How terrible! I'm so glad you were able to help him.''

"He's going to be our coachman. He's wonderful with horses. I assure you I am getting the better of the bargain. This isn't charity by any means.''

Natasha turned a laughing face toward her husband. "Of course not, and I must not say you are being kind because you'll go all stiff and uncomfortable,'' she teased. In her glee at making Cam squirm, she failed to note a rise in her path and stumbled, her unsteady knees giving out on her.

He caught her about the waist with one arm, shoring her up, and now it was his turn to tease. "You are well-served for not looking where you are heading, and you a dancer too.''

She looked up at him, errupting into quick laughter that stilled just as quickly. Cam noted she blinked those fabulous lashes and freed herself gently with an innocuous remark, but not before he had seen the alarm that had leapt into her face. His own features froze into formality.

They entered the house together, but the momentary closeness was gone, destroyed by an instinctive recoil Natasha couldn't disguise. She *wanted* the closeness—that was the stupidest part—and regretted that Cam took care to project an air of impersonal friendliness thereafter, but Natasha was finding her own emotions difficult to understand those first days at Krestonwood.

Everything she discovered about Cam here in his own home deepened her liking and respect for him. She had always recognized his innate kindliness; living with him showed him to be even-tempered and fair-minded with respect to his dependents. As he became more accustomed to her presence and companionship, he responded with occasional flashes of humor, a quality she had once despaired of finding in her brother's serious-minded friend.

On a less exalted plane, she had never denied that looking at him was sheer sensual pleasure. Her fingers itched to explore the bones in his marvelously sculpted face, and her eyes always sought the red sparks sunshine drew out of his thick brown hair. When he really smiled at her, strange impulses chased up and down her spine, and on rare occasions there was a certain look in his eyes that excited and frightened her.

And there was the rub, of course. Part of her was eager to pursue the beginnings of knowledge to its ultimate end, which must be possession on his part and submission on hers. Her initial experience of lovemaking, which struck her as a cruel misnomer, had been physically painful and spiritually degrading. Only an idiot would seek a repetition. And yet . . . she had reveled in dancing with Cam; his arms about her induced pleasurable sensations no others evoked. Her instincts told her that to invite the beginning was to invite the rest, so Natasha tried to ignore the nameless yearnings that were part and parcel of her new association with Cam.

It was at this unsatisfactory stage that the newlywedded pair paid their first visit to Flint Abbey. Harry and Susan had called the week before with an invitation to dine, and Natasha was anticipating a happy afternoon in her old friend's company as they set out in Cam's new phaeton for the four-mile drive. She quizzed her husband about the surroundings and the neighbors, a number of whom had already called to welcome her. He responded good-naturedly to all her questions and it seemed no time at all before they were being welcomed inside the former abbey by the various members of the Flint family.

Some time later the young ladies found themselves alone in a charming saloon. The dowager Lady Flint was resting and all three men had gone to inspect a new acquisition in Lord Flint's stables. Natasha looked up from examining a miniature of Harry as a boy in time to catch a strange look on Susan's face.

"Sue, is something wrong? Are you all right?"

"I," said her hostess wonderingly, "have just been soundly kicked."

Natasha glanced around wildly for some previously unseen dog or cat before the sense of Susan's words came to her. "Oh, you mean the baby? Does he do it often? Does it hurt very much?"

Her friend laughed. "Generally it's more like a flutter, but that was a definite kick. My son is getting bored with his incarceration, and so am I. I am starting to feel so clumsy."

"Well, you do not look clumsy," Natasha said. "You are blooming. When exactly is the baby due?"

"A week or so before Christmas. It seems a long time to wait."

"I don't think I should be in a mad rush," Natasha confessed with a grimace of distaste.

"You mean because of the pain of delivery? Well, women have been producing children since the world began. What others have done, I can do."

"Yes, of course." Natasha felt she'd been less than tactful, and she tried to make amends. "I daresay it cannot be that much worse than the other, just longer."

Susan had picked up her knitting again and was counting stitches. "The other?" she repeated absently. "Oh, you mean the first time? Yes, with some women the rupturing of the maidenhead can be terribly painful, but just as it's worth it for the subsequent pleasure, my baby will be worth all the pain of bearing him. You'll feel the same." She began to cast on the next row.

Natasha, devoutly grateful for her friend's concentration on her knitting, produced an indistinct mumble of assent. It seemed her grandmother had neglected to mention certain things in her little talk about a woman's duty to her husband. Cousin Edwina's premarital advice had been limited to the style of her visiting cards. She had been too enveloped in misery to comprehend anything Cam had said to her following their dismal coupling, though she'd been aware part of it had been an apology of sorts.

Natasha was a trifle distracted for the remainder of their

visit, but the others were such old friends that she need scarcely do more than smile and contribute an occasional encouraging word or two. Her mind was busy with the implications of the knowledge she had just gained.

Back at Krestonwood several hours later, Natasha's preoccupation continued until Cam, noticing her unfocused stare, remarked on it.

"What are you looking at so intently?"

They were in the small family parlor that had become, more or less unpremeditatedly, the room they generally retired to in the evening. Cam had been softly playing on the pianoforte, an activity that usually pleased his bride, but tonight he had sensed her inattention after a time and he turned away from the keys, his glance tracing hers to the two portraits hanging over the fireplace.

"I was thinking about your parents. Your mother was very beautiful, wasn't she?"

"Yes."

"She looks sweet-natured but sad too in that portrait— or at least very sober. Was she?"

"She was of a rather serious nature, certainly; there has been more laughter in this house in the weeks you've been here than I recall during my entire childhood." His wife sat very still, digesting this, but he went on as though making a reluctant discovery. "Perhaps she was sad."

"Why was that, do you think?" Natasha prodded when he came to a full stop.

"I don't know. She was alone here a great deal after I went off to school. She didn't care for society of the sort you've experienced this past Season, and my father was away at sea much of the time. My uncle Humphrey and his family came here often while my aunt was still alive, but we've very few relatives."

"So you more or less grew up with Charles?"

"Not by his choice or mine," Cam said with a dry intonation that wasn't lost on Natasha.

"Tell me about your father. What was he like?"

"I didn't really know him very well, he was home so seldom. He was a large man with a ready smile who liked to gather a lot of people around him. Like most sailors he

187

was happiest at sea, and then, of course, I was quite young when he died—he was killed in the Battle of the Nile."

"No wonder your mother looks sad. It must have been a very lonely life for her. It's too bad you had no brothers or sisters."

"Yes."

Natasha's eyes continued to examine the attractive portraits. "You get your coloring from your mother, though her hair is much redder, but your bone structure comes from your father. You are really a very handsome man, Cam, even more so than your father, who looks like a heartbreaker in his naval uniform."

"Fustian!"

Laughter bubbled up in Natasha. "Now I've embarrassed you, which was very ill-done of me. Never mind, I shan't do it again."

Cam had recovered his countenance by now. There was a teasing gleam in the green eyes that studied her with a disconcerting thoroughness. "And who might you look like, my little witch? Not Peter, that is certain."

"Oh, I'm a throwback," she declared airily, "or so they tell me. According to my father, I'm the image of my grandmother in her youth."

"The Russian one?"

"Yes."

"Small wonder then that Grandmother collected jewels from half the aristocratic sprigs of Imperial Russia."

"Why, Cam, can it be that you are complimenting me? Now, I would have said that your taste ran more to tall willowy blondes." With her head tipped to one side and her pansy eyes sparkling with mischief she was the personification of girlish diablerie.

Cam stared in fascination while warning signals sounded in his brain. "It's time you went up to bed, Natasha," he said when he was sure of his command over his breathing.

"But it's not yet ten o'clock!"

"Nevertheless, if you wish to guarantee your privacy in your bedchamber, you will go now."

And Natasha, most unwilling, heartily rebellious but too unsure of herself to seize the initiative, went.

15

She regretted it the minute the door closed behind her, but the same lack of confidence that had taken her out of the parlor stopped her from turning the handle of her husband's door when she heard him moving around in his room an hour or so later. There was no hurry, after all. They were married, they shared a house, there would be other opportunities as good as the one she had just let slip away from her.

Natasha went to bed that night determined to learn more about the mysterious art of seduction. Surely in that great library downstairs there must be something to the point. She drifted off to sleep trying to recall if there had been anything in her reading of the *Lysistrata* that might be of help.

And in the end no stratagems or education proved necessary.

At breakfast two days later, Cam remarked that the long spell of delightful September weather looked like breaking within twenty-four hours.

Natasha raised her eyes from the plate of eggs and sausages she was demolishing. "Oh, dear, now I regret that I was too lazy to ride with you this morning. If the weather is going to prevent any outings for the next few days, perhaps this afternoon I will ride to that little stream you showed me the other day. It puts me in mind of my favorite spot at home."

"How would you like it if we were to bring some food along in the gig and have an al fresco luncheon there?"

"Cam, that's a wonderful suggestion. I love picnics, ants and all."

The day was so warm that Natasha didn't even bring a shawl along, pooh-poohing her husband's concern that she might become chilled wearing only a short-sleeved muslin dress. He had already complimented her on this highly becoming white garment sprigged with tiny red flowers and its cherry-red sash of satin ribbon whose long ends fluttered when she moved, and Natasha was not about to cover up its glory with a prosaic shawl. She clapped a wide-brimmed straw bonnet on her head, tied its red ribbons under one ear without benefit of looking glass, and declared herself ready.

Cam watched this hit-or-miss operation with a lurking smile in his eyes that his wife noticed and promptly challenged.

"Why are you half-smiling like that? Do I have a smudge on my face or something?"

"You look a picture, my dear girl. I was simply reflecting that you exhibit less concern for your appearance than any other lady of my acquaintance. They all seem to be forever patting their curls or rearranging their ribbons or gloves. You don't do any of those things."

"*I* have heard," Natasha declaimed loftily, "that the great Beau Brummell spends hours at his toilet, especially over the tying of his cravat, but that once he has achieved that *point de vice* appearance for which he is noted, he never gives it another thought."

"And have you just spent hours in front of your mirror, Natasha?" Her husband's smile spread to his lips as she hesitated, deciding whether to brazen it out. "You don't even appear to have your gloves with you."

Natasha abandoned all pretense. "I forgot them," she admitted, acknowledging the hit with a delightful wrinkling of her small straight nose. "Shall I go back?"

"Or send for them perhaps?" There was a softened look on the chiseled features that started Natasha's heart racing, but Cam turned away, saying briskly, "You don't need gloves on a picnic on your own property. Let's be off. The gig is already outside waiting."

His bride's breezy chatter soon put the smile back on Cam's lips and kept it there during the short drive to the crystal stream that meandered through one corner of his estate. They dined simply and deliciously in their private little Eden on chunks of fresh-baked bread, cheese, and fruit, all washed down by a light wine that Cam returned to the stream to keep cool. He had brought along an old quilt to spread in the one small grassy patch that offered, both banks of the stream being generally overgrown with bushes and trees almost to the water's edge.

Natasha kept her husband entertained with tales of the childhood exploits she and her brother had indulged in in Devon. Cam shook his head despairingly after one hair-raising story involving target practice with a purloined coachman's whip.

"I fear you must have been a complete hoyden, my dear."

"Perhaps *then*, but thanks to Cousin Edwina's sterling example and instruction, you now behold the epitome of a young lady of refinement and breeding."

"Oh, a prime example," he agreed, grinning widely at the picture she presented sitting cross-legged on the quilt. She had discarded her hat upon entering the shaded area and her shoes shortly thereafter for more comfort in sitting, and was now placidly eating an unpeeled plum with every evidence of enjoyment. Cam, himself coatless by now, was seated a couple of feet away with one leg on the ground bent at a right angle, his arms loosely embracing the raised knee of his other leg, whose foot was planted firmly in front of him. His head was angled to survey the girl to his left.

"Well, at least *I* know how to eat without wearing the menu," she retorted, leaning over to brush a crumb of bread from his cravat.

"Is that plum juice I see dribbling down your chin, madam?"

Natasha's superior expression dissolved instantly to laughter, but when she would have returned her hand to wipe her chin, he grasped her wrist, pulling her forward until she tumbled into his lap. His arms righted her, cradling her against his raised knee as he stared into startled brown eyes, all amusement vanished from his face.

"Do you know the effect you have on me, Natasha?" he demanded hoarsely. "It starts out as laughter, but it always ends—"

"Ends how, Cam?" she whispered when he clamped his lips together and turned his head to stare off into space.

"Ends in *wanting*!"

"Wh-what are you going to do about it?"

He turned back and the lack of fear in fathomless dark eyes was invitation enough. Cam bent his head and deliberately licked the plum juice from the corner of her mouth, the tip of his tongue lingering and retracing its path. She trembled, and when her lips parted on an involuntary breath, his mouth immediately captured hers. The marathon kiss that ensued sent electrifying impulses to every nerve in Natasha's body. Inexperience didn't keep her passive. Cam's lips moving hungrily over hers evoked an untutored but ardent response that drove him beyond the realm of rational control.

He made a final clutch at sanity and prudence. Releasing her mouth after an eternity that was yet too short for both, he buried his face in the scented warmth of her neck, fighting for breath and control.

"My God, Natasha, we had best get home before—"

"I think we had much better stay right here," she murmured, pressing little kisses along his jawline near his ear, which was all she could reach even by straining.

With a laugh of mingled triumph and resignation, Cam mentally consigned his Hessians to perdition, thinking at the same time that he should be grateful not to be wearing top boots. That was the last rational thought to enter his head for an enchanted interval. Rampant desire and instinct took over.

As for Natasha, she was too far gone on a voyage of discovery to be aware of any hampering conditions. There was an instant of stiffening when, having settled her on her side, Cam slipped his hand up under her skirt and began to caress silken thighs, but she relaxed under the influence of wordless murmurs of reassurance against her lips combined with the excitement generated by his gently roving fingers.

His own needs tightly reined in, Cam didn't seek entry until he felt her readiness. Natasha's eyes remained tightly closed, but he watched her with an aching tenderness and the remorse he had carried with him for his knowing brutality on that first occasion. He felt the jolt of pleasure with which she received him this time into the molten core of her being, and gloried in the strength with which she clung to him as he began to move within her, slowly at first and then with increasing urgency. He took her with him every inch of the way to the peak and launched them off, accepting in the startled gasp that broke from her lips forgiveness for that previous pain. His arms contained her trembling on the long, sweet descent to reality as she nuzzled as close to him as layers of rumpled clothing would permit.

The chuckle of the waters burbling along in the rocky streambed at their feet became audible once more as did the stillness in the midday air, and the threadbare green canopy of branches over their heads came back into focus, permitting glimpses of azure sky above.

"What a perfectly beautiful marriage bed," breathed Natasha as one still under the influence. "So this is what we've been missing these past weeks."

"I need hardly tell you, my darling, that it is not always this wonderful. Will you forgive me for that night?"

"Of course." Natasha turned her face down onto his shoulder, reluctant to dispense with the least portion of the sublime intimacy created by the union of their two separate persons.

"Tell me about that night with Charles, Tasha."

She sighed and complied, relinquishing the lingering magic.

When she had finished, he said on a note heavier with puzzlement than anger, "Whyever would your cousin wish to harm us like that?"

"She wanted you herself, of course."

His embarrassment communicated itself to her in the slight loosening of his arms. "But there was never the remotest chance of that, even if you didn't exist," he exploded.

Natasha knew a moment of real pity for Lucretia as she tried to explain. "People often delude themselves into believing what they wish to believe. It is very human."

"I think it more likely that one is afraid to believe what one wishes most to believe."

Natasha disagreed strongly and was summoning up arguments to refute so unnatural a theory when she fell asleep. For a while longer Cam lay there studying the perfection of her skin and the exquisite modeling of her bone structure. His eyes traced the lovely arcs of her brows and the mirror-image crescents formed on her cheeks by eyelashes so long and thick as to challenge belief in their reality. For that matter, it was beyond belief that he could ever have laid eyes on her and failed to detect the beauty, but though he could no longer summon up his first impression of Natasha, he well recalled that it had not been favorable. Which should teach him to beware of rash judgments, he concluded piously, wrapped in a warm cocoon of well-being as he gazed with awed contentment at his sleeping wife.

Cam nearly dozed but became aware suddenly that the emotional warmth he was feeling no longer included his bare backside, which was registering a cooling in the air and the beginnings of a damp breeze, the latter confirmed by a glance upward to where their leaf canopy was no longer motionless. Nor was there any blue to be seen in the sky through the branches. Carefully he drew his pillowing arm out from under Natasha's head, substituting a few folds of the quilt when she didn't stir. He pulled her dress down, his own clothing up and got back into his waistcoat. Next he laid his jacket over Natasha to replace some of his missing body heat and spent an unrewarding few minutes trying to retie his cravat without the aid of a mirror.

Cam let Natasha sleep as long as he dared without chancing a wetting on the drive back, then shook her gently awake and reluctantly left her to neaten her appearance while he walked back through the trees to the last field to rehitch their grazing horse to the gig.

When he came to Natasha that night, Cam's first action

was to remove the pins that confined her magnificent hair, running his fingers through the luxuriant softness with transparent pleasure. "This is something I've longed to do for ages. Tonight, my darling, there will be nothing between us, no boots—thank heavens—no stays or hairpins, not even this extremely fetching white costume that is, in any case, as effective at concealing your charms as Salome's last veil."

"This afternoon was perfect," Natasha protested dreamily.

"It was indeed, but tonight will be better."

Thanks to his wife's enthusiastic cooperation, Cam had no difficulty in fulfilling his promise. Natasha knew what to expect now and she met him on equal terms, her passion rising to confront and satisfy his.

"You have surprised me continually from the moment we met," Cam murmured into her ear when he was again holding her quietly, "but now you astound me. I never dreamed or expected anything like this six weeks ago."

"Why not?"

He was oddly embarrassed by the innocent question, but Natasha's honesty demanded a like return. "Lovemaking has never been more than a . . . a release before; the women didn't really matter."

"Oh. Do I matter, Cam?"

He gripped her fiercely with one arm and pushed up her chin with the other hand, forcing her to look at him. "How can you doubt it? How can you ask that?"

"Well, I have always felt that you disapproved of me— not as much lately as when we met, perhaps—but I have never been sure that you really liked me."

"My God, woman, you take a deal of convincing!"

"Is that a problem?" The mock innocence of the question drew a shout of laughter, after which he proceeded to demonstrate the positive nature of his feelings for her to the ultimate satisfaction and exhaustion of both.

Cam remained awake long after Natasha went to sleep in his arms. His body was sated and content but his spirit was too uneasy to rest. Their time together was so short. He knew now that it would have been infinitely wiser to have kept her at arm's length, kinder to both. If he had foreseen that it was going to be like an amputation to tear himself away from her, he would have done just that—at least, he hoped he would have been able to deny himself. Even more for Natasha's sake. After today he could not question that she cared for him, but how could he have known that, considering the conditions under which they had married? There was no real excuse for his recent conduct, though. He had been tempted and he had fallen.

Perhaps mortals are not intended to dwell for long in the rarefied atmosphere of the mountaintop. Cam had already plummeted, and Natasha's blazing happiness lasted for less than forty-eight hours.

There wasn't a cloud on her horizon when she awoke, figuratively speaking. Clouds aplenty hurtled across the sky bringing with them rain showers for the second day in a row. Natasha turned from the gray skies that were in her line of vision when her lashes lifted and her eyes collided with her husband's sleeping form. She lay still some moments, savoring the delicious warmth in which she was enveloped, bemused by the near miracle of unity achieved by two such disparate entities as Cam and herself. Stealthily she rose onto one elbow, the better to avail herself of the infinite delight she took in visually feasting on the aesthetic elements that defined her husband's person. If a man could be described as beautiful, Cam was that man. It was a rather austere beauty, to be sure, the marvelously chiseled skull being sparely covered with firm flesh that resembled pale marble, the whole enlivened by the sharp contrast of compelling green eyes, dark brows, and that variegated hair that imprisoned bits of fire and sunlight. She wasn't the only female to be fascinated by this particular work of art, but to her alone belonged the privilege of appreciating it at her leisure from within his embrace.

She was gloating in her privileged state, greedily absorbing the beauty of his mouth, long and finely carved, when Cam opened his eyes. Natasha could feel a blush rising from her throat at being thus caught staring, but she boldly held his gaze, seeing confusion flare into warmth before a shadow seemed to flit across his features. She must have been mistaken in that, though, because the warmth rekindled and she found herself being pulled on top of him and soundly kissed.

"Good morning," said Cam when it became necessary to draw breath.

"It . . . it's raining," Natasha replied inanely. "You won't be able to ride."

"Good."

The lazy satisfaction in his voice brought the heat back to her cheeks and the flame to his eyes. After that, no intelligible conversation was exchanged for an appreciable interval.

They emerged eventually to enjoy a leisurely breakfast in a companionable silence interrupted by intermittent bursts of trivial conversation. Driven by a recently acquired disinclination to allow her husband out of her sight for any length of time, Natasha settled into the library with a book while Cam busied himself with estate business. They were there when Albert came in with the post he had collected at the receiving office. Glancing up to smile at the young footman as he left the room, Natasha saw her husband go swiftly through the pile, setting aside the London newspapers. He abstracted an envelope that he proceeded to hold in a clenched grip for long enough to arouse his bride's curiosity. Becoming aware of her regard, he lowered his eyes swiftly as he opened it, but not before a little chill feathered along Natasha's nerves at the bleakness that crossed his face momentarily.

"Cam? Is something wrong?"

"No, darling, nothing." He did not look up from his reading.

Unconvinced and feeling a touch rebuffed, she bit her lip and went back to her book, but Virgil's poetry had lost its power to charm, though she applied dogged attention to an activity that had changed in a twinkling from pleasure to chore. She concentrated fiercely on *not* watching Cam, but somehow over the last few days she had developed an awareness of him under her skin, an awareness that did not depend on vision or hearing, and this knowledge told her that something troubled his spirit.

Whatever had clouded Cam's horizon in the morning dissipated after lunch. The rain continued and he insisted on playing for her dance practice that afternoon. Any initial consciousness she might have felt at exercising and working under a masculine eye evaporated within ten minutes. Dancing was an activity to which Natasha brought intense concentration and dedication. Before the session was over, Cam had identified these qualities as being of the same order and magnitude as possessed by jockeys, fencers, and other competitive athletes. It was an unsuspected facet of his wife's personality, a dimension he wouldn't have hesitated in terming unfeminine had he discovered it early in their acquaintance. Now he considered that it added immeasurably to the fascination she exercised over him. As Natasha spun around the room, his eyes followed her movements with devouring attention as if to commit every angle and nuance to memory.

Natasha was too engrossed to notice then, but by the time they retired that evening she was convinced that something was troubling Cam despite an able pretense of light-heartedness. Once or twice there had been a fleeting look of sadness in his face and he seemed to receive all communication a split second later than normal, as though her words must penetrate an invisible barrier to reach him. A cold numbing apprehension was rising in her.

Their lovemaking that night contained an element of desperation, the memory of which remained after passion was spent, coloring the lovely languor that had previously followed release. Lying in her silent husband's arms, fulfilled but fearful, Natasha was prodded by the nameless dread creeping over her to ask, "What is it, Cam? I know something is wrong. Please tell me."

His arms tightened spasmodically, then he drew away from her. In the dark she could feel that he was lying on his back, staring upward. She stayed unmoving, afraid to breathe, praying that he would not shut her out. The silence had deepened until she could count her own heartbeats in her throat before he spoke.

"I couldn't have put off telling you much longer, but I hated to tarnish what we have discovered these past two days. Natasha, I have to go away for a time."

"Go away? Where? Why?"

"To Vienna. For the meetings between the Allies."

"But that is not so terrible." Relief overflowed in Natasha's voice. "I know we have only been here a short time, but Vienna should be most exciting just now."

"You don't understand. I cannot take you with me." The clipped words shut off her rising excitement like a hand squeezing her windpipe.

"Why not?" she gasped. "I would not mind the traveling, truly, Cam."

"It isn't that. I've been told Vienna is bursting at the seams. There are no accommodations to be had."

"I would not care if it were only one room. Please, Cam!"

"Darling, I'm sorry, but I shall be just one of the anonymous young men from the Foreign Office; in fact, I'm going out as a replacement for one who took ill before he arrived."

Natasha heard his words through a haze of pain and shock. Argument would be so much wasted breath, she knew beyond doubting; Cam would not have looked so unhappy whenever he thought himself unobserved today had any possibility existed of taking her with him. "How long have you known about this appointment?" she asked dully.

"A sennight." Reluctance sounded in his voice. "I didn't tell you at once because there were arrangements to be made . . . and because some people shirk difficult tasks. I did not know this summer when I started to explore with my uncle the possibility of going right into the Foreign Office that I would be taking on a wife, although," he added hastily when the sound of her indrawn breath reached him, "that would not have been of great concern in the ordinary course of events. This present opportunity has come about purely by chance."

Natasha's instinctive reaction to the distress spreading through her was to hunch over on her side away from him, her knees drawn up. She was the only obstacle to his happiness. If it were not for her and his own quixoticism in marrying her, he would be over the moon with delight at this assignment.

Cam felt her retreat and turned to gather her against his body, spoon-fashion. "Even a sennight ago I believed a time apart might be no bad thing for us, the way matters were between us, but now . . . I should have kept my distance. It wasn't fair to you."

"You . . . you are sorry about what happened?"

"Tasha, my darling, please believe that these past two days have been the happiest of my life, except that now parting is so damnably hard."

"When do you leave?"

"Soon . . . in a day or two. I've been waiting to hear from my aunt Hester Cameron—my mother's aunt actually, though she was only a few years older than Mother. She's only in her late fifties now. I wrote to Scotland asking Aunt Hester to come and stay with you here while I'm gone. I received her answer today. You'll like her, darling; she has a quick wit and a quicker tongue; she's alert and very independent, she never married, hasn't much use for the whole male gender, I fear."

Natasha half-listened to the deep male voice rumbling above her ear. She had no interest in his aunt, no interest in anything, and no strength to spare from trying to hold herself together to make any responses. It wasn't hysterics she feared but complete disintegration.

"Tasha," Cam said desperately, "it won't be for very long. The Congress has already convened, I believe; it will most likely last for six or eight weeks. I could be home by Christmas." He felt her shrink even farther into that protective posture, but she made no sound at all.

Sometime later, when no reaction of any sort was forthcoming, he removed his arms from around the inert form of his wife and returned to his own side of the bed, sadly conscious that she was relieved to be free of his touch.

In the two days remaining before Cam left for London and Dover, Natasha went through the motions of existing with all the alertness of a sleepwalker. She did not again plead with her husband to take her with him and chance their luck at finding accommodations, nor did she weep or reproach him by word or deed, but her wan little face was a constant reproach. She cooperated fully in all the last-minute instructions about the day-to-day running of the estate and agreed readily to consult Harry Flint about any unanticipated problems that might arise. They discussed finances, preparations for winter, and the necessary items to pack for an indefinite stay abroad.

Natasha did less talking as the time for Cam's departure loomed closer. Most of her stamina was expended in preventing the silent screams of protest within her from being articulated. She knew she was stiff and unresponsive when he made love to her at night, but she could do nothing about that. All her energies were directed toward maintaining a decent composure in the face of impending devastation; she had none to spare for simulating a passion that had died within her in the space of a heartbeat.

It would be difficult to say who was the more relieved when the moment of parting finally arrived. Natasha was aware in some remote corner of her mind that Cam felt guilt and remorse at leaving her, but she simply could not rise to the selfless act of removing the cloud by presenting a bright cheery demeanor for him to store in his memory. She would castigate herself for it later, but that degree of heroism was unattainable at the time. When he crushed her in his arms suddenly for a brief savage embrace at the steps of the carriage, her lips remained cold as marble beneath the onslaught of his seeking mouth, and the eyes that stared after him a moment later had the opacity of obsidian.

16

Aunt Hester Cameron arrived at Krestonwood two days later. Natasha was in the stables at the time, having just returned from a long solitary ride. Henry intercepted her on her way back to the house with the information that Miss Cameron had been ensconced in the morning room with a pot of tea while she awaited her hostess. In the space of a few steps Natasha discarded any idea of changing her clothes in favor of presenting herself to her new relative without further delay. The pervasiveness of her despair had left no time for speculation about Cam's formidable-sounding great-aunt; in fact, had she been on the witness stand, she would have been forced to confess that she had completely forgotten about Aunt Hester's imminent arrival and could only trust that Mrs. Hazeltine had prepared a suitable room for the lady.

As she hurried toward the garden entrance of the morning room to save time, Natasha recalled Cam's confident assurance that she would like his aunt, and offered up a fervent prayer that this should prove to be the case. Memories of her experience of living in Cousin Edwina's house rose to torment her, but she quickly closed her mind on that. Nevertheless, her shoulders were a trifle stiffened and she paused to take a deep breath outside the garden entrance, inhaling the scent of dozens of late roses she had passed by without noticing.

Natasha could have spared herself a few anxious moments. The woman who looked at her with Cam's piercing green eyes over a Limoges teacup was a far cry from a fashionable town matron. Even allowing for the ravages of five days of traveling, Miss Cameron's appearance in a voluminous black gown of venerable age could never have been remotely fashionable. She had put off her plain hat on the settee beside her, and when she bent forward to replace the cup on the table, an uncompromising knot of rusty gray hair became visible.

"Miss Cameron, I do beg your pardon for not being here to greet you on your arrival. I was not quite sure when that would be, you see. Cam did not know either and he—"

"Hush, child, there's no call to get so breathless. Come over here where I may get a good look at you."

Natasha obeyed, standing silent and interested under the kindly but penetrating scrutiny of a pair of intelligent eyes in a fleshy, blunt-featured face that had probably not been pretty even in her youth. It was a face to inspire confidence, however, and when Natasha smiled tentatively, Miss Cameron's answering smile revealed strong beautiful teeth and an incongruous dimple in her right cheek.

"Ah," said that lady, nodding with satisfaction, "I was persuaded you'd be a taking little thing if you had a bit more life to you. Sit down, lass, do. Tell me, how long has that graceless nephew of mine been gone?"

"Cam left two days ago, ma'am. He . . . he was very sorry to be unable to remain long enough to welcome you, but . . . but this assignment came up quite suddenly." Natasha's voice trailed off under the unblinking stare of those far-seeing eyes.

"So, you find yourself abandoned after a few weeks of marriage, eh? Typical masculine behavior that—not the best of them ever had a lick of consideration when it comes to women. Females are fine for amusement in their lighter moments; they flirt with us, make love, and swear their undying affection, then leave us without a backward glance the minute more interesting business calls."

Natasha tried and failed to conjure up a picture of the man brave enough to flirt with Miss Cameron. She stared into those shrewd kindly eyes so like Cam's and, to her acute horror and shame, felt her face crumble into tears. She had not wept from the moment Cam made his devastating announcement, but now the frozen misery inside her gave way and she cried as though she would never stop. She accepted the handkerchief pressed into her hand by the practical Miss Cameron and struggled to contain herself.

"I am so sorry, pl-please forgive me. I don't kn-know what came over me." The words were uttered between sobbing breaths as she fought for control.

"Nonsense, lass, cry it out. It won't do any harm and might do some good." While the storm raged in her vicinity the Scotswoman placidly went about the business of preparing a cup of tea, liberally adding sugar and milk. When Natasha had at last brought her sobbing under control and looked up shamefaced, her fingers mangling the sodden handkerchief, Miss Cameron said briskly, "There, now that you've gotten that off your chest we can set about making the best of a bad situation. You may start by drinking this, and then I believe I would like to go to my room to check that my maid has got my things sorted out. I assume Mrs. Hazeltine has put me in the yellow room, as usual." She continued with a rambling monologue of trivialities while Natasha gulped down the sweet tea, ashamed, depleted, but oddly comforted.

Miss Cameron was as good as her word. Natasha, even had that been her dearest desire, was not to be permitted to sink into a lethargy while the indomitable Scotswoman was in residence at Krestonwood.

Aunt Hester scorned the puny little hills of Wiltshire as being unworthy to consider in the same breath as Scotland's rugged mountains, but she liked being out-doors. The two women spent many companionable hours riding and walking in the area while the beautiful fall weather held. Gardening was another of the older woman's passions. She was full of theories on pruning and planting, theories she set about putting into practice to the disgust of the head gardener, a sworn enemy within a week. Natasha's services as peacemaker and diplomatist were constantly in demand that autumn, for Aunt Hester possessed the impetus of a juggernaut and the finesse and diplomacy of an elephant. Indeed, she had no opinion of diplomacy, for all that her nephew had embarked on a career in that illustrious field, being one for direct action and speech in all her dealings. She had a keen intelligence, insatiable curiosity about the world around her, and immutable prejudices against the male of the species. Natasha loved her dearly and blessed the day she came to Krestonwood.

Aunt Hester took over the task of playing for her great-niece's ballet practice. Her touch on the pianoforte lacked lightness and elegance perhaps, but no one could accuse her of not keeping the beat strong and steady. Natasha's dancing was a revelation and a constant joy to Miss Cameron, who had spent most of her life in her father's remote manor in the Highlands of Scotland. She was fiercely proud of being a Scot and no mean performer at the national dances herself, but ballet was an entirely new source of pleasure to her.

The two women spent their days in quiet country pursuits and their evenings in conversation or reading. Though uninterested in personal adornment, Aunt Hester did exquisite needlework. A typical evening would find the two cosily established in the morning room with Natasha reading aloud while the elder lady stitched away on some intricate piece of work by the light of several good lamps. Her eyes were as keen as her great-nephew's and she was content to be employed thus for hours on end.

The colorful days of October in England slipped by uneventfully. They received word of Cam's safe arrival in Vienna and thereafter could count on hearing from him every week or two. The women looked forward to reading his impressions of all the foreign luminaries assembled in the beautiful Austrian capital on the Danube River. His letters were entertaining and informative as he described the extraordinary scene that autumn, where titles were two a penny and beautiful bejeweled woman competed with one another to collect the most illustrious names in their salons.

Miss Cameron, who had spent almost her entire life in one locale, albeit a much-loved one, cherished a secret dream of world travel and fairly devoured her nephew's letters. If Natasha wished there was something more of personal interest to herself in some of these fascinating epistles she kept her own counsel on that subject, readily entering into Aunt Hester's enthusiasm and perfectly willing to track down all the maps in the library to locate the many principalities represented at the Congress.

It was toward the end of October when a thick packet arrived that had been redirected from Manchester Square. Henry brought in the post while the ladies were at lunch. Natasha squealed with delight when she identified the untidy scrawl.

"It's from Peter at last! I have not had word from my brother since he wrote at the end of May while waiting to sail for America," she explained to Miss Cameron.

"Go right ahead, my dear child, and read them; do not torture yourself for form's sake."

Natasha flashed her aunt a grateful smile and tore into the packet, which consisted of a number of sheets dated from early June up to the first of August, she discovered on thumbing quickly through the lot. "This means, of course, that he would not have received Cam's or my letters telling him about our marriage. This last letter was written from Bermuda while they were waiting to sail for the Chesapeake." She looked up. "We have known from the newspapers that the Eighty-fifth Regiment was involved in the assault on Washington. Peter says the soldiers did not learn their destination until they reached Bermuda."

There was silence for a time while Natasha read her brother's letters. At one point she chuckled. "Listen to this, Aunt Hester. To relieve the tedium of the ocean crossing, General Ross invited the officers of the fleet aboard the *Royal Oak* for an evening's entertainment. The officers billeted on that ship put on a presentation of *The Apprentice*, followed by *The Mayor of Garret* as an afterpiece. Peter says the painted scenery was as good as anything he's seen on the professional stage. Cannot you just picture the scene with lamps placed in the rigging and a curtain across the after deck? The sailors watched the performance from the masts and rigging. Afterward, everything was cleared for dancing. The ball was opened by Admiral Malcombe and the Hon. Mrs. Mullins. There are actually a few ladies accompanying their husbands. All this in the middle of the ocean!" She shook her head wonderingly.

Occasional letters were not the only interruptions in the quiet routine of the ladies' life at Krestonwood. Neighbors came to call and replied with invitations to their homes. The family at Flint Abbey made sure the ladies didn't feel neglected, including them in all their social plans. As the weather worsened and November drew to a close, however, Susan, with her confinement less than a month away, ventured from home less often and less far.

By this time Natasha was convinced that she also was with child. Still hopeful of seeing her husband home for Christmas despite no news of progress from Vienna, she kept her own counsel. In any event, she felt completely well, not even being troubled with the occasional periods of nausea many expectant mothers experienced. She said nothing about her situation as November passed into December, her hopes of Cam's early return dwindling as the cold weeks crawled past. Her silence wasn't a considered decision; in fact, Natasha would have been hard pressed to rationalize her behavior. The instinct to tell Cam first was counteracted by a feeling of distance from her husband that was being compounded with each passing week. This could have been overcome had there been anything in his letters that spoke from one heart to another, but, sadly, this was not the case. She ripped open each of Cam's eagerly awaited letters. They were invariably interesting and informative; her receptive mind appreciated his reasoned analysis of the political situation, but invariably she was left with a feeling of blankness. Except for the social notes, she might have been reading an official report to the Foreign Office. In the atmosphere of impersonality created by Cam's epistolary style it proved impossible to introduce into her own letters a note of intimacy such as was required for the announcement of her delicate condition.

It was at this stage that a messenger arrived from Flint

Abbey one day in mid-December with the news that Lady Flint's time had come. When Natasha had asked Susan if she would like her to be present at the birth, her friend had accepted the offer gratefully. She had had a small bag packed for days and was ready to leave with the abbey's coachman within ten minutes, though Aunt Hester advised the flustered girl that haste was unlikely to be essential, considering the well-known propensity of first babies for taking their own sweet time.

Aunt Hester was proved correct, for Michael Dennis Flint did not put in an appearance until some seven hours later. Susan was well-attended by her mother-in-law, Dr. Smythe, and Mrs. Blandings, an experienced midwife, but she was glad to have her old friend's support, though Natasha's usefulness was limited to wiping her brow and holding her hand tightly during contractions and bearing occasional messages of progress to a nervous Lord Flint, who found the waiting trying to the extreme. Not being well-constituted for a passive role, Mr. Richard Flint had removed himself from the scene altogether, going off to visit a friend for the day. It was a normal delivery, and Susan, tiny though she was, bore it with unflagging fortitude. Indeed, it was she who encouraged her friend toward the end, for Natasha cringed at witnessing her friend's pain without being in any way able to alleviate it. She was curiously drained after the birth as she sponged Susan's face and hands while Mrs. Blandings cleaned up the screaming infant and the proud grandmother carried the news to her son.

Susan was tired but radiant as she smiled up at a rather shaky Natasha. "I told you it would be worth it. He sounds strong and lusty," she added smugly.

"He's perfect, Lady Flint," Dr. Smythe assured her, "and you shall do fine too."

Natasha accepted the wrapped baby from the midwife and brought him over to Susan, marveling at the miniature assemblage of features and the soft fuzz covering his head like the bloom on a peach. One tiny fist had already escaped from the wrappings and was waving in front of his mouth.

"Come meet your mother, Michael," she whispered to the now quiet infant, holding him close for a moment before handing him over to an eager Susan. "He's beautiful, my dear. Congratulations. I am so very happy that I was able to be with you today."

Something in her voice alerted the other girl. "Tasha, are you—?"

Natasha nodded. "No one knows yet," she said urgently as Lord Flint and his mother entered the room.

Susan looked at her searchingly for an instant before turning to smile at her husband.

The expression in Harry Flint's eyes as he approached his wife's bedside remained with Natasha long after she left the abbey. He saw no one else, not even his new son at first, and it was clear that Susan filled his world. Natasha left the room silently, sincerely delighted for her friends' happiness but more conscious than ever of the lack in her own life. To have one's husband look at one the way Harry looked at Susan must be the most wonderful thing in the world. Fortunately the dowager joined her before she could sink into a fit of the dismals. Though it cost her an effort, she was able to muster up a convincingly carefree smile to toast the heir's safe arrival with his proud father and grandmother.

At Susan's insistence, Natasha submitted to an examination by Dr. Smythe when he called on the new mother and son the next day. His confirmation of her condition was superfluous, but it was reassuring to hear that the doctor considered her to be a fine healthy female for whom childbearing should not prove unduly hazardous. Still she did not mention her condition to Aunt Hester or to Sir Humphrey and Charles when they arrived to spend a few days with the ladies at Christmastime.

Natasha was pleased with the opportunity thus afforded to improve her acquaintance with Cam's uncle for more reasons than the family connection. Her initial impression of a sharp but sympathetic intelligence allied to a kindly nature was reinforced by the visit. Miss Cameron and Sir Humphrey were old antagonists who enjoyed their interminable verbal sparring thoroughly, though neither would admit this. Aunt Hester had not met Charles Talbot since he was, as she did not scruple to remind him in front of Natasha, "a spotty adolescent with abrupt manners and a deplorable penchant for ridiculous and conspicuous clothing." She allowed as how time had greatly improved his complexion and address but had barely tempered his taste in apparel. Charles, with his keen appreciation of the idiosyncracies of humanity, declared himself charmed with Aunt Hester and demonstrated his good manners by forbearing to point out that her personal disinterest in fashion left her ill-equipped to judge others in this sphere. Her outspokenness amused him and he took delight in provoking an outburst whenever too much harmony reigned for his taste.

Though sometimes difficult to discern underneath the surface noise and combat, a pleasant sort of harmony did characterize the visit. If Natasha could have put aside her longing for her husband's presence, she would have been as happy as she pretended to be that holiday season. Unfortunately, the passage of time failed to dull the physical ache within her. She needed to see Cam, to tell him about the child they were to have in June, but detailed questioning of Sir Humphrey elicited no more information than was in the papers about the progress of the Vienna meetings.

The mood of the country was highly critical of the conduct of the negotiations by Lord Castlereagh. So far the Congress had produced no resolution decrying the slave trade such as a substantial liberal element at home had long advocated, and the problem of Poland was as far from being solved as ever. During his visit to England in the spring, Tsar Alexander had indicated an intention to grant the Poles a constitution, so it was difficult for those at home, given all the misinformation and rumors abounding, to accept that the tsar could be in such an obdurate frame of mind as reported. Sir Humphre could give Natasha no hope of an imminent successful conclusion to the Congress. Indeed, what with Prussia being in a bellicose mood over her greedy demands on Saxony and the Rhineland, there was a threat of renewed warfare in the atmosphere.

Natasha was in a very thoughtful mood at the completion of her relatives' visit in early January. The idea of going out to join Cam in Vienna had germinated with the birth of the Flint heir, or, more accurately perhaps, after watching Harry Flint's reaction to his son's birth. The birth of a child should bind a couple together indissolubly. The bonds uniting Cam and herself seemed gossamer-thin and stretched to breaking point after more than three months' separation. She felt she did not yet know Cam's heart: they'd been parted too soon. She had cross-questioned Sir Humphrey closely, hoping to get an impression of the probable length of the Congress, with no success. The chances were that it would be over—one way or another—before her baby was due in mid-June, but Natasha was loathe to leave her happiness to the mercy of unpredictable political maneuverings.

She was not blind to the numerous factors mitigating against such a long journey, chief among them the additional hazards of winter travel, monstrous expense, and her condition. One by one she considered the obstacles. Having mastered the map of Europe over the past months, she had no illusions that women traveling in a laden coach could hope to achieve anything near the two weeks it took the fastest king's messengers to go between Vienna and London. They would have to be prepared to spend a month on the road. Thanks to her grandmother, she was fluent in French, and she had learned to read and write German under her father's tutelage. Speaking it was another matter, but Cam had managed with less knowledge. As far as dangers on the road were concerned, they would travel only by day and hire an armed outrider. Cost was the problem easiest to overcome because she was prepared to underwrite all expenses herself, not deeming it proper to use her husband's money for a purpose he would certainly disapprove of.

The biggest stumbling block of all was her pregnancy. If it were known, arguments would rain down upon her head from all sides, and she would be forced to desist. Therefore, the time to initiate the project was growing short. She regretted having told Susan because it meant she must effect a departure without informing the Flints, a discourtesy Sue would forgive her before she would herself. So far there were no visible changes in her body except that her breasts were somewhat larger, which she trusted would not draw Aunt Hester's eye during the daily dance sessions. She was going to need clothes, though, not only for the later months but because Cam's accounts of the brilliant social affairs taking place nightly in Vienna made it imperative that she not come to him looking like King Cophetua's beggar maid. That meant taking her jewels too, another problem to consider.

Had Natasha been one whit less determined, the practicalities of the undertaking would have defeated her at the outset. For every problem surmounted, another appeared on the horizon. The first person she actually approached after weeks of mental exercise was Sergeant Beecham, who allowed as how "he wouldn't mind tooling the new carriage all over Europe and was mighty proud to think the major would entrust his lady's safety to him." Trying to suppress a blush of pure shame at the tacit deception, Natasha put the question of an armed guard to him and was relieved when he promised her there were several former comrades in or about London who would be happy to undertake a well-paying mission for the major. She swore him to secrecy to prevent gossip circulating about the neighborhood and prepared to tackle Aunt Hester.

The fire of anticipation that sparked in that lady's eyes when her niece casually broached the subject told Natasha she had won. Aunt Hester did indeed protest that they should write and get Cam's sanction before embarking on such a daring venture, but she subsided gratefully when the younger woman pointed out that an exchange of letters could quite well take six weeks. If Cam thought the Congress might be winding down by springtime, he would be bound to consider the proposed expedition a waste of money and energy, and they would thus miss out on the thrill of having been present while history was in the making.

Miss Cameron, for once in her life happy to be overborne by a stronger will, threw herself into the planning with a vengeance. It was she who came up with the idea of sewing most of Natasha's more spectacular jewelry inside the linings of the fur muffs they would purchase in London for the cold journey. She agreed that it would be advisable to engage a maid in London rather than take one of the local girls away from her family for a period of months. She even agreed with surprising meekness to the augmenting of her own wardrobe while they were cooling their heels in the city waiting for banking arrangements and Natasha's clothes to be ready. She also approved her niece's choice of Dawson to handle the business of managing the household in their absence with recourse to Lord Flint should anything untoward occur.

Natasha took advantage of one of Aunt Hester's rare migraines to go alone to Flint Abbey to take leave of their good friends on the day before they were to depart in mid-January. She informed Susan that she and Miss Cameron were going to London for a few weeks, the same story she had told Dawson earlier. Eventually she would write the whole truth to Harry and leave the letter with someone to post off to Wiltshire at a later date. To save Cam any unnecessary worry, she intended to make sure no letters announcing her intentions arrived in Vienna before she did. Wishing she did not feel so like an unregenerate deceiver but too bent on her course to cavil at the necessity, Natasha returned home, sobered by her own behavior despite constant rationalizations.

In the fortnight the ladies remained in London, Natasha alternated between intense anticipation when everything seemed possible and periods of gloom when her conscience troubled her and she went in fear of imminent disaster in the form of discovery. While completing the necessary arrangements, they resided at a quiet hotel in an unfashionable quarter to lessen the chance of meeting an acquaintance who might inform Sir Humphrey of her presence in town. As the head of the Talbot family he could forbid her to make the trip, and such was Natasha's need to see Cam that she dared not take the risk. She added to her soul's burden by lying to Aunt Hester, telling her Sir Humphrey and Charles were still in the country.

Toward the end of January the news reaching London was much more promising, with the backing down of Prussia from her militant stand over Saxony, and now Natasha's fears were that the Congress would finish its business before she could get to Vienna. It was only by exercising the sternest self-discipline that she was able to conceal her simmering impatience to be gone while she trotted Aunt Hester to all the tourist attractions in London by day so she would be too fatigued to wish to attend the theater or the opera at night. On the one occasion when she had felt compelled to agree to a visit to the opera, she adopted a sham migraine herself to beg off at the last moment. One more sin chalked up to her growing account.

By the time the small party left for Dover on the last day of January, Natasha's nerves were in a highly agitated state and she was convinced she was a monster of duplicity who had forever compromised her immortal soul.

17

Vienna, Austria
March, 1815

The long case clock in the corner struck four, drawing a glance from the room's sole occupant before he returned his attention to the document he was copying. For the next several minutes the soft scratching noises made by his pen were the only sounds in the room until, with a grunt of satisfaction, the writer laid down the pen, flexed his fingers, and pushed back his chair. The clock was striking the half-hour before, having scrutinized the document for errors, Cameron Talbot dropped it on the table and rose wearily to his feet. Both hands went up to his shoulders as long fingers tried to knead some of the stiffness out of his neck muscles while he walked over to the window and gazed out. Below in the Minoritzenplatz, people moved about, churning up the dirty slush of a late-winter afternoon. There did not seem to be an hour of the day or night when Vienna's streets were entirely empty of activity.

At first he'd found the ceaseless activity exhilarating. It was said that one hundred thousand visitors had swelled Vienna's customary population by half again. There were representatives from the Pope and a delegation from Frankfort's Jews to press for relief from repressive practices in Europe. Every minor princeling with a grievance was here with his retinue as well as full negotiating teams from the large powers. A swell of optimism and purpose filled the air. But that had been October, and now it was March. Cam rubbed the back of his neck and remained by the window looking down on the familiar scene with patent disinterest.

Vienna had captivated, fascinated, frustrated, and

exhausted him in return. The entire Congress had never once sat in session. Work was carried out by committees selected by the four Allied powers and France, leaving the vast majority of the visitors with little to do but play. He couldn't speak for his counterparts in the French or Austrian delegations, but the amount of work to be got through by the ten junior men sent out by the Foreign Office was sufficient to dull the appetite for play of any but the most energetic hedonist. And yet a certain amount of socializing was required, especially of himself because of his long association with Lord an Lady Castlereagh. He had rather enjoyed some of the fabulous social affairs of the autumn, but the novelty had long since worn thin. These days the delights of a hermitage had growing appeal and he had to force himself back to the present when memories of those few weeks at Krestonwood with Natasha intruded as they did with increasing frequency. They were making real progress now though, so perhaps . . .

His thoughts were derailed by the appearance of one of his colleagues, who entered and said with a smile that struck Cam as remarkably fatuous, "There are two ladies asking to see you, Talbot."

"Who are they?"

"They refused to give their names. The old one looks like a duenna. The young one is a ravishing beauty, a bit in the style of that dark little dancer who has been throwing out lures to you lately, but this one has a smile that lights up the place. You really are a dark horse, Talbot. Small wonder you've been impervious to the charms of—"

Cam heard no more, for he had crossed the room in swift strides, unceremoniously elbowing his garrulous comrade away from the door. It was utterly impossible, of course, but . . . He flung open the door and paused dumbfounded as a small whirlwind in crimson trimmed with white fur flung herself at him.

"Cam, oh, Cam!"

"Tasha!"

There was only one thing to do in such a situation. Cam

accepted the hurtling body into his embrace, and when parted red lips lifted in invitation, he kissed them, conscious on some level that her skin felt cold at first. He was also conscious that there was an interested audience to this impassioned greeting. Still gathering his scattered wits together, he put Natasha away from him a few inches and said over her head, "Hello, Aunt Hester." Then, the fog clearing, he gripped his wife's arms tighter. "Natasha, how did you get here?"

"Beechy brought us. Oh, darling, I am so happy to see you at last. It took us over a month to get here because of the snow in places. I feared I would go mad from the delays."

"Why did you not let me know that you were coming?"

"I did not want you to worry about us en route. Besides," she added with compulsive honesty, "I was afraid you would forbid it."

"And so I should have, had I the least idea you might attempt such a foolhardy stunt, and in the middle of winter too. It was utter madness, Natasha!"

"Cam," she wailed, "aren't you glad to see me at all?"

"Of course I am glad to see you, but—" A discreet cough behind him pulled Cam up short. He tucked Natasha under one arm and turned to face the avidly curious man in the doorway. "Oh, Birdwell, I'd like you to meet my wife and my aunt, Miss Cameron. Sir Allenby Birdwell, Natasha."

Cam did some rapid thinking while Natasha proceeded to subjugate the goggle-eyed Birdwell, but for once his cool decisiveness had deserted him. "Where am I going to put you two?" he muttered to himself.

"You share rooms with Melsinger, do you not?" said Sir Allenby. "Why don't I call for some tea for the ladies while you locate him? Tell him he can move in with me. Are you promised to Princess Trauttmansdorff tonight?" Turning to Natasha, he continued chattily, "Princess Trauttmansdorff receives on Thursdays. It will be as good a way as any to introduce you into our frenzied little social circle."

For want of any better plan, Cam went off to act on his colleague's suggestion and, several hours later, found himself escorting his wife to her first Viennese reception.

Aunt Hester had flatly refused to attend, declaring her only interest that night was in attaining the comfort of her bed at the earliest moment possible. She had spent an hour before dinner snipping out the linings in their fur muffs to retrieve Natasha's jewels and was well-rewarded by the stupefaction on her nephew's face as he gazed for the first time at his wife *en grande tenue*.

Cam had never seen Natasha wear any jewelry other than pearls or a locket on a thin chain, since only the simplest adornment was considered suitable for a young girl in her first Season. She had mentioned her grandmother's jewels at the time of their betrothal, but there had been no occasion since their marriage to wear any; indeed, he thought she had not even sent for them by the time he had left the country. Judging by his expression when she entered the small sitting room with Aunt Hester, Natasha in full feminine regalia fairly took his breath away. Clad in a deceptively simple gown of a deep rich red whose soft heavy fabric fell in elegant folds to her feet from the high waistline, she was vibrant enough in herself to render any embellishment unnecessary.

"I had forgotten how lovely you are," he blurted, then capped this not entirely felicitous choice of words by adding, "My God, are those rubies real?"

Natasha chuckled and struck a coy pose with her ivory-handled fan under her chin while Aunt Hester nodded with satisfaction. "I daresay she will not look out of place even in the company of all these bejeweled continental beauties we have been forever reading of back home."

"She'll shine them all down," Cam agreed with a solemn wink at his blushing bride as he came nearer to examine the elaborate diamond-and-ruby parure gleaming softly above the décolletage of her gown. Matching hair ornaments winked back at him from the coiled raven tresses. "I shall always regret that I had not the privilege of meeting Grandmother," he said with a faint smile.

"The gown looks just right, lass," commented Aunt Hester, ignoring the byplay. "No one will be able to tell."

"Tell what, Aunt Hester?" Cam asked idly. He was busy arranging a fur-trimmed velvet cloak about his wife's shoulders and thus missed the quick look of disapproval she sent the elder lady.

"That it wasn't made by a fancy French dressmaker," his quick-thinking relative replied with aplomb. "Don't forget your reticule, Tasha."

It was to be an evening of surprises for Cam. The next came when he presented Natasha to Princess Trauttmansdorff and heard her exchange a few remarks with her hostess in hesitant but correct German. There was no opportunity to inquire into her knowledge of that tongue in the next few hours, for social Vienna welcomed a new face with gratifying alacrity. Natasha's geniune friendliness and lack of artifice generally drew strangers to her side, and tonight was no exception. Cam heard her conversing with members of the French delegation in a fluent French that shamed his own and brought home to him again how much he had yet to learn about the girl who had, unexpectedly, become his wife. As he observed the unending parade of gentlemen seeking an introduction to his bride, unfamiliar feelings that he gradually identified as pride and possessiveness rose in his breast. The possessiveness was no longer a surprise; its first appearance in full force on the night he had forced his husbandly rights on Natasha had shocked and appalled him by its very unexpectedness, and still made him vaguely uneasy. Less unsettling was this new sense of pride in her distinguishing charm and intelligence even in a city teeming with exciting and sophisticated women.

Natasha interrupted his pleasant musing to take his arm and whisper nervously, "Cam, who is that elderly gentleman across the room, the one with powdered hair and all the decorations across his chest? He has been staring at me for several minutes, but I cannot tell from his expression whether it is with approval or censure."

Cam's eyes sought the direction of her glance. "That,

my dear, is the Prince of Bénevent, Talleyrand himself, and I believe I am meant to interpret that regal little nod as a command to bring you over to be presented to him. I can claim no more than a nodding acquaintance with one of the foremost statesmen of Europe, and that solely owing to my long association with Lord Castlereagh." As they started to make their circuitous way across the crowded room, Cam attempted some hasty indoctrination. "Are you aware that the Castlereaghs left for England in mid-February and that Wellington has succeeded him as principle negotiator?"

"Yes, Aunt Hester and I bought newspapers everywhere we could find them en route."

"Good. Do not be nervous. Talleyrand says little and is considered an intimidating presence by many, but his manners are always exquisite."

It quickly became apparent that intimidation was the furthest thought from the French minister's mind. After a few civil inquiries into her impressions along the route of her journey, the prince went on to explain that he had been intrigued by Mrs. Talbot's striking resemblance to his niece and hostess in Vienna, Dorothea Tallyrand-Périgord. "Do you not agree with me, Major Talbot, that your lovely wife could almost be taken for a sister of my niece?"

"*Madame la comtesse* is taller than Natasha and not quite so dark in coloring, but I would admit to a certain elusive resemblance."

"Perhaps the similarity is in the sweetness of their expressions, *n'est-ce pas*? But I have brought a blush to Madame's cheeks. You must forgive my candor, Madame Talbot; it is one of the remaining privileges of old men that they are permitted to pay compliments that not the most jealous of young husbands will resent."

"Surely there cannot be many young husbands dull-witted enough to believe that your excellency has reached that state," Natasha returned with well-done innocence.

"Now it is I who would blush had I not long since lost the knack. Take her away, Talbot, before we create a scandal. My niece shall call on you if you permit, Madame?"

"Enchantée, monsieur."

Cam shook his head as they walked away. "Accept my compliments, my dear. Less than eight hours in Vienna and you have made a conquest of one of the most important figures at the Congress."

"Fustian. He was simply being gallant, but I must say I am partial to such old-fashioned courtesy. I had heard that he is one of the most devious personages here."

"True. Also one of the most brilliant and, I believe, sincerely devoted to the best interests of France. Tasha, I would not for the world curtail your first social event in Vienna, but please let me know when you are ready to go home, such as it is. I am of a mind to attempt a bit of conquest myself tonight."

Long lashes sank and her color rose, but she said bravely, "Surely that particular treaty of surrender has been well and truly signed?"

"Home, Tasha?"

The look she cast up at him was answer enough.

Later in Cam's bedroom, which the charitable might call adequate, he aproached Natasha while she brushed her long hair before a small wall mirror. Sweeping the dark tresses aside, he bent and kissed her neck above the frill of her white rail.

"You looked incredibly beautiful tonight, my darling, but this is the way I will always like you best." His hands went to her shoulders and turned her gently to face him. The kiss they exchanged was long and passionate, fueled by months of loneliness. Cam's hands slid down from her shoulders to her waist to pull her closer.

In the next instant he broke off the kiss, and Natasha found herself looking across a gap of a foot or more into eyes that were blank with shock.

"You . . . you're . . ."

"I wondered when you'd notice," she said softly, a tremulous smile on her lips. "This is really why I had to come to you, Cam. I could not tell you in a letter. Yours were so . . . impersonal that I . . ." She broke off, staring in growing consternation at blazing green eyes in a dead white face. "Cam! Aren't you pleased? Don't you want a child?"

"How did you dare?" he said at last, producing each word with a palpable effort. "I marvel at the sheer effrontery it took to come here, to travel all that distance carrying another man's child. Did you imagine I was so besotted that I would accept the situation if you were at hand to sweeten the blow by making yourself available to me also? My God, but you have misjudged your man this time."

Natasha had staggered back as the sense of his bitter words sank into her brain with the force of physical blows. She was as colorless as he by now and she gripped a bed-post for support. "Do you know what you are saying, Cam? How *could* you believe that I would do such a thing, how could you?" It was a cry of agony, but her husband's expression did not soften.

"You would have me believe then that you are—what? almost six months gone? You forget, madam, that I was used to see your friend Susan at that stage. Your condition is scarcely even visible to the eye as yet."

"Your child is due about the twenty-second of June," Natasha said with quiet dignity.

"You must really think that I am simple," he sneered, "but of course I *am* simple! When I consider that I have been living like a monk for months in the middle of this Sodom and Gomorrah while you . . ." He wrenched away as though the sight of her disgusted him, and flung out of the room, stopping in the sitting room only long enough to catch up the coat, waistcoat, and evening cloak he had taken off while Natasha was in the bedchamber.

Cam walked the streets of Vienna for the remaining hours before dawn, equally uncaring of the cold, the state of his shoes, or what Police Chief Baron Hager's secret agents thought of his strange behavior. His feet were propelled by the same ungovernable mental energy that tortured him with pictures of Natasha in another man's arms, spending on another that passion that he had once gloried in arousing. Why could she not have waited for his return? She'd had Aunt Hester and the Flints for companionship and a new home to decorate with a free hand. If he could remain faithful among all the temptations to romantic intrigue existing in Vienna, surely a virtuous woman could exercise the same restraint in the face of far fewer temptations. The answer could only be that she was truly her grandmother's child, a sister under the skin to these highborn trollops who had established themselves in Vienna, openly flaunting their love affairs, sometimes even in front of their lovers' wives as Wilhemina Sagan had done to poor Laure Metternich. Their birth may have been noble, but these women were courtesans at heart, strangers to feminine virtue. Why had he not seen that Natasha, with her unfeminine frankness and easily aroused passion, was of this type? He must have been blinded by her sweetness and intelligence, but the Duchess of Sagan was known for her intelligence and warmhearted generosity too. Perhaps there was simply a class of females that possessed every feminine virtue save virtue itself.

He had falsely accused Natasha once before and had himself behaved reprehensibly in consequence. Tonight he had experienced a near homicidal rage on discovering her betrayal. That had burned itself out quickly, but until the wound caused by her treachery scarred over he could not guarantee his civilized behavior if forced into the close association that living in those few rooms entailed. For the sake of his sanity and self-respect, Natasha would have to go. His was an important function here and he could not afford to jeopardize his efficiency.

Cam returned to his lodgings as dawn was breaking, drooping with fatique but determined on his immediate course. He hoped to be able to change his clothes and shave while Aunt Hester and Natasha slept, thus postponing the final confrontation until he had recovered his equilibrium, but fortune was not on his side that day. A somber-eyed Natasha was sitting up in the bed looking like a drowsy angel with her spectacular mane of hair cascading over one shoulder. Cam would have ignored her presence as he took a fresh shirt from the painted armoire and headed back to the minuscule dressing room, but she said urgently, "We have to talk, Cam."

"Later."

"Now!"

He paused in the doorway. "There is nothing to discuss. I'm sending you home."

Her eyes fell and she bit her lip, but before Cam could close the door, her voice, soft but distinct, reached him. "I am sorry to disoblige you, Cam, but I am not leaving Vienna."

"I will not have you in my house!" His eyes blazed, and Natasha swallowed with difficulty but faced him determinedly.

"If you attempt to send me away, I will go to the duke and tell him the reason. I will also tell Talleyrand and anyone else who will listen to me. The birth of our child will be incontrovertible proof that I speak the truth."

"I am performing an important service here and you are proposing to make us both appear ridiculous. Have you no sense of shame?" His voice cut at her like a lash, but Natasha remained sober and quiet beneath the sting, though her eyes pleaded mutely.

"I am fighting for the happiness of three people. You would destroy us with your idiotic suspicions."

"You have done the destroying, not I. You are not the girl I married."

"You know nothing at all about me" she shot back, "and I fear you have neither the wit nor the will to learn. You lump all women together and do them all a disservice thereby. As for being married, how can I feel married when from the beginning you have made me feel I was only your wife on sufferance?"

Before this tirade was ended, Cam had passed his hand wearily across his face, kneading his temples. "Enough! I am in no case to argue with you today. Stay if you must, but do not expect me to play the adoring husband. And do not expect me to share this room with you. I draw the line there. Move Aunt Hester in here before I return tonight."

"Oh, but, Cam, surely you cannot wish your aunt to know—"

"There is no way to conceal an estrangement in a suite

little bigger than a prison cell. I demand my privacy as my price for letting you remain in Vienna."

"Very well." Natasha's chin went up and her eyes went opaque. "And I expect all the public consideration due to your wife. Do not think to humiliate me by carrying on conspicuous flirtations in my presence."

"I shall be discretion itself," Cam promised nastily, and strode off, leaving her to her empty victory.

He left the suite fifteen minutes later, still in a flaming temper. When Miss Cameron wished him a cheery good-morning as she emerged from her bedchamber, he turned with his hand on the doorknob.

"How could you allow her to travel in her condition? I credited you with more sense than that."

Miss Cameron blinked at the sudden attack. "But, my dear boy, I didn't know she was *enceinte* until we got to France."

"So, no doctor told you when this child is expected?"

"Natasha told me—about the third week in June."

Cam clamped his lips together and departed without another word, leaving his stricken aunt to stare after him uncomprehendingly.

Never one to tiptoe around a delicate situation, she immediately knocked on Natasha's door. "What ails that lad this morning?" she began without preamble. "He near snapped my head off just now." Miss Cameron came farther into the room and peered at her niece. "You are not precisely chirping merry either, by the look of you. What is it, child?"

Natasha looked into the wise, concerned face and her eyes swam with the tears she had not shed in front of her husband. "Sit down, Aunt Hester. I would spare you this if I could, but Cam has made it impossible. He doesn't believe that the baby is his. I am not big enough in his enlightened estimation," she explained when her aunt's jaw dropped. "He wanted to send us home, but I refused to go. I told him I'd let the story be known in Vienna if he tried to send me away, so he capitulated, but only to save face. You are to move in here with me so he can have your room."

"What maggot has eaten that lad's brain? It's daft he must be, if he *is* my own niece's flesh and blood. I'll knock some sense into that thick skull of his, never you fret, lass."

"I don't think so, Aunt," Natasha said sadly. "For some reason Cam has always believed the worst of me in any doubtful situation, and there have been many. I'm not the conventional type of female he admires." She proceeded to relate the circumstances leading to their marriage, though she could not bring herself to divulge the episode that culminated in the unfortunate consummation of the marriage.

"But the lad's in love with you." Aunt Hester's declaration lacked conviction.

"I hoped so when he left Wiltshire, but you've read his letters. There was nothing of the lover in them. I've been doing a lot of thinking on our journey here and especially last night, and I am persuaded that Cam is afraid to love anyone. It seems everyone he ever loved left him. His father died when he was very young and his mother when he grew up. The girl he wanted to marry accepted his ring and then married someone else the moment he left for the war. Except for his mother, no one really returned his love."

"And she, poor soul, was so blinded by love for that worthless husband that she had little enough to spare for her son, though she was a good mother, mind you. And I'm not saying Cedric Talbot was a bad man either, just that he put his career and his comfort and his pleasures first and last, and did not value the devotion Kate lavished on him like a ninny."

"I don't believe Cam understood this with his intellect, but some part of him learned to distrust love, which is why he acts the way he does now. He is determined not to put himself in a position to be hurt again. I must keep on hoping that eventually I can convince him of my devotion. I cannot do that if he sends me away, so I must persevere until he admits that I haven't betrayed him. But it is hard, Aunt Hester; he said such cruel things to me." Tears started to slip silently down Natasha's cheeks.

"There, there, lass, take heart. You have plenty of courage and resolution to see this thing through. Besides," she added with unquenchable relish, "here we are in Vienna at last. There will be much to see and do that will not depend on that maggotty lad's goodwill."

Though she could not rise to Aunt Hester's enthusiasm, pride and perseverance supplied Natasha with a solid substitute as the newcomers toured Vienna during the next fortnight. The smitten Sir Allenby Birdwell wangled some free time to act as their escort while they learned their way around the city. Though Natasha suspected her husband connived to free his amiable compatriot by doing double duty at the embassy, she wisely accepted what the gods provided, willingly repaying Sir Allenby with grateful smiles and a well-feigned interest in his breezy conversation that featured gleeful renditions of all the latest scandals in the town. Miss Cameron, a model of rectitude in her personal life, greedily lapped up the gossip, and her pithy comments were subsequently incorporated into Sir Allenby's stock of dinner-table anecdotes.

He drove them past the Palm Palace whose right-hand tenant, the Duchess of Sagan, vied with Princess Catherine Bagration, who lived on the left side, for the attentions of prominent figures like the tsar and Prince Metternich, among others. Unfortunately, the beauteous occupants had earned themselves such unsavory reputations that the Palm Palace was now forbidden territory to any woman who valued her good name. They visited St. Stephen's Cathedral and drove all around the enormous Hofburg, sparing a little pity for Emperor Francis, who had been sharing his palace with the entire Russian and Prussian delegations for six months. Having to preside over forty tables set up for dinner each night, the seating governed by protocol among a plethora of minor royalty, was not a chore anyone could envy the emperor.

Vienna was not at her best in the dying grip of winter, but the ladies could see that the Prater, the island park in the middle of the Danube, would be a lovely place to stroll when the chestnut trees lining its great allée came into bloom. The narrow streets of the city were full of shops and restaurants that beckoned. Certainly Vienna by day provided sufficient sources of diversion to keep the visitors from Great Britain from becoming bored.

There was no denying that the evenings were difficult. Cam did not trouble to make himself even minimally pleasant to his wife, treating her with cold formality on the few occasions when they dined together. He had nothing at all to say to her voluntarily; the ladies gathered all their information on the daily happenings of the Congress from other sources, even the alarming news, a few days after their arrival in Vienna, that Napoleon had tricked his unwary guardian, Sir Neil Campbell, and sailed away from Elba on the brig *Inconstant*, accompanied by the twelve hundred soldiers of his personal guard in other vessels.

Cam's public demeanor was everything that was correct, even outwardly cordial, but he spent as little time by his wife's side as was necessary to establish her comfortably among the other guests on those social occasions where his presence was required. He never again commented on the dramatic gowns that distinguished Natasha among the fair fat Germanic ladies who thronged the receptions, nor did he blink an eye at the costly array of jewels that she displayed to such advantage. The spectacular jewelry worn by Mrs. Talbot, the untitled wife of a minor English diplomat, aroused some speculation that would have been more widely circulated had Bonaparte's probable whereabouts and intentions not been the overriding concern of everyone that March.

It all washed over Natasha's head in any case. She was performing her part with a sweet dignity and charm, but those who had known her gaiety and spirit in London would have been shocked to witness her conduct in Vienna. It would be dramatically overstating the situation to assert that she was bleeding to death internally, but the personal cost in carrying out her desperate strategy to save her marriage was high. There were times when Cam's unrelenting coldness so wounded her that her craven spirit shriveled in his presence. He conveyed his ladies home from social events but never came in with them, and

Natasha, despite repeated promises to herself to do otherwise, could not prevent herself from lying awake listening for his eventual return, sometimes hours later. Only Aunt Hester's tender concern and robust cheerfulness kept her from sinking into a prolonged depression as the estrangement became firmly established.

Only once did Natasha's resolution falter. Cam sought her out in the middle of March to announce that the duke had decided to put himself at the head of the Allied troops in Brussels in anticipation of renewed war with France if King Louis could not prevail over Napoleon. Lord Clancarty was to remain in Vienna to see the negotiations through, and Wellington had invited Major Talbot to join his staff in Brussels.

"I shall be leaving for Belgium in a few days. You have achieved your objective of averting gossip in Vienna. It is time for you and Aunt Hester to go home before traveling in Europe becomes any more hazardous."

Natasha's spirit quailed as she searched the set features of the man who wielded so much power over her heart, apparently without knowing or caring that it was his. Inevitably, with the birth of their child must come an acknowledgment that he had misjudged her. The increasing strain of opposing her will against his was such that it was indeed a temptation to simply go home and hope for the best when he returned to England. The horrifying possibility that he might never return with the renewed danger of war stiffened her wavering resolution. It would be utterly useless to remonstrate against his decision, of course, but womanlike, she plunged right in.

"Why must you rejoin the army? You have more than done your duty to your country in the Peninsula."

Cam shrugged broad shoulders. "This is an area where I can really be useful, and I am freer than many others to make the sacrifice, if it comes to that."

Natasha flinched at the intended cruelty but clutched her courage about her. "I shall go with you to Brussels, then. Nothing has changed."

"Have done, woman," exclaimed Cam, more shaken

229

than he would have believed at her obduracy. "If you will not think of your own safety or that of Aunt Hester, at least consider the child you are carrying. It is unnatural for a woman to expose her child to danger."

"I shall expect my child's father to ensure our safety."

"What can you possibly hope to accomplish by playing out this charade?" he demanded, his impatience not quite concealing a fatigue that she guessed was the result of the unsatisfactory situation in which they were mired.

Her eyes softened and pleaded. "I am fighting for our marriage, Cam, not my honor. That will be vindicated in due course, but it would mean so much more to both of us if you could bring yourself to believe in me before the child comes. I know I am not the sort of wife you envisioned; on the other hand, I love you with every fiber of my being. It isn't something I have any choice about—I realized that on the night of our wedding. Perhaps I should have more pride than to . . ."

Natasha broke off her plea since she was speaking to empty space. With an inarticulate sound of pain and protest, Cam had spun on his heel and stalked out of the room.

18

Brussels, Belgium
Late May, 1815

Brussels was enjoying an idyllic spring. Hundreds of
magnificent chestnut trees lent her streets an air of
elegance, and beyond the city walls near the canal, the
double row of lime trees along the Allée Verte was in full
bloom. This was a favorite equestrian ride for all the
growing numbers of military personnel gathering for what
looked like an inevitable showdown with Bonaparte, the
hordes of visitors who had come to spend the Season
abroad for the first time in years and the Bruxellois themselves. The parks were gay with flowers and the streets
were made colorful by glimpses of scarlet, blue, and green
uniforms as members of the Allied forces sauntered among
the soberly clad citizens of the town. Feminine visitors
introduced yet another palette into the scene with their pale
pastels and popular all-white costumes.

The Talbot ménage had been in Brussels for nearly two
months by this time. They had had the good fortune to
secure a commodious house off the Place Royale, leased
from a fellow countryman who changed his mind about
the desirability of bringing his young family to reside
abroad at the exact moment when their chosen destination
was likely to be in the path of renewed hostilities. The size
of the establishment was considerably greater than
required by a family consisting of only three persons, but
that was regarded as an advantage by Cam, who thus
managed to avoid meeting his wife except on those occasions when their presence as a couple was socially
inescapable. Now that Natasha's condition was obvious to

all, such occasions became rare as custom curtailed her public appearances.

The situation between the couple had deteriorated rather than improved with time. There were no more angry confrontations such as had occurred in Vienna, but the continuing weight of her husband's displeasure at her presence in his life had gradually taken its toll on Natasha's spirits despite her reasoned intention to wait out this bleak period with fortitude. Recently, she had made a discovery about her own nature that had altered her view of what course the future might take with respect to her marriage. On their level of society there was nothing rare about unions where the parties possessed little feeling of a positive nature for each other. For the most part the unwilling partners contrived to rub along together, patching in various adjustments to the fabric of their lives to enable them to make it cover them as adequately as possible. Often these adjustments consisted in taking lovers or mistresses who, one assumed, supplied the emotional warmth missing in the marriage. Over the past lonely weeks, Natasha had identified in herself a strong unwillingness to live her life on false premises. Much as she loved and longed for Cam, it was becoming increasingly apparent to her that she could not endure the purgatory of spending her life with someone who despised her. The constant punishment to the soul was more than she could knowingly take. Fortunately, her financial independence from her husband made it possible for her to choose to live a separate life with her child and Aunt Hester, if the latter would consent to join them.

These radical ideas had evolved into half-formed plans of late because even in her state of retirement she had learned or, more accurately, deduced from fragments of remarks floating around her drawing room that Cam had been seen frequently in the company of a certain Mlle Marchant, a well-known dancer who was said to have scores of men seeking her favors. She was not shocked—under the circumstances, how could she be? An *affaire* was the most likely choice of retaliation for a man in Cam's imagined position, but she flattered herself that she knew something about her husband's character by now. There was a strong streak of puritanism in his makeup. She did not believe he looked upon infidelity with the easygoing tolerance common to most of their world. If Cam was seriously involved with this Mlle Marchant even before the birth of their child could exonerate his wife, it could only mean that he cared nothing for her as a person, since he did not scruple to act in a fashion he well knew would hurt her deeply.

Natasha was sitting in the park on this lovely afternoon in late May determined to bring the tormenting period of uncertainty to an end. Reportedly, Cam could often be seen strolling here with Mlle Meachant at this hour, after leaving army headquarters in the Rue Royale, which formed one boundary of the park. She herself walked in the park in the mornings with Miss Cameron for the modicum of air and exercise permitted to one in her advanced stage of pregnancy, but she had taken advantage of her aunt's daily rest period today to slip out of the house unaccompanied and walk the short distance to her present perch near an ornamental stretch of water. The only ruse she had adopted was in the guise of a sketching block she had brought along with her. She was prepared to add a few lines to an execrable drawing of a pair of swans should she be accosted by any of her acquaintance. Cam would know this for the farce it was, but at this point it mattered little what he thought. The crucial decision she was contemplating was entirely her own to make, and no words or actions of her husband's would alter it once taken. She would know by his attitude on meeting her while in company with his flirt—to give him the benefit of the doubt—if there was any hope left for saving their marriage.

She had been bending over her stage prop at intervals for nearly half an hour when the sound of her name being enunciated in accents of surprised pleasure by a well-known voice caused her to clutch her pencil so tightly it broke with a loud snap.

"Natasha! Is it really you?"

"Why, Captain Standish, what a pleasant surprise. How do you do?" She struggled to infuse some cordiality into her own voice, conscious that her erstwhile suitor's unexpected arrival at this particular spot was likely to queer her game entirely.

The tall fair officer stood gazing down at her, greedily assimilating the enchanting heart-shaped face framed by a high-crowned bonnet with a wide poke that was lined in a deep-rose color, taking in huge startled dark eyes and smiling red lips, taking in also a charming rose-colored gown that matched the bonnet lining and curved outward below the waist in a fashion that unmistakably proclaimed her condition. His eyes flew back to hers and a surge of red flared into his cheeks.

"I . . . I had no idea . . . I mean that you were . . . are—"

"Why should you indeed?" Natasha replied in a cheerful voice meant to ease his embarrassment, "and I had no idea you were in Brussels. You've rejoined the army, I see." She nodded at his scarlet coat.

"Yes, yes I have. I arrived in the area last week. I am billeted in Ninove with the cavalry. And . . . and you? Is your . . . is Major Talbot back with the military too?"

"We left Vienna in March when the duke asked Cam to join his staff here." Natasha attempted to coordinate her casual chatter with an assumption of easy pleasure in his company, all the while searching her brain for a tactful way of getting rid of him in case Cam should suddenly appear with his dancer. "You must come and call on us soon," she said abruptly, unequal to the task. As she gave him their direction, she groaned inwardly, aware before he opened his mouth of the significance of the frowning look he was casting about him.

"I say, you are not here alone, are you?"

"Not really, my maid is executing a small commission for me," Natasha improvised. "She'll be back directly."

"I'll wait with you, then. May I sit down?"

"It is not at all necessary, Captain. I must not keep you from any appointment you may have."

234

"I'm as free as the breeze at the moment, just here in Brussels getting my bearings, so to speak."

Natasha gave up. "Under other circumstances it would be a delightful city in which to spend some time. Have you been to the theater yet?" she asked, reverting to a social manner while she wondered how long she should wait for her mythical maid's return before making her excuses and effecting an escape.

The problem was taken out of her hands in the next moment when Captain Standish, having answered her query about the theater in the negative, declared in quite another tone, "Ah, that's all right, then."

Puzzled, Natasha raised questioning eyes to his.

"Your husband . . . coming this way," he explained when she looked blank.

The Scots poet Burns knew whereof he spoke when he talked about well-laid plans going astray, Natasha thought wildly as she sat in frozen uncertainty, not knowing where to look or even whether she hoped Cam might change direction without ever spotting them.

Again the matter was taken out of her hands as the man at her side rose to his feet and stepped into the path to intercept the trajectory of Major Talbot and his female companion. Natasha had a brief respite in which to compose her features into a sweet social expression as Cam's attention was drawn to the man in his path holding out a cordial hand.

"How do you do, Talbot? It has been rather a long time since we last met."

"Standish! What are you doing in Brussels? No, ignore that piece of idiocy—I can see by your uniform what you are doing in Brussels." The still figure on the bench impinged on his peripheral vision at that moment. "Natasha, what are you doing here?" Hearing the accusation in his tones, Cam fought to subdue it, saying more softly as he withdrew his hand from the other man's grip, "Natasha did not tell me you were in town."

Captain Standish laughed. "She did not know. I came upon her by a fortunate accident just these few minutes ago. She was so engrossed in her sketching she didn't notice me. I might easily have passed her by, but I would know that profile anywhere."

"I see," Cam said grimly. A tug on his sleeve from the woman clinging to his arm brought his eyes around to meet the expectant gaze of a dark-haired young woman whose daring pink silk headgear featured three ostrich plumes on a huge brim that made Natasha's fashionable bonnet appear almost staid by comparison. "I beg your pardon," he acknowledged stiffly, "I'm afraid my wits have been wandering and my manners lacking. Mlle Marchant, may I present my wife and Captain Standish?"

Natasha had gotten to her feet during the previous exchange. While Cam stood expressionless, the two women murmured suitably and Captain Standish swept the major's companion a graceful bow.

"This is indeed a pleasure, Mlle Marchant."

Cam interrupted the ongoing amenities with ruthless purpose, saying sternly to his wife, "You should not be out here, Natasha, at this hour. I'm going to take you home."

"Yes, Mme Talbot, the air grows colder and you wear only that light shawl." Mlle Marchant added her pleas to Cam's orders, adding with a gay laugh, "We will share your husband, no? An arm for each."

There was genuine amusement in the smile Natasha directed at the other woman. "I think not," she declined gently. "I wouldn't dream of delaying you. Captain Standish will see me safely home, won't you, Captain?"

"Of course, it will be my pleasure," this gentleman agreed with gratifying celerity, gallantly offering her his arm.

"So nice to have met you, Mlle Marchant. *Au revoir.*" A discreet pinch of her escort's arm served to get them moving before Cam could propose any countersuggestions if he were so minded.

The first half of the ten-minute walk to the Talbots' rented house in the Place Royale was accomplished in near silence. Captain Standish's mind was of a pedestrian order, but he was neither stupid nor insensitive; he would have had to be both to have remained impervious to the strange nuances afloat during the scene they had just enacted. A sense of delicacy prevented him from questioning Natasha, though he would have given much to have the situation clarified. For her part, Natasha was too occupied with pondering her own interpretation of the recent meeting to be aware of the silence initially.

Though persuaded that the person of Mlle Marchant was totally irrelevant, only her existence having meaning, she would not have been female had she not seized the opportunity offered by Captain Standish's distracting presence to effect a covert study of the woman Cam was parading in public. She judged the tall slim brunette to be some three or four years her senior and, in a fair-minded spirit, conceded that the dancer was strikingly pretty. That was to be expected; more surprising was a feeling that the other woman was possessed of a pleasant disposition and genuine kindness. Natasha was unable to regard the woman as her enemy. Contributing to this conclusion was the saving relief she was hugging to herself at the moment. She had risked a look at Cam as he had performed the introductions with the inherent good manners that always characterized his demeanor. Steeling herself not to react outwardly if she met triumph or dislike in the cool green eyes, she had caught a flicker of shame or regret that had nearly caused her to lose countenance. Indeed, she had experienced a wave of giddiness that probably gave credence to Cam's subsequent decision to take her home. Perhaps it was not much to build a future on, but she felt rather like a condemned prisoner granted a last-minute reprieve. Her chin lifted and the handsome man plodding silently by her side came into view, bringing her back to the present straightaway. Animated by a sudden sense of release, she devoted her best efforts for the rest of the short walk to entertaining her escort to such good advantage that the once familiar light of pursuit was back in his eyes, a situation she would have to be at pains to correct at their next meeting.

The next morning after subjecting her niece to a prolonged scrutiny, Aunt Hester gave it as her opinion that

Natasha was looking much better, the bruised look around the eyes having faded. The two women were going through the post together in the study. Natasha smiled a brief acknowledgment, then dropped the pile of envelopes back on the worktable, sighing. "Still nothing from Peter. It has been nearly a fortnight since it was announced that the Eighty-fifth had arrived back in England. I will not feel comfortable about him till I learn the extent and condition of his wounds from Peter himself."

There had been a letter from Captain Phillips to his sister and one to his brother-in-law awaiting them on their arrival in Brussels in early April—missives written from Jamaica before he had sailed to Louisiana in November of last year. They had been redirected to Vienna, arriving at the embassy after their departure, and had been included in the first diplomatic pouch that was dispatched to Brussels. To his sister Peter had expressed his great joy and satisfaction at learning of her marriage to his friend, glee-fully confiding that he considered himself a successful matchmaker since he had brought the two together with precisely that end in mind. At the time Natasha could only hope her brother had been less forthcoming in his letter to Cam, but her husband had never volunteered a word about the contents. The disastrous results of the ill-conceived attack on New Orleans were known by the time they left Vienna. A communication from his commanding officer had eventually reached them praising Captain Lord Phillips' bravery and stating that he was making a satis-factory recovery from his wounds, but from Peter they had heard nothing.

Natasha was reading a long chatty letter from Susan when the butler entered to tell her that a young woman wished to see her.

"Who is it, Hillaire?"

"She refuses to leave her name, *madame*," the butler replied. "I was asked to say that you met yesterday in the park and that she wishes only a monent of your time."

Startled, Natasha lowered the letter she held in her hand and stared at the impassive face of the butler.

"That's odd," said Aunt Hester. "I do not recall meeting anyone save Lady Georgiana Lennox in the park yesterday, and she would have no reason to deny her identity. Send the caller up, Hilaire."

"She specifically requested a private word with Mme Talbot, Mlle Cameron."

Natasha had already struggled up from her chair. "I'll see her, Aunt Hester. Where have you put the visitor, Hilaire?"

"In the small front reception room, *madame*."

Curiosity and trepidation competed in Natasha's mind as she slipped into the small reception room a few minutes later to greet her caller in the French tongue with wary courtesy. "Good morning, Mlle Marchant. What may I do for you?"

The strikingly dressed brunette of yesterday had toned down her appearance somewhat today. Her décolletàge was perhaps a trifle daring for daytime wear, but there was no fault to be found with the style of her light-blue gown and accessories; the straw bonnet set at a dashing angle atop her abundant brown curls was positively plain, being trimmed only with blue satin ribbons tied jauntily under one ear. Her rouge had been applied with a lighter hand today also. She had risen from the edge of an uncomfortable-looking carved chair when her hostess entered, and now she began quickly, "Actually, I came here today to do something for you, though I've been of a dozen minds about whether I was being too presumptuous in going where I'm not wanted. But I liked your face right off, so here I am." At that the girl fell silent, twisting her gloves between nervous fingers.

"What is it you wish to do for me?" prompted Natasha after a few seconds, which were spent by Mlle Marchant in studying her hostess's composed countenance as if to reassure herself of something.

"I thought I would tell you that your husband and I have never been lovers," she stated bluntly. A quickening expression in dark eyes acknowledged Natasha's audible intake of breath before she went on, "He likes to be seen

239

with me and he says I amuse him, but that is as far as it goes. Until yesterday I rather hoped for more because there's no denying he's the best-looking man in Brussels and very rich, and I have a mother and two young sisters to support. Not that he hasn't been very generous already," she added hastily.

"I see. Why have you decided to tell me this, Mlle Marchant? Did my husband ask you to do it?"

"*Ciel, non!* He has never even mentioned your name to me. That is why you were such a surprise yesterday. But, as I said, I liked your face and I saw the way Cam looked at you and I thought if I came here and told you the truth, perhaps it might help Cam."

"In what way?"

"Well, what is between you two does not concern me, but it doesn't need a great intellect to figure out that Cam isn't really happy. Now that you know that he's only been trying to make you jealous with me, could you not forgive him?"

"Forgive him?" Natasha echoed, her face a blank.

Mlle Marchant nodded sagely. "For whatever he did that spoiled things between you."

"Oh . . . yes, *mademoiselle*, I can forgive him, and I thank you very much for coming here today. It was a generous act on your part." She rose with a sweet smile and escorted her visitor to the door herself before heading back to the study prepared to hoax a curious Aunt Hester with a hastily concocted tale of a stranger with whom she had fallen into conversation returning a broach she had dropped in the park. Her conscience might prick but her spirit was miraculously lightened.

Several days later a travel-weary Major Talbot let himself into his house in late afternoon and started up the staircase. He had been to Ghent and back with messages to the Bourbon king, and at this moment a hot bath and a drink represented the sum total of his desires. He was proceeding past the slightly open door to the ladies' favorite sitting room with his customary caution, designed to avoid attracting Natasha's notice, when a familiar voice from within stopped him in his tracks.

"No, no tea for me, thank you. What's afoot, Tasha? I've been in Brussels for two days and have yet to set eyes on Cam."

Peter! A surge of emotion rooted Cam to the floor momentarily and he missed Natasha's soft reply. Before he could take a step, Peter went on, impatience coloring his tones.

"I am well aware of how the Duke drives his staff, but there's more to it than that. Don't think to ride on my back, Tasha. There's practically no evidence that Cam even lives here. The butler seemed surprised that day I arrived when I asked him when the master would be home for dinner. And I've already heard talk in the town."

The man in the hall froze, his hand arrested an inch from the doorknob, while Peter paused.

"Look, Tasha, I know it ill becomes me to mention this to you, and I would not, except that in my experience a woman's female friends always ensure that she gets wind of all her husband's peccadilloes. There is talk about Cam being involved with some dancer—I can't recall the name, but I heard it from more than one source."

"Her name is Hélène Marchant and I have met the lady. You may accept my word for it that there is nothing wrong in their association. My dear brother, look at me!" Natasha's voice, rich with amusement, floated out to her avidly listening husband. "Except for the tamest of outings, I am confined to this house, and I fear I am not the liveliest of company these days. You really cannot expect that Cam should be forever dancing attendance on me. I assure you I do not believe that Mlle Marchant is a danger to my marriage, though I am grateful for your concern."

"Spare me the platitudes, I beg you. If you believe 'em, then you're no kin to Grandmother, who would have made short work of this Mlle Whats-her-name! By God, friend or not, if I thought Cam were playing you false, I'd call him out today—and shoot him left-handed."

Cam didn't stay to hear Natasha's soothing response. Peter was *not* going to be permitted to harass his sister in her delicate state! Silently he ran back down the stairs and

241

came up again, letting his booted and spurred feet ring on the wooden treads as he sent his eager voice on ahead, "Tasha? Where are you, darling?"

"In here," came the somewhat breathless rejoinder.

Cam threw open the door and headed toward the woman regarding him in wide-eyed fascination from a rose-colored settee behind a tea table. After a couple of steps he allowed his eye to fall on the tall man standing stiffly near a side chair. His face broke into a wide, welcoming smile. "Peter! How wonderful to see you! Excuse me a moment, old fellow."

He continued his path around the far side of the table to where Natasha sat in wary silence. "Forgive my dusty condition, darling. I feel like I have been gone forever. How are you feeling?" Without giving her time to reply to this tender inquiry, Cam took his wife's pointed chin in one hand and bent to kiss her lingeringly. Her warm mouth was motionless under the pressure of his, and he gripped her shoulder warningly as he raised his head to study his old comrade and new brother with concerned affection. He chose to go on the attack immediately, however, both to hide his dismay at the changes in him and to gain a tactical advantage whle Peter was still assimilating the fond greeting between husband and wife.

"Why haven't you written before this, Peter?" he asked as he approached the other, hand extended. "Tasha has been fretting herself to ribbons over your probable condition."

The worst of his brother-in-law's wounds became instantly apparent as he gestured toward his immobile right arm and extended the left to grip Cam's hand briefly. "I can't write yet," he said shortly, "although the doctors still have hopes of an eventual recovery of most functions." A motion of his head revealed a vivid red scar that ascended from the left cheekbone into his hairline.

"So you are out of the military?" Belatedly, Cam took in the significance of Peter's dove-gray inexpressibles and the beautifully cut coat of burgundy hue. "And very dapper dog too, if I may be permitted to express an opinion."

A reluctant smile appeared for the first time in the young baron's blue eyes, which no longer reflected their owner's happy-go-lucky nature. "Sorry I cannot return the compliment, brother," he retorted, raising a quizzing glass hanging from a black ribbon to one eye and peering with fastidious disgust at the mud-splattered figure presently disgracing his sister's drawing room.

With Natasha's little gurgle of laughter, a sound he had not heard for months, Cam felt some of the tension depart the room. When Miss Cameron returned from a trip to the shops a half-hour later, it was to find a congenial little party drinking sherry around the tea table and exchanging reminiscences.

19

Cam went late to bed that night, having sat up talking with his brother-in-law long after Natasha and Aunt Hester had retired. Their talk mainly concerned the present military situation in the area and Peter's recent experiences. It had taken repeated probing on Cam's part to get him to recount the full history of the American expedition, including the terrible situation in which the army found itself last winter in the freezing swamps of Louisiana.

Going back over their talk now as he settled himself for sleep, Cam hoped the fact that Peter had never questioned him about his marriage was a fair indication that the little scene he had staged today had allayed all suspicions. Fond though he was of his old comrade, it was going to prove deuced awkward to have him living here. Tonight had passed off more smoothly than he would have dared to predict eight hours ago, but how could they hope to keep up the charade indefinitely? Except for a couple of obligatory receptions early in their stay in Brussels before Natasha's situation became obvious, he had not once dined at his own table until tonight. Natasha had projected a sweet serenity this evening that was very appealing, but how long would it be before Peter missed that vital spark that had set her apart from ordinary people? And if her child was not born at the time she had specified, what then?

The thought did not take him unaware; it had been hovering at the back of his mind since the familiar cadences of Peter's voice had reached his ears this afternoon, but for the first time since Natasha's unexpected appearance in Vienna, he didn't instantly rebury it and dash frantically off to do something—anything—that would keep him too busy to confront it with his intelligence. He did indeed give up the attempt to sleep, rolling over on his side to grope for the tinderbox. Presently, with a lighted candle on the table and a lighted cigar in his mouth, he made himself comfortable against a mound of pillows and prepared to examine his behavior over the past months.

It went without saying that he had treated Natasha shabbily. He had done so with full deliberation in order to hurt her in every way possible short of physical abuse, and there had been times when it would have relieved his own frustration to shake her until her teeth rattled and that look of bewildered suffering was replaced by honest pain. The sight of her inflamed his senses and the awareness of her treachery festered in his brain like a wound under the skin. Self-knowledge told him there would be no healng for him until the source of the infection was removed, but all his efforts had proved fruitless; she refused to leave.

Under the circumstances he had been nauseated by her declaration of love for him in Vienna, but it had given him a weapon he hadn't scrupled to use against her when they reached Brussels. Once they were no longer expected to be seen together at evening entertainments, he had begun a public flirtation with Hélène Marchant that his wife was bound to learn of, the nature of the female being what it is. He had marched into the *affaire* without questioning the practical advantage he could hope to gain; by then it would have been medically inadvisable for Natasha to travel despite the provocation.

And she had fought him to a standstill. He had realized the significance of her presence in the park the other day, of course, and had been rocked to find the question echoing in his mind: what would he do if she really did leave him?

He thought about that now as he had during the solitary hours he had spent on horseback these past days riding to and from the exiled king's court in Ghent. Living with Natasha had certainly been a hellish experience these past months, but he literally could not contemplate life without her; it was an impenetrable blank. Which must mean what? That he loved and believed in her?

Cam lay back staring into the shadows beyond the bed until the lengthening ash on his cigar fell onto the sheet and burned a hole before he could brush it away. He had never thought of romantic love as an explanation for his attitude toward Natasha; he had simply moved into her life and assumed responsibility for her. He had not questioned his motives; it seemed clear enough that he had taken over her absent brother's role. Not until her spiteful cousin had cast doubts on her innocence had he seen his attitude as blatant possessiveness, but by then she was his wife and he was entitled to feel that way. Even after the passionate interlude at Krestonwood, he'd left for Vienna with the cheery confidence of someone placing a valued possession in safe-keeping until it was convenient to retrieve it. It would have been more enjoyable to have her with him, certainly, but since that was impossible, they would just have to make the best of it.

Natasha's appearance in Vienna had blasted him out of his comfortable delusion. He had been shaken to the core by the overwhelming jolt of joy that had flooded through him on seeing her again. Before he could begin to understand or accept the implications of this feeling had come the second shock of discovering her condition. In all fairness, he still did not believe his initial reaction was unreasonable. In conjunction with the manner in which she had chosen to break the news, the visual evidence seemed conclusive. But later, when the first tide of shock and anger had ebbed somewhat, why had he continued to resist an explanation that could restore his confidence in his wife, surely a most desirable state? Why could he not have kept his reservations to himself and muddled along until the event proved the case one way or another?

Cam was not normally given to introspection concerning his emotional reactions, and for months he had tried to avoid feeling at all, but now he struggled to make sense of his recent conduct. Looking back, he could see that he had freely acknowledged his anger at the presumed betrayal but, after the first shock, had denied the concomitant pain. All his actions had stemmed from anger and might have been expressly designed to disguise his hurt from himself.

He shifted uneasily in the large bed that was growing colder by the minute as he tried to wrest a clear understanding of his mental and emotional endowments from past events. Sheer cowardice was how he would describe his attitude from a three months' vantage point. He had expected a comfortable surface type of marriage, not at all difficult of achievement, and then had doomed his expectations by choosing Natasha as partner. And make no bones about that! While he was struggling to bring honesty to his perceptions, he might as well jettison the false notion that circumstances had dictated his marriage. The truth was that he had never let Natasha out of his sight, figuratively speaking, from the first meeting, but having chosen someone not fashioned for pale emotions and petty enthusiasms, he had yet lacked the courage to abandon his defenses. He had been unwilling to consign his heart into another's keeping and had reacted violently when Natasha had expressed her commitment to him.

And all to no avail! He had neither avoided pain nor kept his inner core sacrosanct. Natasha had invaded his heart and taken up residence; there was no cutting her out without killing the organism. Even when pointedly banished from his thoughts, she had remained lodged in some corner of his consciousness, the sweet passionate warmth of her tantalizing him unmercifully.

It was a relief of sorts to acknowledge his feelings, but Cam was not so simpleminded as to consider his troubles over. He and Natasha had lost the knack of communicating with each other. Today when he had kissed her she had made no slightest response. In theory it should be no difficult thing to tell the woman who had bravely professed her unconditional love for him that he had, belatedly to be sure, come to the realization that he returned her feelings in full measure, but somehow over the next several days the perfect moment to approach Natasha seemed to elude him.

Rumors of Napoleon's imminent campaign against the Allied armies were flying around during the early part of June, unsettling the transient civilian population of Brussels. Unfortunately, military intelligence was no more reliable than civilian rumors. Cam knew that Wellington placed little confidence in his Dutch-Belgian troops in the face of the flood of French propaganda broadsheets Napoleon had sent into Belgium, and the emperor was estimated to have an army of over one hundred thousand men under his control at present. A number of social events were scheduled in Brussels for the month of June, including a ball the Duke himself planned to host on the anniversary of the Battle of Vitoria. As part of an effort to keep the populace from panicking, scheduled events were not canceled, but by the second week of June a trickle of emigration had become a flood that put a premium on all available horses and conveyances as foreigners fled the area.

Amid conflicting intelligence reports Cam had not tried to send Natasha away even had she been willing to undertake a journey. The presence of his brother-in-law contributed greatly to his peace of mind during this tense period when his duties kept him constantly on the move between military positions. He was scarcely ever home these days except to change his clothes. Natasha maintained her air of calm serenity, but he thought he detected a shade of anxiety in her eyes each time he kissed her goodbye. The only good thing to come of the situation was that her lips now clung to his on these occasions. Each time he left the house, he promised himself a private interview with his wife to sort out their differences, but the long busy days went past without affording him the opportunity.

As his frustration grew at the delay in setting his house in order, Cam mentally fixed on the evening of the fifteenth as the moment to arrange some time alone with Natasha. The Duke and Duchess of Richmond were giving a large ball that night at their rented mansion on the Rue de la Blanchisserie. Peter would be attending and the field marshal's staff would all be there. One officer would not be missed among so many.

He was at headquarters on the afternoon of the fifteenth having an early dinner with the Duke and his staff when the first report came in that Napoleon had attacked the Prussians that morning at Charleroi. Although still suspecting this was a feint and the main thrust would be to the west of Mans to cut off the English from their ships, the Duke sent out orders within a couple of hours to assemble the whole army at its various divisional head-quarters ready to move at a moment's notice. After the campaign of false intelligence Napoleon had waged to conceal his army's movements, he had struck fast, catching the Allies unprepared. Surprisingly, Wellington still planned to attend the ball and curtly advised Major Talbot to do likewise to keep himself in a position to be apprised of all developments as they occurred.

When Cam went home to change, Natasha was resting and Aunt Hester warned him not to disturb her as she had not been feeling quite the thing that day. She still had not awakened when her husband reluctantly departed for the Richmonds', clad in all the splendor of gold lace.

The Richmond ball was to remain in Cam's memory as one of the severest tests of self-control that he had ever been required to undergo. Thanks to his highly visible style during most of his time in Brussels he was expected to partner a number of young ladies and perform full social duties while his thoughts were a few streets away with Natasha. What with the field marshal's late arrival to confirm the persistent rumors of a battle, the news of the army's imminent departure swept through the ballroom even before the message arrived around midnight with the intelligence Wellington had been awaiting—the attack on Charleroi had not been a feint. Napoleon was directing his move at the seam between the British and Prussian positions to divide the two armies that together out-numbered him.

It was now official—the army would march south at dawn to meet the enemy. All over the ballroom affecting scenes of farewell were being enacted as officers of the more distantly deployed units slipped away, leaving anxious loved ones to cope with their distress in public. His own mortality had never concerned Cam in the past except momentarily before his first battles, but now it was rammed home to him that he might never see his wife again and his child might never know its father. By the time the procession had formed to go into supper the need to make his peace with Natasha was a driving urgency that was no longer to be borne.

He walked rapidly home and was admitted to his house by Hilaire. It did not occur to Cam to wonder why the butler was still fully dressed after one o'clock in the morning as he passed him without a word and bounded up the stairs to knock at the door to his wife's suite. It was opened by a servant he'd never seen before, a woman of middle years, formidable size, and unwelcoming aspect, wearing a large starched cap and apron.

"I want to see my wife."

"You can't come in here now, sir," the woman declared uncompromisingly.

"Who's to stop me?" Cam bustled the affronted woman out into the hall and locked the door behind her.

Natasha's sitting room was ablaze with lights and he found her sitting back against the pillows of her bed with her finger holding her place in a book while large dark eyes gravely watched his approach from the outer room.

"Thank goodness you're still awake, darling. I have not been able to get any time alone with you this past sennight and more, but the army is moving out at dawn and I had to tell you how sorry I am for the way I've treated you these last months." At her little cry of distress he sat on the bed and seized her hands, which had fluttered up to her mouth.

"Tasha, I wouldn't fault you if you found it impossible to forgive me; I know I've been as cruel as it is possible to be to someone one loves, but you must believe that I *do* love you, quite desperately. I think I always have, but I honestly did not know it until you came to Vienna, and then I fear I went a little mad. Oh, I can't explain my behavior so it makes any sense; I'm not even sure I understand myself, but I could not leave without telling you this." He brought her hands to his lips and then dropped one to cup her chin in his hand. "You are crying, Tasha," he said wonderingly. "I've never seen you cry before, not even when I've hurt you the most."

"Oh, Cam, I've been praying for a moment like this. At times I really feared it might never happen and I'd have to go away from you." The tears were coming faster now, and Cam gathered her into his arms and held her comfortingly, his heart overflowing with humble gratitude, until the silent weeping abated. He had his handkerchief out and ready when at last she pulled back, saying with a wavering attempt at a smile, "I am sorry to be such a . . . a watering pot. I don't d-do this very often, I promise you."

He watched her lovingly while she blew her nose and mopped her cheeks. "If anyone is entitled to a bout of tears, you are that person. "I . . . Tasha, what is it?" he asked on an anxious note as sudden spasm crossed her features and she drew in her breath sharply.

"Just a labor pain."

"But . . . but how can this be? You said the baby wasn't expected until next week!"

Natasha smiled at the look of horrified disbelief on her husband's face. "Babies have been known to arrive before they are due, you know."

"But how can I go off and leave you in a few hours? I should be here with you at a time like this. Where is the doctor? Why is no one with you?"

There was a touch of the maternal about Natasha's smile as she regarded her agitated husband. "Having babies is women's business, just as fighting wars is men's." The smile faltered but she continued briskly, "It will be several hours yet before the baby is born. I shall do fine with Mme Charbonneau the midwife, who comes very well-recommended. The doctor has been notified and is no doubt on his way. I'll have Aunt Hester and Peter too. You must get some rest before you have to leave."

"Where is this so-well-recommended midwife?" Cam asked truculently.

"That is undoubtedly she, banging on the sitting-room door. What did you do to her, by the way?"

Cam looked sheepish. "I locked her out in the hall, thinking she was an abigail. I believe I hear Peter's voice too. Before I let them in, will you kiss me good-bye, Tasha?"

Two slim arms encircled his neck in a convulsive clasp as husband and wife exchanged a long embrace that had the primacy of a marriage vow.

"God go with you and protect you, my darling," whispered Natasha, her eyes shimmering with tears.

"I'll be back, my heart—never doubt it—perhaps even before the baby is born."

"I hope not!" Natasha gasped as another spasm of pain contorted her face and sent her husband hurrying to let the midwife back into the room.

It was nearly three days before Cam kept his promise. When he left shortly after dawn on Friday after a couple of hours' sleep, the baby had not arrived and he was not permitted to see Natasha, who was in active labor, attended by doctor, midwife, and Aunt Hester. The latter came out to wish her nephew godspeed, and Peter rode part of the way with him until a nervous Cam implored him to return and keep watch over his family.

They fought a limited engagement that day with part of the French army under Marshal Ney at Quatre Bras, a crossroads about twenty miles south of Brussels. Casualties were high on both sides, but nothing like the losses taken by their Prussian allies at Ligny on the same day from the main French thrust. Since the Prussians were retreating north on Saturday, the seventeenth, the Anglo-Dutch forces were compelled to do the same to prevent Napoleon from destroying his enemies' communications and carving them up piecemeal. The retreat had been well-managed with few losses, but extraordinary thunderstorms and an all-night rain had soaked the weary men and turned the fields of uncut rye and corn where they spent a miserable night into quagmires. Most had no heat and some got nothing to eat before the next day's long agonizing but decisive battle fought just south of the village of Waterloo some ten miles from Brussels.

By the time Wellington's forces had barely withstood the final French assault of that horrible day, the carnage was so terrible on both sides as to almost render the question of victory or defeat immaterial at first. Cam's senses were so dulled by the relentless cacophony of artillery and the choking smells of smoke, not to mention the growing horror of seeing friend after friend fall during that seemingly endless afternoon, that he had ceased to be aware of his own raw wounds, quickly attended to as they occurred, since none of them materially impaired his ability to ride or swing his sword when necessary. He had no concern for the frightful appearance he presented by the time the field marshal left the scene with the French army being pursued by the British and Prussian cavalry.

The sight of the empty places set for the staff's dinner back in Waterloo village, places that were to remain vacant, started the process of thawing the numbness in which Cam's faculties were encased, permitting the worry that had surfaced at intervals during the past three days to attack him once more. There had been no word from Brussels about Natasha, though Peter had promised to try to get a message through after the birth.

Sleep was out of the question. He was one throbbing mass of pain, very little of it actually physical. The Duke, engaged in writing his dispatch while Colonel Gordon lay dying of his wounds in his chief's camp bed, was in little better frame, judging by his bleak demeanor. He waved Cam off with best wishes and admonitions on the condition of the roads, which were reportedly choked everywhere with returning wounded and blocked in places by broken-down equipment and supply wagons that had never arrived from Brussels.

It took Cam until the small hours of the morning to accomplish the ten miles or so, even though Walker had a fairly fresh horse for him. Every foot of the way was made difficult by the gruesome realities they encountered, most of which they were unable to alleviate once they had parted with the pitifully small store of food, water, and medical supplies in their possession. Cam's irrational fears for Natasha's safety fed on the horrors and suffering they witnessed on that trek. The fear of death he had not experienced during the interminable costly battle dogged his step now and settled into a knot in his stomach. He knew beyond doubting that his wife was a strong healthy young woman, but women died in childbirth every day. During that entire journey through an interior hell, he writhed in the talons of a superstitious dread that he and Natasha might have struggled through these past terrible months only to have their marriage ended by forces beyond their control. Dimly he recognized that this mental torment was precisely what he had planned to avoid in his personal life, but that was past praying for; Natasha represented his whole hope of happiness in this world. To lose her would be to be condemned to eternal darkness. Of the child he thought not at all.

A fully clad Peter appeared on the doorstep of the Brussels house in time to see his exhausted brother-in-law descend from his horse with much less than his customary agility.

"Cam! Thank God you're in one piece! We haven't known what to expect. Since Friday there have been persistent rumors that Napoleon was about to enter Brussels at any moment. The town is clogged with our own wounded, but they don't know how the battle went after they left the field. I was getting ready to head south looking for you."

"Natasha?"

Peter looked more closely into anxious eyes in a gray face and flung out an arm to assist Cam up the steps. "She's fine. You have a son, by the way. Is it over?" he asked in a reversal of their roles of the previous year.

"Napoleon's retreating, but it was a close-run thing. I must see Natasha. Give Walker some money, will you, Peter? We gave all ours to some of the wounded we met so they could buy food from the civilians."

Lord Phillips caught up with his brother-in-law before he reached the staircase. "Cam, you cannot show yourself to Tasha looking like that; she'll have hysterics. Your left sleeve is in tatters and that bandage on your right arm is caked with dirt and dried blood. As to your head and face—''

"You don't know your sister. Her courage is of another order." He continued up the staircase, concentrating on putting one foot in front of the other.

"At least let me pull off those disgusting boots for you."

"Thank you." Cam sank wearily down onto the stairs and, when the boots were off, accepted Peter's assistance in getting to his feet again with a rueful grimace. Words were beyond him at the moment; only the need to see Natasha kept him moving.

"She'll probably be asleep at this hour," Peter felt obliged to warn, but when he entered Natasha's sitting room with Cam on his heels, she called out anxiously, "Peter? I thought I heard . . . Oh, Cam!''

They would not have to concern themselves with possible hysterics or vapors, Peter reflected thankfully as he saw his sister's face radiant with joy, though two tears slipped silently down her cheeks as she gazed up at her husband.

"Tears, Tasha? How foolish," he chided gently, sinking onto the bed to take her chin in his grimy hand. "I told you I would be back."

"I'll get some water and fresh bandages," Lord Phillips said hastily, though the other two were not even aware of his tactful retreat.

When he returned some fifteen minutes later, the sight that greeted his eyes nearly caused him to drop the basin of hot water he had carefully carried all the way up from the kitchen. Natasha was sitting up against a pile of pillows contentedly feeding her infant while her husband lay sprawled beside her sound asleep in all his dirt and the remnants of his uniform. A glimpse of the old Natasha appeared in the mischievous grin she flashed him.

"The nurse was scandalized to see Cam here. I had to threaten to dismiss her before she would leave the baby. Cam agrees with me that he is going to have green eyes," she continued while Peter deposited his basin and medical supplies on the nearest table.

"I'll carry Cam into his own room and see what I can do about cleaning up his wounds while—"

"You'll leave him right where he is!" she shot back, giving her brother a fierce underbrowed look before returning her gaze to the guzzling infant. "I've waited long enough for this moment," she added so quietly that Peter was unsure of her exact words.

"Well, I . . . I don't suppose a few more hours will matter all that much," he conceded, backing himself awkwardly out of the room and leaving the small family together at last in peace.